The Convergence

Book Two of
The Amulets Trilogy

J. Lawson

Dedication

This one's to everyone who has contributed in *any* and *every* way to the creation of these books.

To those who were there from the very beginning, my mom, Joan; my dad, Ken; my Aunt GeeGee and Aunt Lil; my Uncle Wayne, and so many others who read to me and kept me well stocked with books starting at such a young age. They are the ones who introduced me to a love of reading.

To my school teachers who made the reading fun and meaningful beyond just the ordinary storytelling. They offered me so many more layers to literature and allowed me to deepen my love and appreciation of it.

To those who, more recently, have helped me in my latest endeavors of creating and offering something to the book-loving community from the opposite end of things; by writing my own works. Angie Bee, Jennifer Flaig, Ray Sherman, and Jessica Mueller along with all my other local writing folks have been such an incredible support network. They allowed me to bounce ideas, gave me feedback as well as insight from their own experiences, and motivated me through the entire process. I couldn't have done this without them.

And finally, to the unsung and underappreciated heroes who work behind the scenes; the wonderful wait staff at Perkins and Starbucks in Peoria, Illinois, and The Bartonville Diner in Bartonville, Illinois. A huge thanks to Lynette, Ariel, and so many others. For always letting me camp out in booths for hours at a time, for keeping me well stocked in coffee and ranch dressing, and for keeping me sane, I am incredibly grateful.

Contents

Chapter One
Reminiscence

The rain pattered lightly on the window as Georgia stared up at the ceiling. The only good thing about it, she thought, was that it was finally not snow falling from the sky. The cold winter seemed to have loosened its icy grip on the town of Shamore, and the whispers of spring could be heard at last. Georgia turned over on her bed and looked out a tiny window through which grey light was starting to filter. She shut her eyes and thought back again, as she had so many times, to the events of that winter. People had kept to themselves in their homes, so she hadn't been forced to interact with anyone more than was absolutely necessary on her few outings. The bookstore where she worked had been almost dead. She flinched as her mind processed the word "dead" and she gritted her teeth, pulling the blankets tighter around herself.

It had been one of the harshest winters she could remember; in more ways than one. In a way, the cold temperatures and copious amounts of snow that had kept most of the townspeople indoors the last two months had been a blessing. The lack of human interaction had meant requests to recount the details of Jordan and Sawyer's disappearance, or at least the details that had been organized and put together for the town, had been kept to a minimum. Still, the interactions she *had* been forced to endure, and the inevitable reactions resulting from those interactions, had been tough to stomach.

Georgia sighed heavily and tossed off her blankets. The cold hardwood floor shocked her feet as she stood. She put on her robe and walked toward the stairs that would take her to the bathroom of the Maren home where she was now residing with Jordan's parents. Not long ago, the house had been a source of comfort, laughter, and family. Georgia had arrived in Shamore only a few short months before with her ailing mother. Her mother had been born in and grown up in Shamore, but they had moved to a town a few hours away when Georgia's father passed away. Her mother had attributed their move back to Shamore to her desire to return to the place she felt most at home.

When Georgia had started work at the bookstore, Jordan was the only other person that worked there besides Ryan, the owner. She and Jordan had become fast friends, feeling a connection neither of them acknowledged to the other right away. Not long after, during an ill-fated trip into the woods where Jordan had told Georgia she frequently spent time, Georgia found herself in danger and Jordan had come to her rescue. In doing so, she revealed she had the same ability as Georgia to transform into an animal at will. Both girls had previously thought themselves to be the only person in existence who could do this, and they bonded immediately over their common gift. From then on, they became almost inseparable, spending much of their shared free time with each other.

It was around that same time Jordan had met Sawyer, the handsome grandson of the town grouch and barista at the local coffee shop they both frequented. While there was an obvious connection between Jordan and Sawyer, Georgia never felt jealous or neglected. Nothing could transcend the bond she and Jordan had, and she was happy when Jordan's relationship with Sawyer developed. They became a close trio and settled into an easy routine.

Georgia's heart ached at the memories of "before", when life had been complex only in regard to the secret they kept. Things had been so much easier – and significantly happier. She turned the shower on as hot as she could tolerate it, trying as she had for months to warm the seemingly permanent cold spot in her core that she hadn't been able to shake for months. The Marens' house had been her source of warmth and happiness back then. When her mother had passed away the previous year, Jordan and her parents had been quick to invite Georgia into their home and their family. Judy and Gordon had treated her like one of their children from the very beginning. She had missed her mother, but being welcomed into their family had helped what would have been an intolerable situation become endurable. If only she had known how short-lived that comfort and new-found happiness would be.

Looking through the frosted glass door of the shower, Georgia's mind flashed back to the nightmarish events that had taken place in the woods last December. It played often through Georgia's mind like a bad horror movie trailer.

…Sawyer crashing through the woods toward them with armed men at his heels…

…shots fired…

…Sawyer lying on the ground, bleeding…

…Jordan leaning over him, crying, begging Christian to do anything to save him…

…Christian plunging a knife in Jordan's chest, using his knowledge of ancient magic to place her blood and a potion in Sawyer's mouth…

…Sawyer convulsing through his first and final transformation into a wolf…

…Jordan being fed the potion, her final transformation, and the quiet that filled the woods as they all waited to see if Jordan could survive…

The intense relief Georgia felt when Jordan finally drew a breath had been brief as they all realized the finality of the decision that had been made. No one in the town knew of Georgia and Jordan's transformative abilities, and, especially now with the new developments in a potential war that no one but they were aware of, their secrecy was all the more imperative. This meant that, with Jordan and Sawyer now permanently in their animal forms, a story had to be formulated as to why they had suddenly disappeared and would never be seen again. Not only that, but the story needed to deter anyone from searching for them for any length of time as the woods around the town were becoming less and less safe. The final decision had been tragic but necessary; Jordan and Sawyer had to be believed dead. As no one knew about Christian and Victoria's existence either, Georgia had been the only one left to deliver the news.

Giving the nozzle a rough twist, Georgia turned the shower off and grabbed her towel, attacking her wet hair. The betrayal she felt when Jordan hadn't even consulted her or taken her feelings into consideration before making the decision to leave her human form behind and leave Georgia alone in her hybrid form had been bad enough. But being expected to inform Jordan's parents that their only child had been killed was almost intolerable. They had just settled into a comfortable life with the four of them in the house, and then Georgia had been forced to break their hearts. Two weeks had passed before she had seen Judy not crying. Georgia had even offered to find her own place to live, but the Maren's had shut her down saying she was the only daughter they had left.

That moment had been the first time since the chaos in the forest that Georgia had cried. She knew they did think of her as a daughter, but she also knew every time they saw her, they had to be taken back to the night she told them about Jordan and Sawyer. The pain in their eyes was torture for her. For this reason, she had taken to showering before she knew they would be awake in the morning and, most of the time, she was out the door before they ever came downstairs. She also tried to stay out as late as possible. The few times she wasn't able to leave the house quickly enough, Judy always asked her to try to get home and join them for supper because they missed her. More recently, the request had been because they wanted to make sure she was ok after speaking with the police.

With a soft snort of derision, Georgia quietly closed her bedroom door behind her. That had been another unexpected burden she had been forced to deal with and the event still rankled. The town police had showed up at the bookstore where Georgia worked to question her about the disappearance of her two friends. They hadn't directly come out and said it, but it was an accusatory interrogation in a thinly veiled attempt to get her to confess to knowing more about the disappearance than she claimed. It had been over an hour of aggressive questioning before Ryan had come to her aid and finally insisted they leave so she could get back to work. Their efforts had gained them nothing, but it had reignited the resentment Georgia felt toward Jordan and Sawyer and she didn't want to think about it anymore, much less discuss it with Judy and Gordon.

Georgia looked around the room, making sure she had everything she needed for work as well as her notebook to bring with her to Mama Landry's restaurant after she got off. She had spent a lot of her free time there, writing the bedtime story her mother had told her when she was little and that Jordan had told her she should write down. This, of course, had started before they knew the story was real and that magic and shapeshifting beings really did exist in the world, but she couldn't shake the idea that writing the story down would keep a part of her mother closer to her.

It irked her that she was enjoying doing something that had been Jordan's idea, but she didn't want to lose the one form of catharsis she could find lately. What bothered her even more was how often she wanted to run a passage by Jordan or get her opinion on something, but Georgia hadn't been back to the woods since the night they had come up with the story Georgia would tell, and she wasn't in a hurry to go back. She knew she had a job to do and there were plans to make that necessitated her return to the woods at some point, but she couldn't bear to think about being in their company yet.

In the kitchen, Georgia poured a travel mug of coffee from the machine that was timed to brew every morning. She picked up a pen and scribbled a note to Judy and Gordon letting them know she would be home late that night, but would try to make it for supper that weekend. She knew she couldn't get out of spending time with them much longer, so it would be better to do it sooner rather than later.

She had just gotten to her car and opened the door when she heard the front door slam shut and saw Gordon walking toward her. Her heart skipped a beat, and she was surprised that, along with the regular guilt she felt every time she saw either of them, she was also pleased. It had been over a week since she had seen either one of them and she didn't realize how much she missed them.

"Hey, Georgia," Gordon said, stopping in front of her. "Heading to work?"

"I am," she said, giving a weak smile. "Things have been slow, so Ryan suggested we do a deep clean of the place and get it looking nice before the weather really breaks and more people are out shopping again."

"That's a good idea," Gordon nodded. "It's probably a lot of work with just the two of you, so it's good things are slow and you can get that done."

Georgia's stomach clenched at his mention of it being just the two of them. Georgia and Jordan had worked together at the bookstore until Jordan's "disappearance" and she tried not to mention the store or work because of it. Looking into Gordon's face however, she noticed there was no blame or even sadness in his eyes as he said it. "Yeah, she agreed tentatively. "It definitely keeps us busy when there isn't much else going on, which is good because otherwise the days would drag."

Gordon smiled. "Well, have a good day. I'm glad to see you'll be joining us for supper this weekend. I know Judy misses you too. We've been talking about you and hoping you're doing well after that garbage with the officers last week." Georgia blanched but Gordon pushed on. "Ryan told me about it when I bumped into him at the market. It is completely asinine. They had no right to accost you like that. How they could even think you'd have anything to do with any of it is beyond Judy and me. As if it wasn't enough you lost your best friend. I hope you haven't let anything they had to say bother you too much," he said, squeezing her shoulder and planting a kiss on top of her head. "We'll see you soon."

Georgia sunk into her car and wiped her eyes quickly as he turned to walk back to the house. She couldn't believe how angry he'd been that the police had spoken to her. She had known it was a possibility the police would want to question her, and she could understand why they might be desperate to get some kind of lead as there was really nothing to go on. The story they devised was air tight, but the intensity of the questioning had surprised and hurt her. It warmed the cold spot in her chest that Judy and Gordon were as miffed by the whole thing as she was. As she drove to the bookstore, she realized some of her worries about Judy and Gordon's perceived or anticipated negative feelings toward her might be her own displaced guilt and nothing more. She took a deep breath as she parked in front of the store. It might be time to heal.

Chapter Two
Sightings

Georgia closed the bookstore door and locked it behind her. She had arrived an hour before opening to get a jump start on the cleaning, but now that she was there, she wasn't feeling motivated. She checked the stock room and noticed a small delivery had come in the day before. She pulled the orders and noticed two books that had been special order for a customer. She ran her finger down the list and stopped as it landed on a familiar name: Augustus Toole. It was Sawyer's grandfather. She leaned back against the pallet of books and raised her face to the ceiling, closing her eyes. It seemed like no matter what she did or where she was, she was reminded of those days right after the woods and all the people whose lives she had to irrevocably alter.

Telling Auggie had been a peculiar experience since she and Jordan had spoken to Auggie just hours before Jordan and Sawyer were supposed to have gone missing. They knew when they discussed the plan in the woods that he may suspect their story was not entirely true, but they had to keep everything consistent. When Georgia had shown up at his front door again and asked to speak with him, he had joined her on the front stoop instead of inviting her in. He had listened to her story silently, arms crossed, and had no reaction except for a slight tightening in his jaw. When she finished, she remembered his reaction had been strange. He hadn't shown any true emotion at the news; not that she was particularly surprised. He had never been one to show any extremes in emotion the few times they had spoken before, even when the news had been quite grim. But upon hearing that his grandson and his girlfriend had likely been killed and there was a good chance they would never be found or seen again, he had simply told her it was a shame; he had liked that Jordan girl and Sawyer was a great grandson and he would be missed. Then he had patted her arm, told her to take care of herself, and turned to go back inside. When Georgia had asked if there was anything she could do for him, he simply paused in the door, not turning to look at her, and said "Be careful yourself. We don't want anyone else disappearing out there," and closed the door.

The more she thought about the lack of reaction Auggie had shown, Georgia strongly believed he knew there was more to the story than what she had told him, but he had the decency not to push it. She had been grateful at the time. Now that time had passed, however, she wondered how much he suspected. Shaking her head slightly she looked at the books he had ordered: "Artillery Through the Ages" and "The Magical Compendium: A Guide to True Knowledge." Georgia bagged the order and sat it under the front desk. Normally she would call customers to tell them their order was in, but something inside of her was telling her she needed to pay another visit to Augustus Toole soon.

Next, Georgia put away the general stock orders and took the completed log to Ryan's office. As she walked in, she smiled sadly at the picture on the wall next to his computer. It was one Georgia had taken of Jordan holding a stack of fantasy novels while kicking over a pile of business leadership books. Last year, Jordan organized a store reset to take out a large portion of the business books Ryan was so fond of so they could start carrying more fantasy books the kids tended to enjoy. It was a very successful reset, and it had killed Ryan at the time. Jordan and Ryan always had more of a sibling rivalry type of relationship than a boss and employee relationship. Georgia reached out and touched the face of the Jordan in the photograph. Even with as much grief as they had always given each other, Ryan had been devastated when Georgia had broken the news to him about Jordan. He had hugged Georgia and been apologetic to her, going on about how he knew how close they were and how valuable of an employee she had been. What he hadn't said, but what had shown in his actions since then, was the regret he had that he hadn't been more open about how much he really valued her.

Ryan had picked up most of the slack around the store now that it was just him and Georgia, but he hadn't been able to bring himself to stock the shelves. Georgia didn't know if it brought back too many memories about his and Jordan's banter, or if it was too painful of a reminder for other reasons, but he had left that aspect of the job to Georgia ever since. He had also put up the picture of Jordan in the office, and he had set up a collection and used book sale, all proceeds to benefit the Marens and their expenses after Jordan's passing. Georgia had felt conflicted participating in those activities, but had done so to keep up appearances. At the very least, she was happy to be helping out the Marens in some way.

Georgia left Ryan's office and returned to the front desk. She still had twenty minutes before the store opened, so she pulled herself up to sit on the front counter and opened the town paper that had been left in front of the door that morning. She wasn't usually a newspaper reader, but she didn't want to get started on a book and have to stop just as it was getting good. As she browsed the front page, the photo for an article just below the fold caught her eye. It was a somewhat blurry photograph of the edge of the woods on the north end of town. It had been taken in the evening time and it was a distant shot, but just barely visible at the line of trees was a large, dark shape. Georgia thought there was something vaguely familiar about the shape and she began reading the article.

Increase in Town Sightings of Wild Animals

Town resident Rita Zane captured this picture Monday evening as she arrived home. She stated she saw a bear in her back yard, but by the time she was able to retrieve her camera, it had retreated to the woods. This sighting is the most recent of an increasing number of animal sightings close to town in the past two months. Officers in charge of animal control and safety say they are at a loss as to what could be attracting these animals, but they advise residents of Shamore not to bring garbage out until the day of garbage pickup and caution against leaving anything edible outside. They also suggest not leaving small pets or children outside unattended for any length of time, especially toward evening hours as this is when the majority of the sightings have taken place. Wolves and bears have been the most commonly sighted and, while there have not been any attacks, officers do not want residents to put themselves or others at risk. If you see unusual wildlife near your home, do not attempt to scare these animals off. While wolves and bears tend to be skittish around people and their nature is to flee, they can also be very aggressive if threatened. If any sightings should occur, please go inside immediately and call the Shamore Sheriff's Department as soon as possible.

Georgia closed her eyes and took a deep breath. She knew exactly why the animal sightings had increased in the last two months. Jordan, Sawyer, and Christian were getting restless and they were apparently willing to take risks coming this close to town to potentially catch a glimpse of her, or rather, hoping she would catch a glimpse of them. There had been a time or two she thought she had seen a flash of something moving along the tree line behind the Marens' house, but she had never taken the time to investigate or even think too hard about it. She couldn't help but think about it anymore. If the number of sightings was really increasing so much the police felt the need to put it in the paper, it was a lucky thing there hadn't been any attacks so far. Not that her friends would ever attack anyone; she knew they wouldn't for certain. But the truth was, most of the people in their town had guns, and the fact her friends hadn't scared someone enough for them to go get their gun and shoot to scare them off was amazing.

Georgia glanced at the clock above the door and saw it was time to open the store. She blew out a sigh and walked to the front door, twisting the lock, and flipping the sign to OPEN. As much as she didn't feel ready to see them, she knew she had run out of time. Aside from her anger and frustration at the situation she had found herself in, she had also been reluctant to tell Jordan just how sad her parents were; about how things hadn't been the same and seemed they would never be. But the short visit with Gordon this morning had helped to assuage some of that apprehension. She still may not be happy with her forest friends, but she didn't want them to get hurt, or worse. This weekend, after supper with Judy and Gordon, she would venture out to the clearing in the woods and do what needed to be done at last.

Chapter Three
Potential Danger

Ryan arrived fifteen minutes after the store opened. He dropped a shrink wrapped package of bookmarks on the counter and set a bakery bag next to it. The sweet smell of pastries reached Georgia's nose and her mouth watered.

"Ooo, did the bookmark and breakfast fairy make a visit?" Georgia smiled, opening the bag and looking inside.

"Donuts on the house," Ryan smiled back. "I stopped at the bakery next door and grabbed a few. It felt like a donut and coffee kind of morning. I would had gotten you coffee, but I know you are particular about yours and I knew better than to attempt it. Plus, I know you usually bring your big gulp in anyway."

Georgia looked at her 32oz travel coffee mug. "It's really a shame they don't come bigger," she said, her face completely serious. Ryan stared back at her and they both paused a few seconds before saying, at the same time, "That's what she said," and then burst out laughing. It was a joke Jordan would have normally made, but they apparently both couldn't help themselves. Pretending they didn't notice she wasn't there would never work long term, so bringing a part of her humor back to the store seemed a better way to process her absence.

"The bookmarks look great!" Georgia said excitedly.

She had come up with the idea of theme bookmarks to put in the bags with each purchase. Fantasy, romance, horror, crime, children's, professional, and biographical genres were represented, and each one listed a few books or series in that genre. All of the works listed were books they carried in the store. Georgia had hoped to broaden readers' horizons and possibly increase sales with the extra information. Ryan had agreed and they had ordered the bookmarks a few weeks ago. Georgia opened the shrink wrap and began looking through the different bookmarks, sorting them and putting them in stacks on the shelf under the register.

"I'm going to keep most of the them under here to put in bags, but I'll put a few of each of them out on the table so people can see them all and grab one if they're interested."

Ryan nodded and grabbed the paper Georgia had been reading. He glanced at the front page. "This is getting out of hand," he said seriously, the humor of the previous exchange gone from his tone. "These kinds of animals are dangerous. It's only a matter of time before someone gets hurt. I'm surprised they haven't ordered a cull hunt yet."

"A cull hunt?" Georgia asked, turning from the table she had been straightening to make room for the bookmarks. It sounded ominous, and butterflies began to flutter in her stomach.

"It happened once before when I was younger. There were apparently getting to be so many bears in the woods that they started pressing the boundaries and coming into town. I don't know if they were looking for food or if there just wasn't enough room for them all out there. I find that kind of hard to believe since those woods go on forever.

Anyway, one of the kids in town got attacked by a bear while she was playing in her own backyard one evening. She didn't die, but she ended up losing her leg. The parents in town had a fit about it, and rightly so. They leaned on law enforcement heavily enough that they finally had to do something about it, so they called for a cull hunt. It's what happens when the population of a species of animal gets too high. People were allowed to hunt bears freely for a certain amount of time if they saw them on their own land. They even issued licenses to people to go into the woods and shoot a certain number of them. I guess it worked, because I don't remember a bear sighting ever again after that. Well, up until the last couple months..." His voice trailed off and Georgia looked at him inquisitively. Ryan swallowed hard and looked her in the eyes. "I really hope these sightings don't have anything to do with Jordan and Sawyer disappearing, that's all." He tucked the paper under his arm and walked back to his office.

Georgia watched him as he disappeared through his door. If only she could tell him that the sightings had everything to do with Jordan and Sawyer's disappearance, but not at all in the way he suspected. It was one of the hardest things about this whole situation; seeing people in distress and having the knowledge to put them at ease, but not be able to share it. Georgia picked a donut out of the pastry bag and took a bite. It was still warm and tasted wonderful, but she knew all the donuts in the world wouldn't fill the empty void inside her.

*****

Georgia smiled and waved goodbye to the last customers of the day before flipping the store sign to CLOSED and locking the door behind them. She opened the register and pulled out the till. She grabbed the paperwork from the day and brought it and the till back to Ryan. She knocked gently before walking in.

Ryan spun around in his chair. "Not a bad day, eh?" he said, taking the papers, sitting them next to his keyboard, and grabbing the till.

"It was pretty great," Georgia agreed. "There were more people in the store than there have been in weeks and we had a lot of sales. I guess we really should get that deep cleaning done sooner rather than later before we won't have time for it. I planned to do it this morning, but I put away the shipment and stocked the shelves and ran out of time. I can come in early Sunday if you need me to. Or I can stay late."

Ryan shook his head. "You've been working too much overtime lately. I was letting it slide because I think we both wanted to throw ourselves into our work to avoid thinking about... other things," he said, his voice getting quiet. Then he cleared his throat and resumed his normal volume. "But it's time for that to stop. It's time to devote the appropriate amount of time to work and the rest to other things. You can come in one hour early on Sunday if you'd like, but that's where I'm capping it. We'll get the cleaning done as we can. Go out and do things, Georgia. Rediscover fun," he smiled affectionately.

Georgia smiled back. "Only if you do, too."

"Deal," Ryan said. "I'll count the till and process the paperwork tonight. You go do whatever it is you do with that notebook you carry everywhere."

"I'm writing a story. Kind of. It's just a continuation of a story my mom used to tell me before bed when I was younger. I figured maybe I could turn it into something eventually," she shrugged.

"A story, eh? Well, maybe when you've got it finished we can carry it here in the store. I might even read it. I've been told before I need to broaden my horizons," he said wryly, alluding to the fact Jordan and Georgia had both made many book recommendations to him in the past; none of which he'd ever given a chance.

"Is that so? Well, whoever gave you that advice really knew what they were talking about." Georgia winked before turning and walking out of the office. She heard Ryan laughing softly. She picked up her bag, notebook, and the package with Auggie's books in it. She unlocked the bookstore door, exited, and locked it again behind her. As she got in her car to drive to Mama Landry's restaurant, she couldn't help but think how neat it would be to have a book she had written appear in the bookstore. She smiled in spite of herself. Things may not have been going great in her life, but that small thought was a positive one she could cling to.

Mama Landry's restaurant was fairly empty when Georgia arrived. It was just after five, but the dinner crowd during the week was never quite as big as the weekends. Georgia was grateful for this as it meant she wasn't tying up a table with her hours of writing and coffee drinking, and it also meant there were less distractions, allowing her to get lost in the story.

"Hello, suga." Mama Landry greeted her. "Ya sit right on down in ya booth an' I'll bring ova some coffee in a jiff."

"Thanks, Mama," Georgia answered, matching the big smile Mama Landry always wore when she arrived.

The restaurant had taken the top position of places she felt most welcome and comfortable these days. Mama Landry, the proprietor and often times only server of her restaurant, had taken Georgia under her mama hen's wing once word of Jordan and Sawyer's disappearance had spread. Georgia appreciated that she had never forced her to talk about it, but simply treated her as she always had; like one of her many chicks. It seemed like she knew that a sense of normalcy and not needing to talk about those events was what Georgia needed more than anything at this time. Georgia sat at the same booth she, Jordan, and Sawyer had always sat in when they came to the restaurant. Even though it wasn't the same without them, sitting anywhere else would have felt wrong. Sometimes she could still feel them sitting there with her and it was often hard not to order more than one coffee if there happened to be another server working.

Mama Landry brought out a carafe of coffee and a large mug; bigger than any of the regular mugs the restaurant used. These had been Georgia and Jordan's mugs. Mama Landry had said more than once she had bought them to save her poor legs some walking since she and Jordan had needed refills so often with the regular sized ones, but they all knew the truth was she did it because she loved them. And they loved her.

"How was work ta-day, darlin'?" Mama Landry asked, pouring a mug of steaming coffee and leaning her large hip against the side of the booth. "Did Mr. Ryan work ya inta tha ground?"

Georgia laughed as she reached for the mug. "Oh yes, he was in rare form today." They both knew he had never been able to push her or Jordan around, even if he had wanted to, which he never really did. She appreciated that Mama Landry could always get her to smile, even when she felt like she never would again. "But I put him in his place and now he's there all by himself finishing up the work while I come and drink amazing coffee at Shamore's finest dining establishment."

Mama Landry tipped back her head and let out a warm, deep chuckle. "Well now, that's good ta hear. What can I get ya fo' supper ta-night?"

"I'm in a veggie mood tonight, Mama. How about a salad? Toss anything in it you think I might like and I bet it'll be delicious."

Mama Landry pulled up her chest and looked at her disapprovingly. "A salad o' all things!? Ya getting far too thin, chil'. Most people plump up ova tha winter, but ya wastin' away ta nothin'. Ya need some meat on them bones. Ya sure Mama can't bring ya some nice fried chicken or a ham steak with taters an' gravy?"

Georgia's mouth watered slightly at the mention of fried chicken. The truth was, she just hadn't been hungry for the last couple of months. She knew it was stress and that she was getting leaner than she had been in a long time, but food just didn't taste as good these days. If anything could taste good though, it would probably be Mama Landry's cooking.

"I'm really fine, Mama. But I tell you what, I'll leave it to you. Tell the cook to prepare whatever you think is best, and that's what I'll have. Mama knows best, right?"

Mama Landry beamed at her and patted her hand. "Ya know that's right," she said warmly. "An' I'll do ya one betta. Mama'll prepare it hersef so ya know it's tha best meal ya had in a age. Be back soon, sweets."

As she watched Mama Landry walking away, she could feel her heart warming. It was nice to feel that the cold spot that had become a permanent fixation in her core the last couple months wasn't as present as it usually was. Maybe she really was beginning to finally heal. It was nice to let some of the anger go, even if it was only for short bursts. She missed feeling happy. She opened up her notebook to where she had stopped writing the last time she was here and put her pen to paper, letting the words of the story flow free and easy.

Chapter Four
Spirits

When Mama Landry returned, she brought not one, but two plates of food with her and sat them down on the table. "Mama!" Georgia exclaimed, looking up at her. "There's no way I can eat all that!"

"Course ya can't, chil'! My goodness, ya ain't a mountain lion." Georgia choked on the coffee she was drinking and looked at Mama Landry, almost wondering if she knew something about Georgia's alternate existence, but put it out of her mind as the woman lowered herself into the booth across from her. "It's gettin' late an' I ain't had my suppa yet, so I thought I'd make a little extra an' join ya fo' jussa bit, if ya don't mind o' course."

"Oh, no, not at all!" Georgia smiled. "I'd love you to join me. If you haven't eaten yet, it sounds like your boss is a bit of a terror too. How *do* you deal with it?" They both laughed softly and started in on their food. The first bite of chicken was like heaven on her tongue and she sighed as she settled in to her meal. She had been right, the food was amazing and she tried to force herself to slow down and enjoy it. They ate in silence for a while before Mama Landry spoke.

"So Miss Georgia, how ya doin' these days? Ya seem ta have settled inta a nice rhythm at tha store, but it seems like ya always there. Don't ya do nothin' but work an' sleep?"

"Of course, I do," Georgia answered. "I come here and see you a few times a week, don't I?"

"That's true enough, an I'm sho glad ya do 'cause lawd knows ya need ta eat. But ya know what Mama means. Somethin' else gotta occupy ya time or ya gonna burn yaseff right out."

Georgia looked at her and smiled. With anyone else, this line of questioning might put her on the defense, but things had been feeling a little better with her today and plus, she could never accuse Mama Landry of anything but caring.

"I do know what you mean. And you're right. Ryan said the same thing to me today actually. He forbade me from doing more than an hour of overtime this week and said I need to go find something else to occupy my time." She pushed her notebook to the center of the table. "I've actually been working on expanding a bedtime story my mom used to tell me. It feels good to have a part of her still here. Jordan was the one who thought of it so… yeah."

She trailed off and looked back down at her food, moving her mashed potatoes around on her plate but not eating any of them. It was the first time in months she had been the first to bring up Jordan's name and, while it didn't hurt as much as it used to, it was still an uncomfortable feeling. She had a feeling it would open a dialogue she wasn't sure she was ready for.

"Well, Miss Jordan had a good idea then. Souns like a lovely way ta remember ya mama. What's tha story 'bout?"

"Oh, you know, just magic, royal families, life, death, conflict, that sort of thing."

"Well, that soun's a lot like real life, don' it? Ya mama must'a been getting ya ready fo' tha real world, wasn't she? She was a great woman, ya mama. Was always a sweet chil' an' a good woman. I 'member when she moved away it was so sad. Lotta folks missed her somethin' awful. It's hard losin' a ray a sunshine in tha storm o' life. But she needed ta go. And when she came back with ya, it was like things came full circle. Ya just as pleasant an' wondaful as she was, ya know?

Georgia filled with relief that the line of conversation hadn't gone in a negative direction. Hearing about her mom had always been comforting to her and, while it was a little odd that Mama Landry thought magic and royal families was preparing her for real life, she thought it was probably more the life and death and conflict parts of the story she had been referring to.

"Thanks, Mama. That means a lot. I miss her, but I do feel like she's close to me when I write. I hope she'd be happy with the choices I'm making. I just wish she was still around to talk to."

"Oh honey, she is! Goodness, chil', the ones we love don' eva really leave us. Ya go right on 'head an' talk ta her; she can hear ya. Ya tell her anythin' an' everythin' that's on ya mind. An' if ya need someone ya can look at while ya talkin' to her, Mama Landry's always here with a spare ear an' shoulda any time ya need, no judgement an' no unsolicited advice if ya ain't askin' fo' it. An' I'm sure Mr. and Mrs. Maren'd say tha same thin'. We all jus love ya to pieces, suga." She smiled warmly and Georgia smiled back.

"I know. And I love you all too. I may just take you up on that some time. I haven't been in the mood to talk for a while, but recently I've been thinking it's probably necessary to the healing process. Whether I think I'm ready to or not, it needs to happen soon."

"It sure 'nuff does," Mama Landry agreed. "An' while ya doin' ya talkin' to whoeva it is that needs talkin' to, ya might wanna talk ta Miss Jordan and Mr. Sawyer while ya at it."

Georgia's head snapped up from the chicken she was about to bite into.

"They ain't gone neitha, ya know. They spirits're still close. I feel 'em all tha time. They can hear ya too, an' ya may need ta jus' get some things outta ya system ta set it all right in tha world."

Georgia nodded but didn't say anything. The look in Mama Landry's eyes as she was talking about Jordan and Sawyer's spirits had been too knowing. Realistically, she knew Mama Landry had to have been talking about remembering them and feeling like they were still around in spirit, not reality. But something about the way she had looked at her and the tone in her voice made her question if she may know more than she let on. Georgia decided to prod a little further.

"Mama, do you really think people's spirits stay around even after they pass away? Or is it something we make ourselves believe just to make it feel like they are nearer to comfort ourselves?

"Oh no, suga, they still here. When I was a lil girl, my mama always told me tha ones we love neva really leave us.

They spirits're all 'round, guidin' us, givin' us gentle pushes in tha directions we need ta go. Think 'bout it; haven' ya eva' been at a loss fo' what ta do an' ya think 'bout what ya mama would do? That's her givin' ya a little nudge. An' it's most always gonna lead ya right."

"I suppose so," Georgia agreed, feeling a little better. It seemed obvious Mama Landry was thinking about the memory of people more than their actual current presence in the world. "I guess the memory of how people acted and how they taught us how to act does have a lot to do with how we live, doesn't it?"

"Sure do. 'Course, then there's tha spirits o' people that ain't with us no more, but ain't really gone neither."

Georgia held completely still, waiting for Mama Landry to continue. For a few long moments, they seemed to be waiting each other out, seeing who would speak first.

"Well... how can someone be gone but not really gone, Mama?" Georgia finally asked cautiously.

"There's all kindsa gone, honey," Mama Landry responded. "I dunno if it's a great subject for us ta-night, though. Things still raw in ya heart an' I don' wanna eva be tha one who makes ya sad or upsets ya. I stayed away from tha topic on purpose. I don' wanna cause ya no more pain than ya already had ta bear."

"It's fine, really. I feel ok talking about it with you." She saw the look of doubt on Mama Landry's face and she added, "I promise, I'll let you know if I get too sad and we can stop."

Mama Landry pushed her plate to the side and leaned forward over the table. There was no one else in the dining room of the restaurant anymore, but it was as if she didn't want anyone to hear what she was about to say. Reflexively, Georgia leaned in as well.

"I know everyone's sayin' Miss Joran an' Mr. Sawyer was killed in a accident out in them woods last December. But it ain't neva felt right. It don' feel like they gone at all. I still feel like Miss Jordan's right here an' even like I might see her if I turn 'round quick enough. Course, I neva' do. Same with Mr. Sawyer. I sometimes think they still out there an' they just stayin' away 'cause…" she trailed off.

"Why?" Georgia encouraged, leaning so far forward the table top was pressing into her ribs. "If they were still alive, why would they stay away?"

"Well, I don' know fo' sure," Mama conceded, leaning back. "But maybe they got somethin' they need ta do an' they don' wanna involve no one else. Or maybe they lookin' fo' somethin'. Could be lotsa reasons keepin' 'em away. But I jus' don' feel like they gone, Miss Georgia. I hope that don' give ya some kinda false hope they'll be walkin' inta town again at some point," she continued on, seeing the interest in Georgia's face. "Somethin' tells me they ain't comin' back neither. I just don' think they's dead. Not completely."

"Not completely?" Georgia asked, truly incredulous at how close to reality Mama Landry was treading.

"Not completely. They might be gone fo' good from our lives an' we'll neva see them again, but I think they gotta be out there some otha way. I get a feelin' when people die. I feel like they left us an' there's a sense a closure. But I don't feel like that with them two. It ain't tha same is all." She seemed to come out of a deep thought then. She looked at Georgia's face. "I hope I ain't scared ya with this talk. It's just tha ramblin's of a spiritual old woman, Miss Georgia."

"You haven't scared me at all. In fact, I'm kind of inclined to agree with you. It doesn't feel like they're gone to me either. I guess maybe that's why it's been so hard to be around people who are mourning them. I am sad they aren't around anymore, but it feels like I don't feel as bad as I should; as bad as others do. It makes me feel guilty. And I feel like they see me and it just reminds them of what they don't have." Her eyes threatened to tear up again, but she took a deep breath and bit into the roll that had come with her plate.

"Ya talkin' 'bout Mr. an Mrs. Maren, aren't ya?" Mama Landry asked. When she got no argument from Georgia, she continued on. "Chil', them folks love ya jus' like ya was one-a they own. They may be sad 'bout Miss Jordan, but havin' ya there can only help them. Gives them a purpose, ya know? They be focusin' on ya and it lets 'em get outta they own heads a bit. Ya doing nothin' but good bein' there fo' them, be sure-a that."

A new kind of guilt spread through Georgia. Was that true? Were the Marens actually more upset that she wasn't around instead of being upset when she was around? Was she making things worse for them by distancing herself from them? Were they lonelier because of it? She had been trying to make things better for them, but now she worried she was just compounding the issue.

"Ya know," Mama Landry said in a lighter tone. "I always get a feelin' like Miss Jordan's near when I'm lookin' out my back winda doin' my dishes. I just stare off inta them woods and it's almost like she's sittin' with me while I'm washin'. It's strange, but maybe them woods is where them two's spirits decided ta hang 'round. Tha three-a ya spent some time in them woods not long ago, ain't that right? Ya been back there since?"

Georgia shook her head, but didn't trust herself to speak. Even when being interrogated by the police or listening to the sounds of Judy's sobs coming from the living room after she had told Jordan's parents she had been killed in the woods, she had never so badly wanted to tell someone that Jordan and Sawyer really were in the woods. They weren't the same, but they were alive and cognizant that people were missing them. She hadn't thought about it much, but she knew they had to be missing people too.

"Well, maybe that's what ya need ta be doin'," Mama Landry said as she stood up and grabbed their mostly empty plates. "Weatha's getting' betta these days. Get yaseff on out there an' commune with nature an' whateva else might be out there. Maybe that's where ya healin' lies."

As she walked away, Georgia slid her notebook back in front of her and flipped to the last page she had written. Her pen paused over the empty space where the next word would go, but she didn't write. After a minute, she let out a sigh, closed her notebook, and gathered up her things. She wrote a quick thank you and see you later note on the back of the receipt, tossed down enough money to cover the bill with enough extra to make Mama Landry chastise her the next time she came in, and walked out the door to her car.

It was early enough still that she decided to make one more stop for the evening. She felt like she was dangerously close to opening a can of worms with all the discussions she'd had that day, but while she was in a talking mood, she decided she might as well pay Augustus Toole another visit.

Chapter Five
Auggie's Stories

Georgia parked her car in front of Auggie's farmhouse and turned off the ignition. Even when she had a good reason to be there like tonight, she always felt awkward and nervous going to see him. He had never been outwardly mean to her, but in the past he'd made it clear visitors weren't his favorite thing. Still, she needed to get this out of the way or she would always have questions in the back of her mind. She sat up straight, grabbed the bag with Auggie's books, and got out of her car.

The front door opened before she even had a chance to knock.

"Heard you pull up. Figured I'd meet you out here. What can I do for you?" Auggie was dressed in dirty farm clothes. He looked like he hadn't shaved in weeks and may not have bathed in as long. Georgia did her best not to stare at him opened mouthed and held the books out in front of her.

"Hi, Mr. Toole. I saw some books you ordered had come in today and, since you prepaid, I thought I'd bring them to you so you don't have to make a trip into town to pick them up."

Auggie took the package and opened it. He turned the books over and read the backs. Georgia stood there, not entirely sure what she should be doing, but she was there now and wasn't going to leave until she had at least tried to have a conversation with him. Finally, he looked up from the books. "Well, that was right nice of you. Much appreciated."

"Oh, it's no problem. You aren't out of my way at all heading home, so it's the least I could do."

"Well, thanks again. You have a good evening," Auggie said taking a step back into his house and reaching to close the door.

"Wait, Mr. Toole!" Georgia said, reaching forward to put her hand on the door before he could shut it. "I'm sorry, but I was wondering if you had a few minutes to talk."

Auggie looked wary, but opened the door a bit wider and stepped to the side. "I suppose I can spare a few minutes. Come on in if you want. I'll grab some glasses of water."

"Thank you, Mr. Toole," Georgia said, stepping inside and closing the door behind her.

"That's enough of that Mr. Toole business," she heard Auggie grumble from the kitchen. The sound of glasses being taken from a cabinet and water running reached her ears. He came back in to what appeared to be the living room and handed her one of the glasses. "Might as well just call me Auggie like everyone else. Go on and have a seat. What is it you need to talk about?"

Georgia sat and considered a moment before she spoke. Just jumping into a conversation about his book choices seemed a little aggressive and she didn't want to press the good luck she seemed to be having. She took a drink of water and turned a bit to face Auggie directly. "I was wondering if you could tell me what you think about these wild animal sightings. I spoke to Ryan today and he said it had happened before when he was little, but he couldn't remember much about it. Just that there was a cull hunt and the sightings seemed to stop after that."

Auggie nodded. "Not much more to the story than that, I don't think. After that poor little girl got hurt, people weren't taking any chances of letting anything come close to town again. People shot quite a few animals on their land. Bears, wolves, foxes, mountain lions. I shot a bear myself. His skin is the rug in my sitting room. Anyway, the hunt seemed to work since there were hardly any sightings after that."

"Why do you think there are so many again lately?" Georgia said, urging him to continue.

He looked at his water glass and didn't answer for a beat. Then he replied quietly, "Oh, I don't know. Population boom again, I reckon." He took a drink of his water and Georgia didn't believe for a second he thought that was the reason.

"Oh, yeah. I guess that could be why," Georgia said, playing along. "I mean, what else could it be, right?"

"Right," Auggie said, eyeing her suspiciously. "Is that all you wanted to talk about, Miss? Animal sightings from forty years ago and now again?"

Georgia set her glass down and leaned forward. "I saw one of the books you ordered was about artillery. I thought maybe you were worried about the sightings as well. Maybe you were preparing for another cull?"

"Artillery is something I've always been interested in. I figured I'd look at some of the historical artillery is all."

"And the magic?" Georgia asked. "Another interest? Maybe a hobby?"

"What is it you're getting at exactly?" Auggie asked gruffly, setting his glass down as well.

"Before Jordan and Sawyer disappeared, you said a lot of things about the mill; a lot of things about what went on there. None of it was good. I was wondering if you were planning on defending yourself and the town against bears in the woods, or if you were thinking there might be other things out there to defend against. If you have a feeling about anything like that, I'd love to hear your insights as it could potentially save a few lives other than your own."

Georgia could hardly believe her words as they tumbled out of her mouth. She hadn't intended to lay everything on the table quite so bluntly, and yet, there it was. Now, all she could do was wait to see if he had anything to say about it, or if she was going to be kicked out of his house.

Auggie looked at her for what seemed like an eternity. She wasn't going to be the first to move or speak this time. She held still and kept eye contact, not even daring to blink, although her eyes were starting to dry out. Finally, he leaned back in his chair and picked up a pipe he had sitting on the end table next to him. He took his time lighting it, and shook out the match when he was done, setting it in an ashtray.

"There's a lot of things you don't know about this town, girlie. Things you shouldn't want to know about." He took a pull from the pipe, exhaled, and eyed her through the cloud between them.

"That might be true," Georgia conceded. "But there are a lot of things I do know about this town, Auggie. And if some of the things I know could help you, and some of the things you know could help me, maybe we should be sharing these things with each other instead of keeping them to ourselves, wouldn't you agree?"

Auggie let out a soft grunt and gave a small nod. "That may be so, Missy. But I doubt there's much either one of us can do about any of it."

"Probably not on our own," Georgia agreed. "But we won't know for sure until we have all the facts."

"Ah, well facts are hard to come by. Notions, guesses, gut feelings, theories… that's all I've been working with for a lot of years."

"Those are good places to start. Especially if you have some sort of evidence that lead you to them. Why don't you just start from the beginning and tell me what you know, what you think, and what it means to you, and then I'll do the same?" She sat back and waited.

Auggie puffed on his pipe a few times and shifted slightly in his chair. "Well, you know some of it already. I told you before, when I worked at the mill all those years ago, people would disappear. If anyone thought something seemed odd or sounded off, we all knew better than to talk about it or question it. Sometimes the family members of the missing workers, folks who didn't even work in the mill, would disappear as well. Those were explained away as relocations to other parts of town where they still worked for the mill; cabins in the woods, a town down by the ravine they said. Generally, it was places folks don't normally go because it's barren and isolated, but since everyone in this town seems to think the mill's a great place that takes care of their workers, they believed the stories that claimed the mill gave the relocated people all the provisions they needed to survive there.

Feelings about the mill were much different from the inside than they were in the town. Once inside the mill, it was all fear and subservience. Flying under the radar seemed to be the name of the game. If you were too productive, you disappeared. If you were insubordinate, you disappeared. The way the disappearances were explained inside the mill versus to the town often didn't match up, but no one from the mill ever contradicted the stories told to the townsfolk. They all feared what would happen to them if they spoke against the heads of the mill."

"How long did this go on?" Georgia couldn't help but ask. "And were any of the people who disappeared ever seen again? Jordan always told me no one ever left this town. It sounds like a lot of people left the town!"

"That's a lot of questions, Missy," Auggie said, holding up a hand. "As far as how long it went on, I don't know that it ever stopped. When I retired, I signed a piece of paper saying I wouldn't discuss the inner workings of the mill with anyone that didn't work there. Until very recently, I kept that promise. At ninety-two years old, I really don't know that I have much time left, so what are they going to do to me, eh?" The side of his mouth twitched in what Georgia had to assume was the closest thing to a smile he was capable of. She smiled back, and shook her head. "Anyway, they gave me a lump sum as my retirement instead of those fancy pension plans you hear about people getting in the big cities. It was enough for me to live on, and since I like to stay busy, I used some of it to update this farm. I've worked here ever since.

To answer your second question, on very rare occasions, one of the people who disappeared would be seen in town here and there, but they seemed… changed. They were antisocial… jumpy… cold. They did whatever business they had and then moved on again. The few times I remember seeing people I'd worked with, they either came back to get their family, or they traded in vehicles or equipment of some kind for an upgrade. But more often than not, once someone disappeared, they weren't seen again.

And lastly, your friend Jordan wasn't entirely wrong about people never leaving. The people who weren't seen around town anymore were still thought to be living in town, just in areas no one ever went. We were told they were still around, but being taken care of by the mill. No one ever heard anything about them leaving the area. I guess that means her story checks out in most respects."

"Ok, but… if people who worked there before you and with you disappeared…" Auggie raised one eyebrow at her questioningly as she paused. "Well, I mean… not everyone lives to be ninety-two, Auggie. Wouldn't it have seemed strange that there were all these people who were supposed to be living in other parts of the town, but none of them ever died? That there were never any deaths of any kind? Old age? Sickness? Accidents?"

"Oh, there were plenty reports of deaths. It was explained to everyone that it didn't make much sense to take the effort of transporting them back to town, so they were said to be buried in a cemetery near where they lived and a small memorial service would be held here in town for them so people could gather to pay their last respects and what have you."

Georgia sat back. "Huh," she said after a minute of thought. "I guess they kind of have that all tied up in a neat little bow, don't they? If you have people on the inside so scared that they'll go along with any story, no one on the outside is going to have much of a chance to suspect anything shady going on, are they?"

"Nope," Auggie agreed, knocking the burnt tobacco out of his pipe and taking a fresh pinch from a pouch on the end table. "Far as I know, only a few people ever suspected anything, but it wouldn't serve anyone well to raise much of a ruckus about any of it."

"I know this probably sounds random and off topic, but you said you saw a well in the mill offices when you trained. You also said people were taken there when it was time to be replaced, isn't that right?" Georgia asked. Auggie nodded. "Do you have any idea what the well was all about or why it was there?"

Auggie looked confused at the question. "I don't, no," he said, and she believed him. "It's probably been there since the mill was built. Maybe even before. I reckon if they use it at all anymore, they pull buckets of water to clean. The mill has running water, so there'd be no real reason to have a well system, too. Why do you ask?"

Georgia paused before she answered. "Well, I guess my questions about the well fit in to part of *my* story about the strange things about this town. Before I go into it, though, is there anything else you want to tell me? Anything that might be pertinent to the conversations we are or will be having?"

The old man leaned his head back and looked at the ceiling, puffing on his pipe. "I don't know that it really matters, but talking about the article in the paper earlier and talking about this sketchy business with the mill just now made me think of something. Looking back, it was about the time when there was a large rush of turnover in the mill, people getting transferred and promoted and lots of new workers coming in, that the last cull hunt ended up happening. I remember thinking it was odd so much activity was happening at once.

Some people speculated the men who moved to other parts of town must've been doing some secret hunting on their own, and maybe even some of the boys who were being hired so that, when everyone left or got busy working in the mill, the secret hunting stopped and the animal population rose quickly. It never sounded quite right to me, though. I don't remember any of those men having much time to do any hunting. When you worked at the mill, it kept you plenty busy and when you got home it was time to rest up to do it all again. As for the boys, I guess they could've hunted some to put food on the table, but most of them boys were fresh out of school. I don't think they'd have had much spare time to do the amount of hunting it would've taken to keep the population in control."

Georgia's heart rate amped up as she put some pieces together. There were still more questions than answers at this point, but a few things were starting to make sense. Auggie seemed to pick up on the change in energy, because his eyebrows raised a notch.

"I think our having this talk tonight was a very good idea," Georgia said, excitedly. "Between the things you've said and the things I have to say, we might be able to get a little bit better of an idea of what we could be dealing with.

Chapter Six
Magic

"Why don't you go ahead and start your stories then, Missy. Let's see what you've got to say." Auggie said, a note of interest in his gruff voice.

"I'd like to know one more thing before I start in on my list," Georgia said. "Why did you check out a book about magic?" Auggie seemed a little uncomfortable at the question and Georgia tried to dial down the interrogative energy. "There isn't anything you can say that would make me judge," she said softly. "I think we're beyond that at this point, don't you?"

Auggie took a deep pull on his pipe and as he spoke, the smoke escaped his nose and mouth like an old dragon. "There are a lot of things in this world I can't explain, missy; not even after over ninety years of searching for answers. Sometimes when there's no logical explanation, the illogical is the logical step."

Georgia had never felt closer to the surly man sitting across from her as she did in this moment. "I couldn't agree more. And actually, hearing you say that makes what I have to say a lot easier. I just hope your mind is still as open to all of this when I get going." She laughed lightly.

"I'm not here to judge, either. Remember; we're past that," Auggie paraphrased her words back to her. She nodded, folder her legs under her so she was comfortable, and took a deep, steadying breath.

"I really don't know the best place to begin with what needs to be told, but I'll start with what applies to the things you've told me. Magic, or at least magic in the loosest definition of 'a way to explain things that can't be explained any other way', *does* exist." Auggie's eyes widened perceptively at this statement.

"Does it now?" he whispered.

Georgia swallowed, nodded, and continued. "Jordan and I have experienced it first-hand. Information we've gathered from other rather reliable sources has lead us to believe that this town is basically a hot bed of magic. We believe one of the main players in a potential magical war is somehow linked to the mill and the suspicious activities that go on there. We think the well is a significant tool in his arsenal."

Auggie looked at Georgia, dumbfounded. She paused in her story while he processed the information he'd just heard. She hoped he was able to accept or at least absorb what she'd just told him because it was about to get even more intense. Finally, he whispered, "What have you seen?"

"You believe me, then?" Georgia asked, incredulously. "You don't think I'm insane?"

"I don't know what to believe, but what you've said makes as much sense, if not more, than anything I've heard in ninety-two years. Besides, I figure if we're beyond judging each other, we're probably beyond lying to each other."

Georgia's eyes shone, but she kept the tears harnessed. She didn't think becoming overly emotional would help her cause at this particular moment. "You're right about that," she agreed. "Jordan and I haven't just seen magic, Auggie. We've experienced it."

And she gave a brief recount of her and Jordan's history; Jordan's first transformation, her own childhood learning to control it, and how they both thought they were the only ones in the whole world who could do it, until they met each other, and then Christian and Victoria. She then touched quickly on Sawyer's discovery of their abilities and how his love for Jordan allowed him to accept them and eventually join in their hunt for answers about what had been going on in the town. Finally, she relayed the events of the awful evening in the woods, trying not to go into too much detail. Auggie was Sawyer's grandfather after all and she didn't want to cause him more pain than was necessary.

"So you see," Georgia finished, "Sawyer and Jordan aren't actually dead. But they aren't able to come back. We came up with the story I told you and everyone else in town to keep them safe in the woods and so no one would go looking for them and stumble across something potentially even more dangerous. And in the meantime, we still have to try to find out more details about what's going on in the mill, who the main players are, and what we can do to potentially stop this once and for all."

As she watched the man's face, she worried she may have just unloaded too much information on him. He seemed to be overwhelmed with thoughts and he hadn't spoken or reacted the entire time she'd been speaking, except to puff more or less furiously on his pipe, depending on the tension level in her story. When she was about to ask him if he was ok, Auggie suddenly stood up. "I need a drink. Can I get you some more water?"

"Um, sure. Yeah. More water would be good I guess." She was completely thrown by the direction the conversation had taken. She'd been prepared for disbelief, any number of questions, even anger at not being told about all of this before and being lied to about his grandson. But to not say anything about it at all and completely change the direction of the conversation towards beverages was not something she had prepared for. "Auggie, you heard everything I said right?" she asked, grabbing her still-full glass of water, getting up, and following him into the kitchen where he was pouring himself what appeared to be about three fingers of whiskey.

"Oh, I heard you fine," he tossed back the amber colored liquid, blew out a loud breath, and poured another three fingers. "I'm just trying to sort through it all and a stiff drink tends to calm the nerves and lets me focus."

Georgia couldn't help thinking alcohol didn't usually have the greatest effects on focus with most people, but she couldn't blame him after all the information he'd just taken in. She set the glass of water down on the small table and pulled out a chair to sit. Auggie didn't chug the next drink. He stood, leaning against the drink cart that was along the wall in the kitchen. Georgia sat, looking at the table. She didn't want to rush him. She felt lucky he was listening to her at all. She was surprised how cathartic it was to talk about all of this again. It had been months since she'd done more than just thought about it, and the momentum was hard to control. Still, out of deference to Auggie's sanity, she waited.

His drink still in hand, Auggie walked over and sat at the table across from her. They were much closer at the table than they had been in the living room. She could see the deep lines in his face and the amount of grey in his hair, but even so, he didn't seem anywhere near ninety-two years old. There was still a lot of life in him; a drive, a purpose. She found herself liking him despite the many traits that seemed to repel a lot of people in the town; his surly nature, his gruff countenance, his general solitary nature. Beyond all of that, however, he was just a man searching for answers, just like she and her friends were. "So," he finally spoke, looking into Georgia's eyes, "The boy's still alive."

Georgia smiled in spite of herself. "Yes," she said, nodding softly. "Sawyer's alive. He's with Jordan. It was the only way they could be together."

Auggie nodded, the lines at the edges of his mouth relaxing a bit. "He loved that girl, I could tell. You do whatever you can for the ones you love. I'm glad he found her; that they found each other." He took a sip of the whiskey and set it down. "Magic, huh?"

"Magic," Georgia repeated. "Old magic. Centuries old. And very likely linked to the mill and the well."

"I want to hear more about that well of theirs, but I need to ask you to do something for me before we keep on with this."

"Sure," Georgia said, bemused. "What do you need?"

"I need you to satisfy an old man's curiosity, if you would."

"Curiosity? Curiosity about what?"

"Well, I think I'd like to see some proof of this magic, Missy. I'd like to see the shapeshifting in person, if I could. It'd be easier to move on if I didn't have any of this skepticism left in me."

Georgia's stomach clenched in a knot. She should've expected this. She couldn't blame his curiosity, and the "prove it" mentality would probably have been one she operated under as well in similar circumstances. There was really no reason not to show him, other than a slight fear of giving him a heart attack. He may not seem as old as he was, but numbers didn't lie. There was also the fact that she hadn't transformed since leaving the woods that night. Over two months was a long time to go without visiting her other form, and yet she wasn't really worried about being able to. Ignoring it hadn't made the cool sensation that was so strongly present the last few months any weaker; any less close to the surface. She looked at him.

"Are you sure you want to see this?" she asked.

"No, not at all," he replied. "But I think it's something that needs to happen." Georgia stood and walked to the other end of the kitchen where it was more open. "Now hang on, Missy. You're doing it here? Inside?"

She looked around. "It's as good a place as any. No one else will see if we do it in here. It won't wreck anything, and I promise I'm housebroken." She couldn't help trying to lighten the mood. Things were already serious enough.

At that, Auggie gave her a genuine smile, the first she had ever seen from him, downed the rest of his whiskey, and rubbed his hands on his thighs.

"Alright, then," he said. "What do you need me to do?"

"I just need you to watch and not panic," Georgia answered. She sat on the ground to make the transformation seem less intense; going from a five-feet-seven-inch biped to a three-feet tall quadruped would be lot of movement. If she was on the ground already, she'd just change shape, not as much in height.

"Now, when it's done, I'll still understand whatever you say, but I won't be able to talk back; at least not in a way you'll understand. Talk through whatever you need to. You can touch me if you're comfortable. It's completely safe. I'll be in the same mind, just another form. Are you ready?"

Auggie nodded. Georgia closed her eyes and reached into the cool place inside of her, letting it spread out through the rest of her body. She was surprised how easily her body shifted into the form she had avoided for so long; almost as if she had subconsciously missed it. Once she felt herself settle onto all four paws, she stretched and opened her eyes.

Auggie was stock still except for his chest rising and falling and his fists clenching, so there didn't seem to be any signs of the heart attack she feared. She assumed a submissive position and laid on the floor, her furry bobcat's face over one of her paws. Her tail swayed back and forth lazily. She made a rattling sound in her chest similar to the purr of a house cat, if that housecat was over twenty pounds. Finally, Auggie leaned forward ever so slightly and squinted his eyes. Georgia lifted her head a few inches off the floor and looked back.

"Your eyes," he whispered. "They're the same. If I saw you from much further away I wouldn't know any better. I'd think you were wild. But the eyes give it away."

He leaned forward and, with an ease of movement she wouldn't have expected from such an old man, he slid off the chair and knelt onto one knee. He reached out to touch her shoulder. She didn't move at all as he stroked her fur. He reached down and touched then lifted one of her paws. The thick claws remained seated where they usually were. He pushed toes to the side and felt them. Finally, he sat back on the floor and continued looking at her.

"It still feels like you're here. Maybe that's why I never really believed Sawyer was gone. If he's an animal, he's still around. Do you think that's it?" She looked at him and he nodded his head gently. "Right, you can't talk to me like this." He stood and sat back on the chair. "You want to come back now, Missy?"

Georgia pushed up onto her haunches and closed her eyes again. She felt her limbs stretching and the fur retracting back into her skin. When all that was left of the cold feeling was in her core again, she opened her eyes. Auggie's soft smile greeted her and she smiled back.

"Yes," she said, standing slowly and walking back to the table. "I think that's exactly why it still feeling like he's here. And I'm willing to bet he's been coming close to check on you now and then. I think they all are."

"The sightings," Auggie stated, comprehension setting in. Georgia nodded. Auggie slapped his thigh. "So that's what all the sightings have been about. It's not a lot of animals.

It's the same ones over and over. Those youngsters are checking in on us."

"I think they are. And it makes me wonder if that was the case all those years ago. So many people were disappearing and then all of a sudden the animals were appearing. I'm willing to bet it was the same people who were disappearing that were coming back as animals, whether to check in on loved ones, or to scout out new recruits."

"How do you reckon this Edmund fella' is changing the workers?" Auggie asked.

"The well," Georgia answered. "The water from the pond that's keeping Victoria alive is the same water that changed Jordan all those years ago. And we think that pond's connected by an underwater spring to the well in the mill."

"I'll be damned. It's no wonder they never took that thing out. It makes sense now."

"Auggie," Georgia said, reaching across the table for his hand. "I really need to know everything you can tell me about who ran the mill back then. Knowing how it worked in the past might help us to figure out how it is running now; maybe even who is running things now. Can you help us?"

Georgia realize she was speaking as if there was already a plan in place, even though they hadn't discussed anything about a plan beyond the story to tell their families and the town. They would be discussing it eventually though, and if Auggie believed he was helping his grandson as well as her, he may be more inclined to share more and help.

Auggie squeezed her hand quickly then let it go. "There isn't much to tell I'm afraid, but I'll tell you what I do remember. Let's go back in the other room where it's more comfortable."

Chapter Seven
Shared Knowledge

"The thing you have to understand, Missy," Auggie said, settling himself back into his chair, "is that we never got to meet the people in charge. We dealt with the supervisors on our shift, and that was about it. When we got hired we met the hiring manager. They told us about the job we would do. Then we met the trainers and they taught us what to do. After that, we were pretty much on our own. The shift supervisors kept an eye on things and it was them we talked to if an issue came up."

"Right. And can you tell me again just what they told you about the people who left and never came back?" Georgia asked.

"They'd tell us they were either promoted or reassigned to a different position that was more suited to their strengths. There were a few locations they discussed. Out by the ravine Northeast of here was the location they talked about most. There's a town they built out there specifically for the workers of those jobs. Apparently, the workers who were supposed to be working at that town were relocated out there and provided a place to live free of charge. The only thing they had to pay was utilities and for their food, as well as any entertainment they wanted. They even had a doctor in the town specifically for those people. I assume they were allowed to move their whole family out there, since the family members would usually disappear as well; mostly none of them were ever seen again. Seems like it'd be hard to turn down free lodging for the whole family."

"It sure would. Sounds like an incredible deal," Georgia said.

"That's part of how they got people to excel at their jobs. The idea of a free house would appeal to a lot of people. Of course, never coming back to town was a deterrent for some as well. Myself, I never much wanted to live anywhere but here, so I did the job that was asked of me, but I never gave more effort than I needed, so I was passed over for promotions and transfers, which was fine by me. There were, of course, the people who got hired on and couldn't cut it. Those people they either let go or had them come back to work somewhere in town or..." He paused here, the creases in his brow deepening. "Well, now, I don't really know what happened to the people who couldn't cut it but ended up disappearing anyway. It doesn't give me a good feeling; I can tell you that. But some of the slackers were said to have been relocated somewhere else they could possibly be more successful, and we never saw them again either."

"I agree, that doesn't sound good." Georgia said.

"Nope," Auggie said, shaking his head. "And those were the majority of the times the other workers in the mill were told not to talk to the town about anyone going missing. Whatever story the mill came up with, we just went along with it. It's also why no one wanted to get into too much trouble in the mill. You never knew if you'd be the lucky one they'd let go back to town, or if you'd end up who knows where doing who knows what."

"That would be terrifying," Georgia agreed.

"Anyway, when I got too old to do the job well, they offered me my severance and I took it. Before I got it though, they took me back to that room with the well and told me that, in order to keep my severance, I had to sign an agreement promising complete discretion about anything having to do with the mill. If I spoke to anyone about the things I saw or heard inside, I'd be expected to pay back the money and, if I couldn't, I'd be put to another use in order to pay it back. I didn't want anything more to do with them, so I signed the agreement. Until now, I kept my word, and I haven't heard from them since."

"I'm sorry to have made you break your word, but I hope you know how much I appreciate your sharing this with me. I think it'll be extremely helpful," Georgia said earnestly.

"It's not a problem, Missy. Like I said, I'm old enough now I wouldn't be any use to them for anything. And from what you told me, it sounds like there's something far worse than I ever expected going on in that place. It needs to stop. Families have been torn apart by that mill long enough."

"Auggie, can you tell me any names of the supervisors? Any names of people in a higher position at the mill? It would be a great place for us to start our investigation."

"Most of the people in charge didn't live in town. I'd never met or even seen any of them before I started working at the mill. I do remember Dale Neff's daddy and granddaddy were both supervisors, though. It didn't look like Dale was going to follow in their footsteps for a while since he got the job doing construction in town. He always liked woodworking and carpentry. But then he got hurt on the job and couldn't return to his line of work. It appears he did end up getting a job in the mill he could do even with his bum leg. So it seems like it runs in that family. Multiple generations worked in the mill. That's really the only name I know. I stopped working there a long time ago. I imagine it's almost an entirely new lot in there now."

"That name is a great place to start, Auggie. I really appreciate it!" Georgia said enthusiastically. "Between the town by the ravine and that family name, we have a few things to investigate. Maybe more will turn up when we do."

"I sure hope they do. You could check out the cars in the lot to see if you know who any of them belong to. That'd give you an idea of people you could try talking to. If they just started, they might not be scared enough yet and they'll still talk to you. That'd probably be your best bet at getting any current information about who's running things."

"That's such a great idea! Thank you!" Georgia pulled out her notebook and began scribbling a to-do list so she wouldn't forget anything.

"I need you to promise me something, Missy," Auggie said quietly and Georgia paused her writing to look up. "I need you to promise me you and your friends will be careful about who you talk to. The people at the mill aren't ones to be trifled with. It's a nasty organization and they don't take betrayal lightly. The second you go poking around, you're already in danger. Try to keep that danger to a necessary minimum, eh?"

She was touched with his concern for them. "We'll be careful, Auggie. I promise that. But you have to understand, if things are truly headed toward a war, things are going to get ugly no matter what we do."

"Oh, I know that," Auggie nodded. "But no reason to get to that point until absolutely necessary."

Georgia stood and put her notebook back in her bag. "That's true. You have my word."

Auggie stood as well and followed her to the door. He opened it for her and, as she stepped through, he grabbed the strap on her bag, stopping her short. "Why don't you go ahead and check in now and then? Let me know how things are going; how everyone's doing. And if you need anything else from me, I'm here."

Georgia decided to take the risk. She reached out and hugged him lightly. He stiffened, but didn't pull away. "Thank you," she whispered in his ear. "I promise I'll keep you up to date. And I'll try to send you messages now and then as well."

She let go of him and turned to walk to her car. As she got in and closed the door, she looked up and saw Auggie hadn't gone inside. He'd walked off the porch, around the side of the house, and was gazing into the woods beyond his property. She knew he was looking for a trace of Sawyer. She smiled and turned the engine over, backed out of the drive, and started home. Home, she thought. Yes, even with all the negative energy surrounding her the past few months, she was still lucky enough to have a place that felt like home.

Chapter Eight
The Meeting

Saturday evening at five o'clock Georgia was sitting cross-legged on her bed, looking through the to-do list again.

1. Go to mill lot and find who owns cars – possible new worker to talk to
2. Look into Neff family – see if any are still in town other than Dale
3. Ask Mama Landry if she's seen Dale Neff lately
4. Widen search of the woods to include ravine town to the Northeast

She chewed on the end of her pen as she considered the list. There was no way around it; she was going to have to go back into the woods, and soon. There was too much ground to cover for her to do everything alone, and since everyone thought Jordan and Sawyer were dead, plus no one knew Christian and Victoria even existed, she would be responsible for doing all the talking to people. That meant she needed Jordan, Sawyer, and Christian to do some scouting. She found herself wondering if they had found anything in the months she had been away. Before she could get too deep into her thoughts, however, she heard the oven timer go off. She had been smelling whatever amazing food Judy was cooking for the past hour, and her stomach rumbled.

"Georgia! Dinner's ready!" she heard Gordon call from the foot of the stairs.

She got up, opened her door, and called out, "Be down in a second!" She gathered up her bag and closed the door to her room behind her. She planned on biting the bullet and going to the woods right after supper and figured if she had everything with her, it would be less opportunity to talk herself out of it. She walked into the dining room and saw the table filled with food. Her eyes widened and she looked at Judy, who was setting a bowl of mashed potatoes in one of the last available spaces.

"Holy cow," Georgia exclaimed. "This is an amazing spread! Wasn't Thanksgiving a few months ago?"

Judy and Gordon laughed and Gordon pulled out a chair for Judy, pushed it in behind her, and pulled out a chair for Georgia. She sat, and he scooted her chair in as well before settling himself at the table. "No, but it's been too long since we've all sat down and had a meal together, so I believe Judy's trying to make up for two months' worth of meals."

They all laughed at this, and Georgia was relieved to feel almost no awkwardness. Jordan's chair was empty, but there was still laughter at the table. Before she could even let herself feel guilty, she reached out, grabbed the corn, spooned some onto her plate, and passed it to Judy.

"How's the store looking?" Gordon asked as he took the plate of ham and selected two pieces before handing it across to Georgia.

"Not too bad. Ryan and I decided we're going to pull less overtime now. We're going to clean during the slow times, and we're going to allow ourselves to have a life outside the store."

"I think that sounds wonderful," Judy said, handing the bowl of corn to Gordon. "You've been spending way too much time there. It was ok over the cold months, but it looks like the weather is breaking so you should be getting out more and having fun." She picked up her glass of water and took a drink.

"I think so too," Georgia agreed. "It's a really mild night tonight so I figured I'd go for a short walk through the woods and stretch my legs some after dinner."

Judy's glass banged loudly against her plate as she set it down quickly with a trembling hand. The sound made Georgia jump, and she looked at Judy's face. It had gone white as a sheet. She looked quickly across the table at Gordon who also looked a little pained, but reached over and grabbed Judy's hand, squeezing it.

"Um, Georgia, we know you loved spending time in those woods before, but given the events of this winter, I think it'd make us feel a lot better if you didn't go into them anymore. It is not the safest place to be these days. The paper even put out an article about the increase in wild animal sightings and advised everyone to stay out of them."

Georgia broke her eye contact with him and grabbed a roll out of the basket just to have something else to focus on. She should have thought of how they'd react to her wanting to go to the woods. She'd hadn't been thinking. Of course the idea of her going to the same place where Jordan and Sawyer were killed would terrify them. She looked up apologetically.

"You're right, I'm so sorry. I wasn't thinking. It's just natural for me to want to go there since I spent so much time there before. I'm sorry. Of course I'll stay away from the woods. I can find somewhere else to walk outside."

"During the daytime," Judy added, selecting a piece of ham from the plate for herself.

"Right," Georgia agreed. "During the daytime."

The rest of the supper passed pleasantly enough with them talking about neutral topics like how they had been spending their time and the gardening Judy wanted to do when the weather was nice enough. After supper, Georgia helped clean the table and put the dishes away after Gordon washed them. They all sat in front of the fireplace for a while afterward; Judy reading, Gordon doing a crossword puzzle and Georgia writing in her notebook. Finally, Judy and Gordon decided it was time for bed.

"You two go ahead. I'm going to write a little more. I'll take care of the fire and check the locks before I go to bed."

"Goodnight, sweetheart," Judy said, leaning down and brushing a kiss over her cheek. "It was great spending time with you tonight. I hope it happens more often."

"Me too," Georgia agreed. Gordon leaned over, kissed the top of her head, and smiled as he followed Judy up the stairs. Georgia heard their door shut and the sounds of them getting ready for bed. She stared into the fire, the familiar feeling of guilt creeping into her once again. She knew she had promised them to stay away from the woods, but they didn't know the truth about them. The only danger she was in was nothing they could know about, and she had to meet with her friends in order to put a plan in motion to try to stop that danger. She would wait until she was sure they were asleep, and then she would slip out.

*****

Georgia gently pressed her ear against the Marens' bedroom door. The rhythmic sounds of breathing were faintly audible and she sighed in relief. They had stayed up talking much later than usual, but it sounded like they were finally asleep. She had arranged her pillows under her comforter in case one of them woke up at some point and decided to pop their head in to check on her. Her bag and notebook were in her room where they always were when she was home. She raised her head in silent hope that they stayed asleep long enough for her to get back. She then carried her shoes down the stairs, making sure to stay to the far side of them so they wouldn't creak.

When she got to the front door, she put on her shoes and jacket. It was still a little cold at night, but she couldn't take her winter coat in case they came downstairs for some reason and saw it missing. She didn't plan to be in her human form for long anyway, and the cold didn't matter as much once she transformed. She pulled the door closed gently behind her until she heard it click, slipped put her keys under a rock by the front steps, and took off at a run toward the tree line.

She navigated the woods easily, as though no time had passed. As she arrived at the brush that lead to the clearing where she and Jordan had spent so much time and where the unfortunate events of December had happened, she paused. She still had time to turn around, she thought, although she was sure they would have heard her approach. Still, if she stayed in this form, she wouldn't have to hear them. She shook her head. It was time to do this. Too much had to be done and too much was at stake. They couldn't afford to wait any longer. She closed her eyes and felt her body transform as the cold washed over her and then disappeared. She opened her eyes. Through the brush, she could just make out the edge of the pond in the clearing. She slowly pushed through the bushes.

"Where the hell have you been!" a voice shrieked through the sound of a wolf howl. Georgia's back arched slightly as Jordan's hulking wolf form bounded from the far side of the pond toward her.

"Jordan, stop!" called a familiar voice as another wolf followed closely. Sawyer overtook Jordan and cut in front of her, forming a barrier between her and Georgia. "You need to calm down. We talked about this."

"Oh yeah, we've talked." Jordan growled. "For months, all we've done is talk. We've sat here, helpless, ignorant, unable to do anything or know anything about what's been going on in town. All while she was able to go wherever and do whatever she wanted because she had the freedom to do it! My parents lost their only daughter and I haven't been able to see them or see how they're doing, but she knows! Your ninety-two-year-old grandfather lost his grandson and is working his farm, essentially alone, and you haven't been able to know how he's coping, but she knows! There's a war approaching with enemy troops whose numbers are increasing at a rate of which we have no idea. And all this time, she's been in town, doing whatever she wants, working her job, and writing whatever she thinks is important at the time in that stupid notebook of hers, knowing full well we're stranded out here without any kind of bridge to the community without her. It's obvious she didn't care enough to come before now, so I'm *very* interested to know what it is she needs from us so badly that she had no alternative but to traipse back to us." Jordan tuned her head to Georgia. "Well?"

Georgia sat, frozen. She knew they would be upset, but she hadn't expected the explosion of anger and the shame she felt. She didn't blame Jordan for being angry, but she hadn't taken much time to think beyond her own anger. In fact, being yelled at was starting to bring back some of that anger. Sure, Jordan had every right to be mad. But making it sound like she had been having a comfortable little vacation in town while purposely leaving them in the dark was beyond unfair, not to mention inaccurate. She stood and took slow steps toward Jordan and Sawyer while speaking softly and praying her voice wouldn't shake.

"I've been in town doing whatever I want, have I?" She hissed. "I've been having an easy time of it, is that what you all think? You have no idea the position you put me in. I had to tell the people who love you most that you are *dead*! I had to watch your mom sob for weeks. I had to watch your dad try to comfort her while trying to keep himself together. I had to watch Auggie turn away from me and tell me to be careful because we don't need anyone else dying, while I knew full well a lot more people could be dying at any moment. I had to watch Ryan suffer intense guilt and regret. I had to watch this entire town mourn you both. I had to be practically eviscerated by the police during a two-hour interrogation because they couldn't find anyone else to question or blame for the whole thing. I've sat alone every night, alone in the room that's supposed to be *our* room, and think about all the people I had to emotionally destroy. There isn't a day that's gone by I haven't thought about you; all of you. And I'm sorry if you're mad, but I'm pretty damn mad myself, and that isn't going to go away in just a few weeks. You all expect a hell of a lot from me, but you can't expect that."

She stopped inches away from them. She was breathing deeply, but she felt better having gotten it out. They were all silent for a while, no one saying anything, no one moving. Finally, Sawyer stood up, leaned sideways to bump Jordan affectionately, and took a small step toward Georgia. They stared at each other for a moment, then Sawyer moved forward, pushing his shoulder and chest against hers, in the closest thing to a hug they could manage. Georgia paused for a second, then turned her head into his side, returning the sign of affection. She opened her eyes to see Jordan standing a foot away. Sawyer moved away, and Jordan took his place.

"I'm sorry," Jordan whispered in a soft whimper. "I know it has to have been hard on you, too." She leaned back and sat on her haunches. "But you have to understand what torture it was sitting here for so long and not knowing anything. Of course I know you didn't keep us in the dark on purpose. I shouldn't have said that. I was angry." She hung her head lower and eyed Georgia. "Please tell me how mom and dad are," she whispered.

Georgia took a minute to steady herself.

"They're devastated, Jordan. But they're healing. Everyone is. I tried staying away to give them some space; less of a reminder of the bad. But Mama Landry said maybe I should be there for them instead. We had supper for the first time in a long time tonight. It was nice. They're going to miss you forever, but you have to know you won't ever be forgotten."

Jordan heaved a deep breath. "I'm glad they have you. And Mama Landry's right. You need to be there for them. Thank you for doing that."

"How's Auggie holding up?" Sawyer asked from his seated position behind Jordan.

"He's doing really well, Sawyer," Georgia answered. "In fact, he and I spent a few hours talking together the other night."

"Really?" Sawyer asked, clearly surprised. "Hours? How did you manage to get him talking that much?"

"Well, that's kind of an interesting story. I have a few of them actually. But I feel like we should all be together for them. It pertains to all of us."

A loud rustling sound could be heard by the willow tree next to the pond. The hulking form of a bear appeared followed by a beautiful white swan in the water next to it. Georgia smiled to herself. "Christian. Victoria."

"It is nice to see you again… finally," Christian growled from deep in his throat. "We thought maybe you had decided to renege on our bargain."

"Not at all. After these past few months, I can honestly say I'm more motivated than ever to get everything taken care of and to possibly never have to worry about any of this again. I don't want to have to exist in dual worlds. I don't want to have to be the go between." She looked at Jordan and Sawyer. "I love you both, you know I do, and I would do anything for you. I think I've made that pretty clear. But it's too much to exist this way forever. You have each other, Christian and Victoria have each other. I really just want to exist in one world and try to make my way."

Jordan and Sawyer didn't say anything, but Christian responded. "That is understandable and more than reasonable."

Sawyer stood. "I know we haven't been friends for long, but it's hard to imagine never talking to you again. I always knew you'd come back here eventually, but if you aren't able to transform anymore…"

"Mama Landry said something the other day that I think you'll find interesting," Georgia interrupted. "She said there are different kinds of being gone, and that she doesn't believe you two are really dead. She says she has sensed you near her at times, especially when she's outside, almost like if she turned around fast enough, she'd see you out of the corner of her eye. Any idea why that might be?" she asked, wryly.

Jordan and Sawyer looked at each other but still remained silent. Christian let out a low chuckle. "It looks as though you have been caught," he said.

"You all have!" Georgia responded, exasperatedly. "Well, except Victoria. The newspaper printed an article saying there's been a drastic increase in the number of animal sightings near town the past few months. Big animals. Wolves and bears specifically." She looked at Christian. "None of you have been particularly stealthy it seems. They're talking about a cull hunt." Victoria flapped her wings in alarm and Christian swore. "Yeah, that's kind of what I thought when I found out what it was."

"They had one of those hunts a number of years ago," Christian growled softly. "Back when there was a recruiting inundation. There were many soldiers learning about their transition and they were not smart about it. They would come into town to see to their loved ones or to spy to get information. Finally, the town had enough. They were scared for their children and themselves. They ordered a free cull hunt. People could go wherever they wanted within reason and shoot any threatening animal they came across. Once a day, they would meet at the city hall building and record their numbers. No one ever made it into this clearing; I worked hard to keep them away, but I was shot twice for my efforts. A number of the soldiers were killed in the cull, and when the hunt was lifted, it seemed Edmund either slowed his recruiting, or took the time to teach his soldiers the dangers of going into town. I do not like the idea of having to defend against the townsfolk in addition to Edmund's forces."

"Hopefully if you all stay away from the edge of town, the sightings will stop and they won't go through with it. I'm sorry if you feel like I forced you to come looking for me, but I'm here now. And I promise to come back regularly. We have a lot of work to do." Georgia said.

"It wasn't just you they were looking after," Victoria interjected. "They checked on that nice Landry woman and Sawyer's grandfather as well."

"Yes, and about that," Georgia said uncertainly. "I have something to tell you about Auggie."

"You said he was ok, right?" Sawyer said, sounding worried.

"Oh yeah, he's fine. He's really good actually. But the other day an order he placed came in and the books were about artillery and magic." Sawyer's ears pricked and Jordan tilted her head. "Yeah, I was intrigued, too. So I decided it was time to go and see what I could get out of him. Turns out, with the right persuasion, he's a wealth of information."

Georgia relegated the tale of their conversation from the other night; all of the information he had told her about the mill and Mr. Neff's lineage.

"How in the world did you persuade him to give all of that information?" Jordan asked, stunned. "Even when we told him we thought Sawyer's life was in danger, he didn't give us that much to go on."

"Well, that's what I've been trying to figure out how to tell you. I know we said discretion was of the utmost importance, but..."

"You didn't!" Sawyer barked.

"I had to! You have to know I had to. He already suspected. He knew something was going on that couldn't be explained by logic and science. I started out just telling him about us; about what we could do. He believed me, but he told me he needed to see it firsthand so he wouldn't have any skepticism. It was important to him."

"God, Georgia, you showed him?!" Jordan exclaimed.

"I did," Georgia said, notching her chin up ever so slightly. "And I'm not sorry I did. He deserved to know. He gave me more information than all of us have gotten combined. He gave me a name to look into as well as an idea about how to find people to possibly interrogate about the internal workings of the mill. He's on our side. And you should have seen his face when he heard you were ok; that both of you were ok. When I left, he went outside and stared toward the woods, almost like he could sense you out there. It put him at peace."

Sawyer shook himself and Jordan sat again. "I guess it's nice to know he knows we're out here," Sawyer conceded finally.

"This situation may have turned out well," Christian said. "But I must urge you not to make a habit of disclosing this to people without our discussing it first. Our safety will be compromised with the more people who know."

"Of course," Georgia agreed. "I don't intend on telling anyone else. Well, maybe Mama Landry. She seems to basically already know and she's kept very quiet about how she feels about it. I think I'm the only one she's talked to about any of it."

"I can't think of anyone I'd trust with it more than Mama Landry," Jordan concurred. "She'd be safe, if you decide to do that. But Georgia, I don't think you should tell my parents. As much as I'd love them to know we're still alive, I don't think they could handle knowing I'm here but not being able to see me or talk to me. It'd hurt them."

"I know," Georgia said softly. "I won't tell them. Things are… comfortable… for lack of a better word. I want them to stay that way. The trouble is, they made me promise not to come into the woods anymore, what with all the animal sightings and it not being safe. So getting here is going to be hard. But I'll make it work."

"That is good to hear," Christian said. "Because we have a lot of work to do now. Shall we get to it?"

Chapter Nine
Game Plan

"Ok, so what needs to be done and who is doing what?" Sawyer asked as they all sat in a semi-circle at the edge of the pond. "As the only one who can speak to the people in town, or really even go into town for that matter, Georgia's the logical choice for finding someone who works in the mill and interrogating them."

"I agree," Christian said, turning to Georgia. "But I would ask you to bring the list of candidates back to us for discussion so we can decide who is the best choice."

"Agreed," Jordan, Sawyer, and Victoria said.

Georgia nodded. "I plan on taking Auggie's advice and going to the mill parking lot to see if I recognize any cars. And I think what he said about finding someone new there makes sense. We should find someone who hasn't had their loyalties sealed as strongly."

"That's a good idea. And if you have the chance to take pictures or write a really good description of the cars, you can bring them with you and I might be able to remember and recognize a few extra," Jordan added.

"I'll do my best. I don't know if a camera would have the level of discreetness we're going for, but I can probably get a good description down from memory," Georgia said.

"Then that is settled. As for the Northeastern ravine, that is close to where one of Edmund's compounds used to be. It was abandoned long ago and was dormant for quite some time, so I ceased checking on it. I know it well, however." Christian paused here as if caught in an unpleasant memory. He seemed to realize he hadn't spoken for a while, and a rumble came from him as if clearing his throat. "I can take Jordan and Sawyer with me to investigate the areas I am familiar with and we can expand the search if necessary."

"That sounds good," Georgia said. "And it'll keep you away from the town, which is also important."

"Victoria, have you had any luck finding where the pond is connected to the underground spring leading to the well in the mill?" Georgia asked.

"I have found two places the water can escape the pond; however, I do not know which is the one leading to the well."

"Does anyone have ideas as to how we can figure that out?" Christian asked the group.

"Putting something in the water is the first thing I can think of," Jordan offered. "Maybe a dye? But how to tell if it's getting to the well is the real issue."

"That kind of takes us back to the idea of finding someone who works in the mill we can trust. If we find someone, then they can check it for us," Georgia said.

"The last time we tried to put a mole in the mill, it didn't work out the greatest," Sawyer said quietly. No one had an immediate response to that.

"This wouldn't be exactly the same," Georgia finally chimed in. "Like we said, if we can find someone who already works there, they wouldn't throw up such a red flag. Once we decide on the person, I could talk to them, provide whatever information we deem is necessary for them to know, then ask them to check the well. If they accomplish the goal without getting caught, great. If not, well…"

"Casualties of war are often necessary," Christian interjected. "The loss would be unfortunate, but our investment would not be great."

"Sadly, I must agree with Christian. It is the best idea we have and it will yield the fastest results, whether it is a success or a failure," Victoria stated.

"Not to be a downer, but what happens if we pick the wrong person? What if instead of doing what we ask, they decide to tell someone what I've asked of them?" Georgia asked. No one seemed to have an immediate answer for that either.

"Georgia, I know you feel like we ask a lot of you," Jordan said in a voice so quiet it was barely more than a whisper. "And I hate putting you in danger. But the fact is, you haven't been in town as long. A lot of people who hang out in town know you, but you won't know many people who work in the mill, and they won't know you. That's why I'm hoping when you bring the description of the cars, I might know one you don't. That way you'll basically be talking to a stranger. You could even give them a fake name at that point. Then, if they do decide to tell someone, there won't be much to go on other than a description and a fake name."

Georgia nodded slowly. "It makes sense for me to do it. I'm not disagreeing. I'd just feel better knowing we have a plan if things don't work out like we want them to."

"If the plan breaks down, we will keep you far from the mill and I will do whatever scouting I can around the area at night," Christian interjected. Victoria ruffled her feathers, but did not argue. Christian continued. "It is not ideal, but if the worst happens, we will not be dealing with ideal conditions anyway."

No one could think of anything better, so they all nodded slowly.

"So, it looks like I'll be name gathering, car describing, and doing some research on the Neff family," Georgia said.

"And we'll do some site research near the ravine and see what, if anything, we can hear," added Sawyer.

"When shall we meet again?" Victoria inquired.

"The research might take me a bit. How about we meet sometime around next Sunday or shortly after?" Georgia suggested.

"That sounds reasonable," Jordan said. "It might take us some time to find a good place to scout near the ravine, plus we should check a few locations. We'll also need to find the best position for listening to people, if we find any.

It's a lot harder to be covert during the day when people are out and about."

"Clearly," Georgia said, and they all laughed. It was nice to have the air a bit lighter between them all.

"Then it is decided. Sometime after Sunday, preferably not long after, we will reconvene and go over what we have discovered." Christian rose. "Now, if you will excuse me, I think tonight might be the first time in a long while I will be able to sleep well. Tomorrow, Jordan, Sawyer, and I will form a plan and begin our research. Good evening to you all." He turned and walked slowly through the curtain of willow branches and out of sight.

"Georgia, it is truly wonderful to have you back," Victoria said sweetly, and Georgia could hear the sincerity in her voice. The swan turned and swam back through the willow curtain and out of sight.

"I guess we should be getting to bed soon, too," Jordan said, stretching as she rose. "I think he's right. I feel more relaxed than I have in weeks. Sleep sounds good right now."

"Where are you both staying now that you're out here?" Georgia asked, rising as well.

"We found a cave not far from here," Sawyer answered. "It goes pretty far back, so the wind doesn't reach us. We brought in a bunch of soft greens to lay on. Plus, we have each other. It's actually pretty cozy."

Georgia took a minute to think about her nice warm bedroom waiting for her at home. "Is there anything you guys need? Anything I can bring you?"

"We're fine, Georgia. I promise," Jordan said, walking over to her and bumping her gently with her head. "Things aren't bad here. Sawyer and I have each other, like he said. I miss you like crazy, but he keeps me sane."

"It's a full time job, let me tell ya," Sawyer joked, and they laughed again.

"I just want you to be happy," Georgia said quietly. "I want to know it was all worth it."

"We *are* happy," Jordan said earnestly. "And it was more than worth it. I so badly want you to find someone you feel this strongly about. You deserve that."

"She will," Sawyer said confidently. "You're amazing," he said to Georgia. "The hard part will be finding someone deserving of you."

"I love you guys." Georgia backed up a few steps. Just as she started her transformation, she heard a faint whisper of "We love you, too." When she opened her eyes, they were all gone.

Chapter Ten
Reconnaissance and Research

Georgia looked at the clock over the door of the bookstore and groaned. She would have sworn it had been twenty minutes since she last looked, but it had only been five. She planned to go to the mill lot after work. She got off at two and figured it would be an odd hour with not a lot of traffic expected going in and out of the mill. She had made a somewhat incomplete list of people in town whose cars she knew, and she found herself watching out the front window of the bookstore to jot down car descriptions and if she knew the person who owned them.

For such a small town, she was astounded at how many people she didn't know. She guessed Jordan had been right about that. Part of her was tempted to start taking pictures of people in their cars, but she didn't want someone to catch on to what she was doing and think she was being a creeper. It was a shame too, because she could take all the pictures to Mama Landry and she would probably know every one of them. Maybe if she could describe them well enough, that would work too.

"Georgia," Ryan's voice said from behind her and she jumped, knocking her notebook to the ground.

"Geez, you scared me," she said breathlessly, taking the notebook Ryan had stooped down to pick up.

"Sorry. It feels weird being on the other end of that. Jordan used to scare me to death all the time," Ryan smiled.

Georgia noticed that ever since she had visited the woods the past weekend, hearing her friends' names didn't hurt as much. Apparently the visit had been even more cathartic than she had anticipated. It was nice to feel a notch closer to normal again.

"She was good at that for sure," Georgia agreed with a laugh. "Nice to know you're picking up the slack."

Ryan smiled too. "Things are really slow here. You head out if you want. I can take over."

"Really?! Oh, that would be great," she exclaimed, grabbing up her stuff. "If I can do the same for you sometime, just let me know."

Ryan waved her off as she rushed out the door, unloaded her things into the passenger seat, and drove off toward the mill. It was just after one and she hoped most of the lunch traffic, if there even was any, would have filtered in and out of the mill lot and she wouldn't be too conspicuous driving around looking at the vehicles. She had also packed a hoodie and jacket that had been Jordan's in case driving around the lot wasn't possible and she had to be content with just walking along the perimeter.

Fifteen minutes later, she pulled slowly into the lot. She remembered the last time she had been there. It was with Jordan and they had been hoping to warn Sawyer away from the mill to keep him from danger. They hadn't been successful. She bit her lip and turned down one of the rows of cars. She needed to stop thinking about that night and focus on what was going on now. She looked around to see if anyone was outside who might see her and wonder what she was doing. Not seeing anyone, she gave a look inside the cars close to her to make sure no one was sitting in any of them. Confident she was alone, she pulled forward and continued down the aisle.

Her plan was to make two passes. One pass would be to look at each car and determine if she knew who owned it. The second pass would be to write down any easily describable cars to jot down for Jordan. She figured she would also ask Mama Landry if she knew who owned them.

It took under ten minutes to complete her first pass and she had a list of six cars whose owners she knew. It wasn't many, but it was something. She had just started her second pass when a young man who looked close to her age came out of the mill and began walking to the parking lot. Georgia swore under her breath, put her notebook down on the passenger seat, and calmly drove out of the parking lot. She tried to look as nonchalant as possible and hoped she hadn't raised his suspicions.

Five minutes after leaving the lot and heading back toward town there was still no one behind her and she sighed in relief. She looked down at her notebook and frowned. She only had two cars she had made note of, and maybe two more she had seen and could write down once she stopped. It wasn't what she had hoped for, but between those two and the six she knew the owners of, she had somewhere to start. Tonight she would visit the restaurant and see if Mama Landry wanted to have supper together again.

It was too early for supper when Georgia arrived back in town, so she decided to stop at the library. Wireless internet had never been a common thing in Shamore since the ravines and ridges made it almost impossible to get a clear signal, but the library had a periodical archive section she thought she might be able to make good use of. She figured she could look for hidden clues in any articles she could find about the last cull hunt or anything to do with the mill. She also wanted to look into the Neff family.

When Georgia walked in, she scanned the circulation desk for Judy. Jordan's mom worked at both the school library as well as the public library, and it was never set which days she worked which. Part of her hoped Judy would be working at the public library today so could get her help with navigating the archives. The other part of her hoped Judy wasn't there so she didn't have to try to come up with an explanation for what she was doing. The second part got her wish as the circulation desk and the nearby aisles yielded three librarians Georgia didn't know. She walked up to one of the ladies who looked friendly and saw her name tag said Barb.

"Excuse me, ma'am. I was wondering if you could show me where to go to look at the town's newspaper archives?"

Barb smiled pleasantly. "Oh, sweetie, you can call me Barb. I'd be happy to help you." She scooted out from behind the desk and walked toward the back of the library, gesturing for Georgia to follow her. "Anything after nineteen-ninety can be accessed through the computers here. There are keyword searches or date searches available to help you narrow it down. All of the town's newspapers from before nineteen-ninety have been put onto microfilm and can be looked at with our microfiche machine. It's not the greatest quality, but they're legible. Microfilms are organized by the date of the newspaper and then by page number for each issue." She walked her over to the microfiche machine and explained how to put the microfilm under the reader and slide the pan around to see the whole card.

After going through a few of them, Georgia sat back and looked up. "Thanks, Barb, I think I can take it from here."

"Wonderful," Barb smiled. "I'll be at the circulation desk if you need any help. Please remember to remove the film from under the light if you're going to look for something else. If they're left under there for too long, the heat will distort the images permanently and we don't have any way to replace them unfortunately."

"Oh, I promise to be careful with them, for sure," Georgia promised and Barb left her to look on her own.

Georgia spent over two hours looking through thousands of articles. She only found two about the previous cull hunt. One article had been written almost the same as the one from a few days ago. It stated the animal population was thought to be escalating which was pushing animals closer to town, people were advised to stay indoors as much as possible, especially at night, and it alluded to the potential for a hunting order.

A few weeks later, another article stated a cull hunt order had been issued and let people know the dates of the hunt and instructions and locations for reporting their numbers. The hunt had to take place at least a half of a mile from the populated areas of town and could not be done on another person's property without their permission. Also, if people were going to hunt in the woods, they were required to wear bright colored vests to prevent accidents. Georgia had gone a few weeks out from the closing date of the hunt, but nothing had been written about the results, nor had any more articles about animal sightings appeared.

Georgia had noticed there were two pages missing out of a paper three weeks after the hunt. She figured they must have gotten damaged, probably by someone leaving the film under the light too long. She went back to the front page of that paper and looked at the bottom where it referenced the stories that could be found on the inside pages. She had missed it the first time since she wasn't looking for it, but there was mention of a story titled "Weekend tragedies lead to mass funerals". The story had been on the pages that were missing from the microfilm catalog. She stared over the top of the computer, her eyes unfocused. If the cull hunt had eliminated a lot of animals, and those animals had actually been people in their animal forms, it would make sense there had been a lot of people who were thought to be dead. She wished the pages were still there to help her confirm her suspicions.

Georgia removed the film from the reader, put it back in order, and turned off the machine. She walked back to the circulation desk and found Barb again.

"I was wondering if there was any other way I might be able to read certain pages of a specific paper." She handed her a piece of scrap paper on which she had written the issue date and page numbers. "There are two pages missing from one of the papers and there's an article I was interested in reading."

Barb shook her head sadly. "I'm sorry, miss, but there are no backup copies of the microfilms. I wish we had a better archive system, but sadly, this is all we have."

Georgia gave Barb an understanding look. "That's totally fine. Thanks for all your help today. It was great." They smiled at each other and Georgia walked toward the door.

As she reached for the handle, the door swung open. She backed up quickly and saw a young man standing behind the frosted glass. She waited, but he motioned for her to go ahead. She thanked him as she walked through the door he held open for her. She passed over the threshold and was able to see him clearly. Something about his black hair and the sharp angles of his face struck her as familiar. She looked at him a second longer before recognition slammed into her. It was the same guy she had seen leaving the mill when she was in the parking lot. Her stomach tightened with fear as thoughts of being followed entered her mind, but then he smiled warmly at her, nodded an acknowledgement to her whispered thanks, and walked into the library.

Georgia tried to look natural and forced herself not to look over her shoulder as she walked back to her car and got in. She drove slowly to Mama Landry's restaurant, trying to talk herself out of a panic attack.

It was probably a complete coincidence running into the same guy at the library. He couldn't have been following her or it wouldn't have taken him over two hours to get to the same place she was. He didn't look threatening at all, but rather friendly. Her mission was making her paranoid. When she pulled to a stop in front of the restaurant, she was much calmer and even felt a little silly for worrying so much. She grinned and shook her head at herself as she walked through the door to the restaurant.

Chapter Eleven
Leads

"Evenin' suga," Mama Landry said as Georgia sat down in her booth. "How ya doin' ta-night?"

"Fine, Mama, how are you?"

"Oh, I'm just peachy darlin', thanks fo' askin'. Ya just wait right there an' Mama'll bring ya out some coffee."

Georgia smiled in thanks and pulled out her notebook. She didn't know why, but on the back of her list of cars she started writing down everything she could remember about the guy she had seen leaving the mill; appearance, clothes, build, etc. She wasn't feeling as paranoid as she had been earlier, but something in the back of her mind couldn't let go of the idea this guy might be important somehow.

Obviously he worked at the mill and, bonus, he didn't seem to be as unpleasant as most of the people who did. In fact, Georgia thought back to leaving the library, his smile had seemed very genuine. She wrote more about how the corners of his mouth turned up a little extra and the dimple in his left cheek. She pulled herself out of the memory and pushed on. Not only did he seem friendly, but he had come into town during the day. That wasn't very common for mill workers. Yes, he was someone to keep an eye out for.

Mama Landry set Georgia's mug in front of her and the smell of the coffee made her sigh with contentment. "Thanks, Mama. It smells great." She took a sip and did a dramatic eye roll and squeezed the coffee mug to her chest. "It is amazing. You're a coffee goddess."

Mama Landry let out a loud, deep laugh. "Lawd, ya make an ol' lady happy, chil'."

"The coffee really is good, Mama. It's exactly what I needed. I've had a busy day. Is there any chance you'd want to join me for supper again? I have a couple things I'd like to talk to you about if you have time to spare."

"Well, I'd love ta!" Mama Landry exclaimed. "What should we have ta-night? Fish? Steak?"

"How about roast and veggies?" Georgia suggested. "I smelled it when I walked in and it smells fantastic."

"It did turn out pretty good ta-night, sho' 'nuff," Mama Landry agreed. "Roast fo' two it is. I'll be right back, honey."

Georgia looked around the restaurant while she drank her coffee. The place was always so warm and inviting. There were pictures on the walls of events in town spanning back decades. Mama Landry was in most of them and she hadn't changed. She still had the same big smile, same dark hair pulled back in a tight bun, maybe a bit more of the grey hair now, and the same plump figure. She was the quintessential mother hen, and it was obvious everyone in the pictures with her was happy to be in her company.

In the far corner of the restaurant, she saw a picture of Mama Landry with a group of about a dozen young boys, maybe nine or ten years old. From this far, Georgia couldn't tell for sure, but it looked like it must have been at some sort of festival.

She got up and walked over to get a closer look at the picture. She gave a soft laugh as she saw the details she had been missing from across the room. A couple of the boys were wearing bibs and their faces were covered in red slime. Other boys were holding hot dogs in buns in both hands. Still other boys were holding ears of corn. Three of the boys had medals around their necks. Mama Landry was standing behind them, her hands on the shoulders of two of the boys, her face frozen in laughter.

Georgia looked at all the boys and her eyes fell on one in particular; jet-black hair, angled face, dimple in the left cheek. She sucked in a sharp breath, her eyes widening. It didn't seem possible, but the longer she looked at the picture, the surer she was. It was a much younger version of the guy she had seen twice that day. How in the world did this guy kept showing up? She wasn't usually one to believe in signs, but this was too much to ignore. She turned around and walked back to her booth. She had only been sitting for a minute before Mama Landry brought out their plates of food and a basket of bread. She settled into the booth and looked at Georgia.

"My goodness, ya white as a sheet! Somethin' wrong, honey? Ya feelin' sick?"

"Oh, no Mama, I'm fine, I swear. I've just had some really weird things going on today and something in one of your pictures made me remember some of it." Georgia said, grabbing a slice of bread and spreading butter onto it.

"One-a my pictures?" Mama Landry asked, confusion in her voice. She looked around at the dozens of pictures on the walls. "Well, I'm sure sorry if one-a 'em vexed ya."

Georgia almost laughed. Even when she had no way of understanding the problem, Mama Landry was always trying to make people feel better. "Oh, no! It's not the picture that affected me, Mama. It's just… well, can you tell me what this picture's about?" She got up, took the picture off the wall, and brought it back to the table.

Mama Landry looked at the photo and her face broke into a wide smile. "Why, I ain't looked at this picture in ages! This is from close ta twenty years ago, now. We had a festival on main street. This was a eatin' relay. Three ta a team. Tha first kid had'ta eat two hot dogs fast as he could, tha second had'ta eat two ears a corn, an' tha third had'ta eat a whole cherry pie contest style; no hands. Them kids was so excited!"

Georgia smiled. The story made the photo make complete sense. "Do you remember all these kids, Mama?"

Mama Landry looked at the picture again. "I s'pose I do. Why d'ya ask, suga?"

"Well, I think I saw one of them earlier. He seems to be showing up everywhere I go today, and it seems a little strange because I've never seen him in town before. Ever," she emphasized, pointing to the dark haired boy.

"Him?" Mama Landry asked. "Why, that's Austin Neff! One-a tha sweetest boys ya'd ever wanna know. I ain't seen him since shortly afta this picture happened. Ya say ya saw him ta-day?"

Georgia stared at the picture. Neff! The boy's name was Austin *Neff*. This was getting weirder and weirder. The one family she was supposed to try to get information on but had no idea how to even begin doing so was the same family of a guy she had never seen before and yet somehow had seen three times in one day, one being in a photo from twenty years ago.

"Miss Georgia?" Mama Landry's voice brought her out of her thoughts. She looked up at the woman across from her.

"I'm sorry, Mama. What?"

"Ya' say ya' saw Mr. Austin ta-day?"

"I'm pretty sure it was him, yeah. He had the same hair and face shape. He's significantly taller now of course. Why haven't you seen him since this picture, Mama? Where did he go?" Georgia asked.

"Oh, I dunno that he went nowhere s'much as he jus stopped comin' 'round this side a town. Austin an' his folks lived out near tha ravine town far as I knew. He din' come ta town very often, but sometimes he come visit his uncle, Mr. Dale Neff."

"Mr. Neff who lives by you?" Georgia asked.

"That's tha one. He'd stay with him a weekend here an' there, or sometimes over a summer. Not long after tha festival, I think his daddy and his uncle had some kinda'

88

fallin' out, 'cause he never came back ta visit after that. Was a real shame. When he stayed with his uncle, he'd come ova when he saw me out on my porch in tha mornin's an' we'd have tea an' muffins an' chat away tha mornin'. His uncle'd come ova once he got up an' sometimes he'd have a muffin too 'fore they'd go off doin' whateva it was they done. Those was nice times," Mama Landry said nostalgically.

Georgia still felt anxious that this young man she'd been running into was a Neff, but the stories Mama Landry told about him coupled with the friendliness he'd shown when they ran into each other at the library eased her worries a bit. After all, how could someone who would have tea with an old neighbor lady and who held doors for strangers be all bad? "He sounds nice," Georgia offered.

Mama Landry nodded. "Was a young gentleman, he was." She handed the picture back to Georgia. "I'm sorry, sweets, ya said ya wanted ta talk ta Mama 'bout somethin' an' I plum led ya down mem'ry lane instead, din' I? What was it ya wanted ta ask me?"

Georgia was startled to realize she had almost forgotten why she had come into the restaurant in the first place.

"Oh, yeah, I did want to ask you a few things." She pulled out her notebook and flipped to the page with the car descriptions. "Do you know who drives these two cars? I saw them in the mill parking lot when I turned around there earlier today and they didn't seem to fit in with the other beat up trucks and rusted out cars in the lot." She turned the notebook to face Mama Landry, and the old woman read over the descriptions she had written.

"Well, now, tha green one prob'ly belongs ta Miss Heather Moss. She does some-a tha bookkeepin' fo' tha mill an' I think she helps with orders fo' tha warehouse too. Her husband used ta work at tha mill, but he passed quite a few years back. She neva remarried, poor thin'. This black one I ain't sure 'bout. I never seen a car like that 'round town. I s'pose it could belong ta one-a them boys from tha other side-a town; ova by where they say tha ravine town is. It'd be a lotta rough drivin' fo' a car that nice though."

Georgia's eyes widened. So, Mama Landry knew about the ravine town. It shouldn't surprise her, she thought, since Mama Landry knew just about everything in town. Except, it seemed, who owned the sleek black car she had seen at the back of the lot. "Do you know where the ravine town is or how to get there?" she asked.

"Oh, no sugar. I neva been there m'self. I just heard talk 'bout it from Mr. Austin an' his uncle now an' then. I know it's quite tha jaunt an' it's through lotsa woods an' some-a it's nothin' more'n dirt paths. S'why not many folks from there come ta town ever. Can I ask why tha curiosity 'bout tha ravine folks an' tha mill cars all-a a sudden? Is there somethin' ya tryin' ta find?"

Georgia took a drink of her coffee and debated how much she should share at this point. "Oh, nothing specific Mama. Like I said, those cars just jumped out at me when I turned around there. I notice things like that. And the ravine town is something I just heard about recently and it struck me interesting is all."

Mama Landry gave her an appraising look and then picked up her fork to continue eating. "Tha ravine town's interested lotsa people in tha past. It's not a great place ta go explorin' though, if that's what ya thinkin'. Not safe at all. Ya be careful now, ya promise Mama?"

Georgia looked into the woman's eyes and saw the concern there. "I promise to stay careful," she answered, trying her best to give the most reassuring smile she could.

Mama Landry reached over and patted her hand. "That's a good girl. Now, tell me, is Mr. Austin still as handsome as he was when he was a young'un?"

Georgia blushed at the question and looked down. "Um, well, he's not bad looking, no."

"Tha Neffs are a mixed lot. Some-a 'em so mean they make Augustus Toole look like Santa Claus. Tha rest-a 'em is nice as can be. I sure hope Mr. Austin came out like tha nice bunch. It'd be sucha waste ta have them nice looks on a ugly soul." They both smiled and finished their supper in relative silence. When they were done, Mama Landry cleared their plates and took them to the back.

Georgia found herself looking at the young Austin Neff and wondering what had happened to him between the picture and now. Everything she had feared about the Neff family being evil seemed to be only partially true and she wondered if Austin might be the key to getting some inside info about his family. Not only that, but if she could get on friendly terms with him, she might be able to get significant information about the mill as well; information that could go a long way to helping her and her friends in their quest. She wasn't convinced he actually worked at the mill, especially since he had been coming out in the middle of the day. Perhaps he had just been visiting someone there; his uncle even. But if he could come and go from the mill, there was potential there. She was still lost in thought when she saw movement out of the corner of her eye and jumped in her seat as Mama Landry reappeared at her side.

"Oh, I'm sorry sweets," she said, noticing Georgia's jump. "I didn' meant ta give ya a fright. I was jus' gonna put this back up on tha wall if ya done with it."

"That's all right, Mama. Yes, I'm done with it. Thanks for everything tonight; the conversation, the friendship. I enjoy our suppers together."

"I do too, chil'. Ya come in 'round this time any day an' ya got yaseff a date. Oh, an' Miss Georgia?" she asked as Georgia stood and gathered up her things. "Please 'member what I said. That ravine town's dangerous. Please don' go getting' ya self hurt lookin' fo' whatever ya might wanna look fo'. We already done lost too many people in these last few months."

It killed Georgia that she was causing Mama Landry to worry, but it wasn't her specifically who would be going to investigate the site, so she didn't feel like she was completely lying.

"I know, Mama. I appreciate what you're saying. I will do everything I can to stay safe. I don't plan to get myself into any danger."

"That's good ta hear. If ya happen ta see Mr. Austin again, ya tell him Mama said she misses him an' hopes he's doin' fine."

"Oh, I've never even spoken to him, Mama. I think it'd be a little awkward to walk up to someone I've never talked to and let them know someone misses them, don't you?"

"Not at all! I'm someone ya have in common. I want him ta know I think 'bout him an' it'd be a nice conversation starter, now wouldn't it?"

"I suppose," Georgia said reluctantly.

"Besides, ya both is summa tha sweetest youn'uns. Ya should know each otha'."

Georgia gave Mama Landry a sideways glance. Mama Landry smiled at her and winked before she walked away. Georgia gave a small eye roll and a grin as she picked up the rest of her things and walked out the door. Always an agenda, she thought affectionately. Still, maybe Mama Landry was right. Maybe an easy ice breaker would be just the thing to start getting to know this Austin guy and see what kind of shot she had at getting some good information.

Chapter Twelve
An Important Visitor

Georgia spent the next two days trying to discreetly figure out some of the routines of the workers whose car she had recognized at the mill, but she had run into a frustrating series of dead ends. The cars were either at the mill or at home and the people were never seen around town. She couldn't tell what kinds of errands they were running, if any, and she didn't have any idea of the activities they might engage in outside of work; again, if any. No one seemed to have seen any of them if Georgia asked, and she feared she would start to sound like a weirdo if she kept asking people about random townsfolk. She was getting irritable about it all and the lack of help she had, but she knew she was flying solo going into it, and she knew getting upset about it wouldn't help the cause.

During her current shift at the bookstore, she had been stacking books on tables doing a new series set and trying to think about anything other than the mill and the workers. It seemed to be working because, when the bell over the door jingled, she looked at the clock and it had been over two hours since she had started the project. She brushed some of her hair out of her face and walked to the end of the row to see who had come in. She didn't see anyone, and figured they must have known what they wanted and walked to that section of the store.

She went back to the service desk and waited in case whoever it was needed help or wanted to check out. As she waited, she picked up the current newspaper and browsed the contents. She had been checking it daily to see if there was any more information about a hunt being organized. Jordan and the rest of them would need to know if that were the case so they could be on extra high alert for people in the woods and to guard the clearing. So far, nothing had been said about it, which was good because keeping people out of the clearing would mean less time investigating other sites.

She folded the paper back to read a small article about the potential beginnings of an energy crisis reported by the mill and plans to begin work building a hydropower dam somewhere in the northern ridges to help with the issue. It also alluded to the idea of blast mining for gold to help raise the funds.

"It's crazy about that energy shortage, isn't it?" a voice said and Georgia jumped and dropped the paper.

She looked across the counter and up into a pair of familiar, dark eyes. The young man in front of her was well over six feet tall, athletically built, and his skin was the color of a naturally perfect tan. His black hair was long and the front came down to brush his eyebrows. She was looking into the face of Austin Neff.

Georgia stared, not saying anything, until she realized she must look like a complete idiot and hurriedly said, "Um, yeah. It's, uh, yeah, it's really something."

She knew she sounded moronic, but she didn't know what to say. She remembered Mama Landry telling her to let Austin know she missed him and she hoped he was doing well, but this didn't seem like the right time to just come out and say it. She swallowed and stooped to pick up her paper. When she stood back up he was still standing in the same place, smiling the same smile at her. She swallowed hard and attempted a small smile back.

"So, uh, did you find what you were looking for?"

"Actually, no. I was hoping to find a book about the history of technological advances in engineering, but I realized I didn't really know where to look, so I came up here to see if you could point me in the right direction."

"Oh, sure," Georgia said, sliding around the opening in the counter and walking toward the industrial science section. She stopped in front of a double bay of shelves and turned to Austin. "The section's separated by the type of industry, then it's broken down in alphabetical order within the section."

"Got it," Austin said. "Thanks." Georgia nodded and began walking away.

"Hey," Austin called after her and she stopped and turned to face him again. "Didn't I see you the other day? At the mill? And then again at the library?"

"Oh," Georgia said, feigning a look of deep contemplation. "That might be right. I think I remember you from the library, yeah."

"I held the door as you were leaving, right?"

"That's it, yeah," Georgia agreed. He didn't say anything so she nervously followed up with "Uh, thanks for that."

Austin let out a soft laugh. "Hey, no problem. Anytime you need a door held again, just ask." Georgia smiled a genuine smile at that. He was very easy going and funny too. He extended his hand. "I'm Austin."

"Georgia," she replied, taking his hand. A cold zing shot up her arm as they shook and she let go quickly. "Just let me know if you need anything else."

She turned and walked quickly back to the service desk. The last time she had felt that sensation was when she had met Jordan for the first time. It had been a hand shake that time as well, and the sensation had come from being in contact with another shapeshifter, although they hadn't known that was the reason for the sensation at the time.

Her initial contact with Jordan hadn't been so intense of a cold shock, however. It was probably just some static discharge this time. She stood behind the counter again, gathering her thoughts and trying not to be so weird about things. She needed to be more personable if she wanted to have a chance to talk to Austin. All of her other leads were getting her nowhere and this was the only potential she had going.

"I think I can use this one," Austin said when he returned to the counter a few minutes later. He set a book titled "Harnessing Water: A Guide to Hydroelectric Power" on the counter and reached into his back pocket for his wallet.

Georgia picked up the book and looked at it before scanning it and reaching for a bag. She took a slow, deep breath and looked up at Austin, smiling as naturally as she could. "So, Austin you said?"

"That's right," he said, smiling his same smile back at her.

"That wouldn't be Austin Neff, would it?"

His eyes widened a bit and he leaned his hip against the counter in a relaxed kind of way. "It would, actually. How did you know that?"

"Well, I spend a lot of time over at Mama Landry's restaurant. We have dinner together every now and then. We've talked about a lot of things during our visits, and the other night we were discussing the pictures she has hanging in her place. There's actually one with you in it. I think you were about nine or so and it was an eating contest at a festival here in town."

Austin ran his hand through his black hair and rubbed the back of his neck, laughing. "Oh, that one," he said and the faintest blush appeared in his cheeks. "I remember that contest. We would've won, too, but Billy couldn't bring it home with the pie. We came in second though so, I guess it's not too bad. That had to have been close to twenty years ago. I can't believe she still has it up."

"Well, I think it's probably the last picture she has of you. She said you and she used to visit now and then when you'd stay with your uncle and she really enjoyed those times. I'm sure she misses you." Georgia said softly.

He met her gaze and then, for the first time in their few encounters, was the first to lower his. "She's a great lady. I didn't have a great relationship with my own mom and she was definitely like one to me."

"She definitely is just like a mom," Georgia agreed. When she saw Austin looking at her curiously she rushed on. "When I lost my mom last year, she was always there without being too pushy. I've gone through a bunch of stuff this past year, actually, and I can't imagine getting through it all the same without her being there."

Austin nodded. "I should really go see her again one of these days." He paused for a moment, his eyes looking down toward the counter. So," he said, seeming to come out of a deep contemplation. "What do I owe you?"

Georgia took a beat and decided to press her luck. "That's going to come to $18.64. You know," she said as off-handedly as she could while taking the twenty dollar bill he handed her. "The restaurant isn't that far from here and she isn't usually too busy this time of day. You should go over now if you don't have to get back right away. I plan to do the same when I get off in about a half hour."

He gave her an appraising look as she placed his change in his hand and handed him his bag. She held her ground and didn't break the silence or their eye contact. Finally, Austin pocketed the coins, slipped the dollar in his wallet, and grabbed his bag.

"I just might do that," he said. "Or… and this is just off the top of my head… but if you're going to be there, and I'm going to be there, maybe we should just go at the same time. I'll even treat if you'd like to stay for supper."

She thought about that for a second. She had been hoping he would suggest they go together, but she hadn't been expecting a dinner invitation. Still, she didn't see a way she could turn down the dinner but still have him wait to go to the restaurant with her. "Sure," she said. "That sounds nice. Although, you don't have to pay."

"I know I don't, but if I'm asking you to come with me, it's the least I can do. I'll just go wait in the car and start on my book until you get done."

"There are a couple of sitting chairs over by the mystery section if you want somewhere more comfortable to sit."

"That sounds even better," he said, picking up his book and walking that direction. "Just holler for me when you're ready to go."

Georgia nodded at him and watched him walk away. It was times like these she wished she could communication in a more real-time fashion with Jordan. She missed not having someone to talk to immediately about everything. Even in the woods, she had a feeling it would always be them talking in a group from now on and, while she liked Sawyer a lot and didn't really have anything against Christian and Victoria, it just wasn't the same.

Ryan came in about five minutes before Georgia was supposed to leave. He was carrying a large box that barely fit through the door and, as he slid through the entrance, he yelled "Ow, my fingers! Georgia! Georgia, I saw you through the window and I know you aren't helping anyone so can you come help me? *Now!*"

She ran to grab the door and push it open farther and, once he was through, she reached out and grabbed one side of the box so they could both carry half. "Ryan," she said in a harsh whisper. "Just because I'm not helping anyone doesn't mean there isn't anyone in the store. Can you chill out and be a little more professional?"

Ryan lowered his voice a notch. "Fine. But honestly, who parked their fancy car in two spots out front? Are they worried about door dings? There's no one else out there! Who's going to ding it?"

Georgia looked out the front window and almost dropped her side of the box when she saw it was the fancy black car from the mill parking lot. She had an idea she might know who it belonged to and that just made things even more surreal. What were the odds all of this was coming together so quickly? She had started the week so frustrated with the number of leads she had to try to chase down. Just a few hours earlier she had been frustrated with the number of leads that had went stone cold. Now, she was running into a potentially chatty mill employee right in her very own workplace. They got the box to the back and set it on the table.

"What's in this thing?" Georgia asked, bending backwards to stretch out her back. The box had been heavier than she thought and she was kind of impressed Ryan could carry it as far as he did on his own.

"It's the new... what did you call it? Shag? Snag? Whatever you call those bracelets and buttons and hats and gloves for the new book."

"God, Ryan, the word's 'swag' and I'm almost positive you've never heard me use it. Are you trying to sound hip or something?" she couldn't help but laugh. He looked at her with what appeared to be a mixture of embarrassment and contempt, pulled the tape off the top of the box, and started pulling things out onto the table.

"Whatever it's called, you were the one who suggested it, so here it is. Are you going to help me sort it and get a display ready, or what?"

"I absolutely will. Tomorrow. Today, I have plans for dinner so I'm going to have to run. I was supposed to be off a couple minutes ago."

"How convenient," Ryan said, rolling his eyes, continuing to pull out the merchandise.

"Hey, you were the one who said no more overtime, go have a life, do things that make you happy and that you're looking forward to," she called over her shoulder as she walked back down the hallway to the sales floor. "I'm going to do that. I'll see you tomorrow." She turned around and ran into Austin.

"Whoa," he said, grabbing her arms to steady her. "Sorry, I didn't know you'd be coming out so quickly."

"No, I'm sorry," she said, taking a step back. "I just knew you'd probably be waiting and I didn't want you to think I'd forgotten about you out here. I'm just going to grab my stuff and we can go if you're ready."

"I am. I wouldn't want to keep you from doing something you're looking forward to."

Georgia's face flushed red and she stammered, "What? Looking… um, forward to…?"

"Supper at the restaurant, right? You like eating there with Miss Landry. I figured you were looking forward to it."
"Oh, right, yeah. That's what I'm looking forward to."

Georgia turned and made a big production of putting on her jacket and getting her things together. She was acting like a moron and she needed to get it together or he was going to write her off as a head case and have nothing more to do with her.

When she turned back around, she tried to make her voice sound a little more normal as she smiled and said, "Are you ready? I'm starving."

"After you," he said, holding the door open as they walked out together.

Chapter Thirteen
Reacquainting

Georgia noticed she was right about the car belonging to Austin as he shut her driver side door for her before walking over to get into the black car. It really was pretty, but who would have the money to have a car like that in this little town? She put it out of her mind as they drove the short distance to Mama Landry's restaurant. After they parked, she waiting for him to join her before walking in. Mama Landry wasn't in the seating area, so Georgia walked over to her booth and Austin followed. They took their jackets off and sat across from each other.

"So, what's good here? It's been so long, I can barely remember the last time had anything to eat here," Austin said, taking one of the menus from the basket by the wall.

"Everything is good," Georgia said honestly. "I don't think I've ever eaten something I don't like here. Most of the time I don't even pick. Mama Landry just brings me what she thinks I need."

"What you need?" Austin asked. "Not what you want?"

Georgia let out a genuine laugh. "Honestly, half the time what I *think* I want would never have been as good as what she ends up bringing me. I've learned to just trust her instinct. She hasn't been wrong yet."

Austin grinned and looked back at the menu. She couldn't help but take advantage of the opportunity to really study his features while he wasn't looking directly at her. His eyes wrinkled at the corners when he smiled, like he must do it a lot. The dimple disappeared when his face was at rest, but it seemed to reappear any other time. She felt the urge to reach over and touch her thumb to it softly.

"Austin Neff, as I live an' breathe! Get ya scrawny behin' outta that chair an' give Mama some love!" Georgia snapped out of her daydream as Mama Landry came out of the back room with two coffees, one in Georgia's oversized mug and one in a regular mug. Georgia took them both from her and watched as Austin rose to greet Mama Landry.

"Miss Landry, it's so great to see you again!" he managed to say before she pulled him into a crushing hug. They stood together for a full minute, Mama Landry rocking him back and forth ever so slightly and talking in his ear.

"Don' ya 'Ms. Landry' me. It's Mama now jus' tha same's it's always been. Chil', I missed ya somethin' awful all these years. Ain't seemed tha same since ya been away. No one ta drink my tea with in tha mornin'. No one ta come keep me comp'ny while I garden or prune my bushes. No one ta try out my bakin' before I take it ta church. Let me look atcha!" She held him out at arm's length and gave him an appraising look. "Lawd, if ya ain't nothin' but skin, bones, an' a dimple! Ya been away far too long. Ya sit right back down in that booth right there an' Mama'll bring ya out just tha thing! Hello, suga," she said to Georgia, squeezing her hand and rushing off to the back to put in their order.

Georgia beamed at him as he sat back down and smoothed his wavy hair. He was flushed, but she could tell he was pleased at the reception. "I told you she missed you." They both laughed.

"I don't think I've ever had that welcome of a reception even in my own family. It felt pretty good. And you were right, I guess there's no need to look at this." He put the menu back in the basket. "So, I can't help but notice a difference in the drinkware here." He pulled his cup to him and sniffed the steaming liquid. "She must like you better."

"I think we know that's not true. Just look at that greeting you got!" He winked and nodded, his mouth full of coffee. "No, but seriously, Jordan and I used to come here a few times a week for a long time. I still come here all the time. She knows the regular mugs of coffee won't cut it for me. I think she'd give it to me in an IV if she had access. I'm a big fan of coffee." She took a long drink out of her mug and held it up. "Big fan." Austin laughed and she smiled.

"I'm a fan myself. Apparently I'll need to prove my worth before I'm considered for the mug upgrade."

"Either that or you'll have to drink enough that she gets tired of giving you refills every ten minutes. It's really a self-preservation thing."

"Ok, now, here's jus' tha ticket ta fatten ya both up a lil' bit," Mama Landry said, setting down heaping bowls of beef and vegetable stew, a large basket of bread, and a dish of butter. Austin's mouth dropped open at the amount of food and he looked first to Mama Landry and then to Georgia.

Georgia picked up her spoon. "Think you're up for this?" she asked.

Austin picked up his spoon as well. "I guess I'm giving it a shot."

They both took their first bites at the same time. Georgia wasn't surprised at all when the food made its way to her core and she felt warmed from the inside out. She looked at Austin and saw the look of satisfaction on his face as he moved on to his next bite. She looked up at Mama Landry and saw the woman's face full of radiant happiness. Clearly, nothing pleased her more than feeding her children.

"Well, now, whatd'ya think? That hit tha spot?" Mama Landry asked, expectantly.

"This is amazing, Mama," Austin said thickly, his mouth half full of stew. "I feel like I'm nine again! I don't think I've had food this good since then."

"Now, if ya hadn't stayed away so long, ya couldn't say that, could ya?" She ruffled his hair and then smoothed it for him. She looked at Georgia. "How 'bout it, honey, ya likin' Mama's stew?"

"Do you even need to ask?" Georgia said, playfully. "There's nothing you make I don't like. Tonight's no exception." She reached for a piece of bread just as Austin did the same. Their fingers bumped and she pulled her hand back at the shock of cold again. He picked up a piece of bread and held it out to her. She reached for it gingerly, smiled in thanks, and picked up her knife to get some butter.

"So, what brings ya two youngun's in here ta-getha' ta-night? I got tha impression tha otha' night ya didn' know Mr. Austin," she said to Georgia.

"I don't," Georgia answered. "Well, I mean, I didn't. He actually came into the store today and I remembered you telling me to tell him you missed him if I saw him, so I did."

"And I invited Georgia to come with me to say hello when I found out she was already planning on coming here," Austin finished. He drank the last bit of coffee in his mug and set it down.

"Well, ain't that nice?" Mama asked, a knowing look on her face. "Nice, nice, nice. Let me go back an' get ya s'more coffee an' then I'll let ya two visit. Two-a my most fav'rite people gettin' ta know each otha does my heart good." She walked away and Georgia saw Austin smirking. She raised an eyebrow.

"One cup down. If I keep up this rate, do you think I could get a bigger mug as soon as next time?" Austin asked, hopefully.

Georgia laughed as she picked up her spoon again. "You just might." She couldn't help but wonder if he meant the next time he was there, or the next time they were there together. Either of those options sounded good to her. If he went without her, at least he'd be in town and she'd have opportunities to try to run into him and get some more information. If he went with her, the information gathering would be that much easier. Plus, she thought, he wasn't bad company. He was funny, friendly, and easy to talk to.

"So, you said you and your friend Jordan used to come here all the time. Why doesn't she come here anymore?" Austin asked, continuing to shovel stew into his mouth.

"Oh," Georgia said. She wasn't even aware she'd mentioned Jordan. The question surprised her, but she rebounded quickly. "She, um… she actually died a couple months ago. Her and her boyfriend. Accident in the woods." She grabbed another piece of bread and busied herself buttering it. She reached out to set her knife back on the plate and, as she did, Austin reached out and took her hand lightly. She looked into his face and fought the urge to pull it away. The look of genuine sympathy in his face was sweet.

"I'm so sorry," he said, and she had no doubt he meant it. "I've lost friends and family too. It's never easy." He squeezed her hand gently and let it go. She pulled it back and put it in her lap with the other one. It didn't feel cooler to the touch, but inside the difference was significant. "I think I actually heard about that," he continued. "It sounded like people think they were attacked by an animal in the woods and fell over a cliff trying to get away?" Georgia nodded, still not looking at him. "Not a lot of news from town makes it out to us, but sometimes it makes it through the mill staff. How are you doing now?"

"It's still hard, but we're all trying to just keep living life. It's what they would've wanted." Georgia gave a small smile. "So, do you live far from here?"

"It's a jaunt, yeah. We're out by the Northeast ravine. It's close to an hour drive because you can only go around thirty-five miles per hour for most of it and it's all winding dirt roads and hills. It's a pain."

"I couldn't help notice that you have a really nice car. I wouldn't think those roads would be good for it. I'm surprised it still looks so nice." Georgia prodded.

"Oh, yeah," he looked toward the street even though it was getting darker and they could barely see the details of the cars outside through the restaurant window. "I actually keep that car in a shed at home most of the time. When I come into town, I drive the car like a snail through the woods until I get past the worst of the roads, then I can open it up when I hit the main roads. I don't get to drive it very often."

"If you don't get to drive it, why have it?"

Austin smiled sheepishly. "It's my toy. I've always been interested in cars and I wanted that one for years. I saved and was finally able to get it. Haven't you ever bought something frivolous just because you wanted it?"

"I guess," Georgia answered. "Nothing like a car. But, I spend money on things I don't really need all the time; mostly books and coffee."

"Sure," Austin said, returning to his food.

This wasn't good. She wanted information and instead she appeared to have insulted him. She thought quickly about a way to get things back on track; something that would sound friendly but also had the potential to lead her down a road of information. "So, tell me about where you live. Is it anything like town?"

Austin snorted gently and shook his head. "Not at all. This town is a bit behind the times, what with no real signal for internet, cell service, or cable and all that, but our town is straight out of the 1800s. We have a well system, spotty electricity when it works at all, and most of the ladies in town make all the clothes and blankets for everyone from wool we get from our own sheep."

"But it's only an hour away!" Georgia said, shocked. "Why not just make trips into town for what you need? You could run electric lines from here to you."

Austin shrugged. "We do come into town to pick up supplies sometimes. Or the mill will send supply trucks in. But since the mill pays for our homes and all the buildings and big equipment in our town, we all try to cost them as little extra as possible. Plus, we don't have a lot of time. Work hours are long, and days off are spent with family or catching up on house work or sleep."

"It sounds rough," Georgia said, sympathetically.

"It's not too bad. You get used to it." Austin said. "I haven't been to town for longer than a quick errand in years. Have things changed a lot?"

"Oh, I'm not really the one to ask about that, actually," Georgia said. "I've only lived here for a little less than a year. My mom and I moved back here when she got sick and wanted to come back home to where she had grown up. She passed a few months before Jordan and Sawyer."

"So much loss in such a short amount of time," Austin said softly. "Again, I'm sorry."

"It's ok," Georgia said lightly, eager to change the subject. "She was happier than she had been in a long time before she went. And I'm glad we came back here." Austin smiled at her and she pushed on with the subject change. "So, do you work at the mill then?"

"Yes and no," Austin said and she thought she could see the hint of a tension in his face. "I run errands for them. I work on deliveries and transport. But I don't work inside the mill very much, no."

"Oh. Well, that sounds good. Does that mean you have a little more free time if you don't have set hours? Do you just work when they need you?" Georgia asked, thinking this was great. If he was running between the mill and the ravine town, he would know about both. He would also have a lot of inside info if she could get him to share it.

"I suppose. Although, I feel like I'm needed all the time," he said softly and continued to eat the last few bites of his stew.

"I've been there," Georgia sympathized. "Sometimes I feel like I'm being pulled in twenty different directions and everyone expects something from me. It's hard."

Austin nodded but didn't reply. Georgia decided not to push any further for the moment and they finished their meals in a mildly uncomfortable silence.

Mama Landry appeared just as they both finished off their third piece of bread.

"All right now, who wants dessert?" They both groaned at the same time and all three of them laughed. "Well, now, that's what I like ta' hear! I'll be back with more coffee. Keep on visitin'."

"Actually, Mama, I have to be going soon," Austin said. He pulled out his wallet and took a few bills from it. "Please keep Georgia in coffee as long as she needs, though." He smiled, stood, and handed Mama Landry the bills. She put them in her apron pocket and pulled him into another hug.

"Don'tcha stay gone so long this time, hear me? Ya break an old woman's heart if ya stay away so long again." She looked at him wistfully as she held him at arm's length.

"You have my word, Mama," Austin said seriously. "I won't stay away. I shouldn't have stayed away so long, but things were hectic and… complicated. I'm sorry. I really did miss you, too. You're more than enough reason to come back, and I have a few others in mind, too." He darted a quick glance to Georgia who blushed again and looked back at her coffee cup.

"Now weren't them some pretty words, Mr. Austin. Ya keep to 'em." She pinched his dimpled cheek gently and grabbed their plates before walking away. Just before she walked through the doors to the kitchen, she turned. "Ya take care now, hear? We had 'nuff sadness 'round here fo' a while. Seein' ya back's a ray a'sunshine in this stormy world." She pushed through the doors and was gone.

Austin turned back to Georgia. She couldn't tell for sure, but she could almost swear his eyes were misty.

"Well," he said. "I really should be getting back. I have kind of a long drive." He paused for a moment, then continued on. "I'd like to see you again sometime, if you're interested that is."

"I'd like that," Georgia said, and she meant it. Aside from getting information, she was enjoying getting to know him. She pulled out a bookmark from her bag that had the bookstore's phone number on it. She flipped it over and wrote her schedule for the next week on it, then handed it to him. "The store's the easiest place to reach me. Either call or come in any time I'm there. We can go from there."

He took the bookmark and put it in his back pocket. "I definitely will. I had a nice time visiting tonight." He held out his hand and she put hers out as well. Instead of shaking it, however, he turned it over, brought it to his lips, and kissed the top softly. "G'night, Georgia," he said, letting her hand go and putting on his jacket. He walked toward the door, looked over his shoulder and smiled before pushing it open and disappearing into the evening.

Chapter Fourteen
Check In

A week after their first meeting, Georgia found herself heading back into the woods after making sure the Marens were asleep again. She was much more anxious to get there this time and was excited about all the information she had to share. She didn't have many leads that had panned out, but she did have a significant new source of information that could end up being a pretty big deal. She had transformed not long after she got into the woods because she could travel much faster as a bobcat and she was in a hurry to get to the clearing. She crashed through the brush and skidded to a stop, nearly plowing over Christian who was in his human form. He jumped sideways to avoid being hit and swore under his breath.

"Permit me one minute," he growled, not sounding much different than he did when he was a bear. He walked to the edge of the pond, waded in, and disappeared under the surface.

Alarmed and slightly out of breath, Georgia looked to Victoria, Jordan, and Sawyer who were grouped together a few feet away at the edge of the pond. "What's going on? What in the world is he doing going into that water? It has to be freezing!"

"We need someone to feel around and find exactly how the two paths out of the pond are laid out," Jordan answered, walking over and bumping her shoulder against Georgia's in an affectionate greeting. Georgia flicked her tail in happiness. "Victoria doesn't have the dexterity to be able to tell how large the passages are or whether they can be blocked easily."

"Alas, it is true." Victoria agreed, floating above the spot where Christian had disappeared. "I was only able to use my beak and neck to feel along the edge until I found holes large enough to possibly be tunnels which would lead to the well."

"It's the middle of the night. How is he going to be able to see down…" Georgia trailed off as half of the pond illuminated from beneath. She shook her head. "You know, even with the fact that all of us are currently talking animals with human brains, magic is still so foreign to me I wonder if I'll ever get used to it." Jordan and Sawyer laughed.

"It should not take long," Victoria said, not taking her eyes off the water where Christian had submerged. They could feel her tension, and they remained silent until finally the glow faded and bubbles rose, followed shortly by Christian's head which bobbed toward the edge of the pond. The rest of him emerged as the pond got shallower, and he finally stepped out, shivered, and transformed into his hulking bear figure.

"Well?" Sawyer asked him expectantly.

"As Victoria stated, there are two places water can enter and exit the pond. Upon my investigation, I found water was flowing in and out of both. They are of adequate size to place a container of dye inside each of them; each one a different color. Once that is achieved, we will need to seal both tunnels tightly, at least temporarily, so the dye may leech into the streams and, inevitably, into the well's water.

If we have someone in the mill who is able to check the well, we should know within a day or two which tunnel is the connector by the color of the water. Once we know, we will leave that tunnel blocked and unblock the other, letting fresh water continue to flow into the pond."

"That sounds reasonable," Jordan said. "Now we just have to find someone in the mill we can ask to do that." They all looked toward Georgia.

"I may actually know someone we can ask," Georgia said, excited to be able to share her news. She told them all about the leads she had found in the parking lot, and how all of them had gone cold. She told them about asking Mama Landry about the two unique cars in the parking lot and her only knowing who one of them belonged to. Then she told them about seeing Austin leaving the mill, seeing him again when she was leaving the library, and again in the picture at Mama Landry's restaurant. Finally, she told them about Austin coming into the bookstore, his being the one who owned the other car, and how they had dinner together and talked about a number of interesting things. When she finished her story, they all made noises of approval.

"You have done well," Christian said approvingly. "This Austin seems to have the potential to be someone able to check the water from the well. If he does not truly work there, he is not likely part of any army. He should not have a deep seated loyalty to their secrecy or know of the power the water may generate."

"I thought the same thing," Georgia said. "I was worried at first when I found out he was a Neff because Jordan and I were pretty certain Dale Neff was one of the newest recruits to the army and Dale is Austin's uncle. But it sounds like he doesn't have much contact with his uncle anymore and hasn't for a while. What?" Georgia asked as Christian rose to all fours at the mention of Mr. Neff and a faint rumble emanated from his throat.

"Did you say 'Neff'?" he asked in barely a whisper. Victoria ruffled her feathers.

"Um, yes," Georgia replied nervously. "Is that a problem? He really seems a lot different than his uncle."

Christian didn't reply for a while. Instead, he began pacing the clearing, huffing now and then. They all remained still and watched him, letting him pace through whatever he was dealing with. Finally, he turned and faced them.

"After the first war, most of the remaining relatives of Edmund Nephyrion believed him to be dead. They changed their names so as to escape persecution by Onirus vigilantes who sought to continue the eradication of evil. The Neff family line is believed to be directly descendent from the Nephyrions. Neff… Nephyrion. If that is true, your Austin may very well be Edmund Nephyrion's very distant great nephew. This makes him potentially significantly more dangerous."

Georgia was stunned. How could the person she had grown to almost enjoy spending time with, who seemed so genuinely kind and compassionate, who Mama Landry had adored as a child, be evil? She had been so excited just a few moments ago; they all had. And now she might have just involved herself with someone who could be a major enemy; a main player for the opposite side. Evil. She couldn't wrap her head around the idea.

"Just because his name is Neff, doesn't mean he has to be an enemy, does it?" Georgia asked, almost pleadingly. "I don't get any kind of negative feeling around him, and I'm usually a pretty good judge of character. Not to mention, I have been more paranoid than ever lately. I mean, look at you," she said to Christian. "Your entire family came from that side too, but you didn't want anything to do with the evil of that family, and you left."

"Yes, and look at all it has cost me," Christian said quietly. "The people I left behind know what I gave up to leave. Many believe I left for my love and lost her, just like I lost my family by leaving them behind. I do not believe many would be anxious to repeat my choices and make the same sacrifices, especially believing I failed in my attempts at freedom."

"Do you think most people on that side even remember you or your story?" Sawyer asked.

"Perhaps not," Christian conceded. "However, there very well may still be people in the court who were present when I was. They will know what happened and how I was able to elude them; the ways in which I was able to escape will not be able to be replicated. But," he said, with a slightly more positive tone, "these things have been true since we started this plan. The family young Austin Neff belongs to and comes from does nothing to change these facts. What we need to determine now is how deep he is involved with the mill directors, how much information he has and is willing to share, and how much of that information we can believe. I am cautious but optimistic. I feel it is suspiciously fortuitous he has presented himself to us just at the time of our greatest need, but perhaps the fates are smiling on us." They all nodded slowly, digesting what he had just said. Georgia broke the silence. "So… did you guys get a chance to observe the ravine town? What's going on there?"

"Oh!" Jordan said, rising. "We sure did! That place is nuts," she said, her tail wagging in excitement. "It's straight out of an old west novel or something. They use water wheels to generate their electricity, they wash their clothes in a river, they use candlelight mostly at night, they sew their own clothes. It's really something to watch."

"Ok," Georgia nodded. "That's definitely interesting and fits with what Austin told me about the place. But how does that help us?"

"Ah, yeah, well… I guess it doesn't." Jordan said in a dejected manner. "We did see some people who looked to be in charge, but we couldn't hear their names. We are too big to be able to get close enough during the day when people are out to hear their conversations."

"How are we going to be able to overcome that barrier?" Georgia asked. Everyone sat quietly. No one offered suggestions. "Were you not able to come up with any ideas we could try once you figured out the issue?" she asked incredulously.

"We came up with one," Christian replied flatly. "We do not believe you will be fond of it."

Georgia tilted her head up and closed her eyes. She had a feeling she knew where this was going, and he was right; she didn't like it. She had enough on her plate to overwhelm her; she didn't have any desire to add more.

"Georgia, we are truly sorry. You have been burdened with much as of late and I hope you do know we greatly appreciate your efforts. You are serving a great purpose and should be very proud. We are proud of you." Victoria said softly from her pond. Georgia looked at her and took a deep breath. The words were less comforting than her tone. The tone reminded her a bit of her mother's voice. A pang hit her and she realized how much she was missing her lately.

"Ok," she said with some reservation. "So I need to go there and hide somewhere close so I can hear what they have to say. Do you have a place you'd suggest I hide based on what you observed?"

"The trees." Sawyer answered quickly. "During the day there are so many people out walking around there would be no way you could sneak around on the ground anywhere close enough to hear. But in the trees, you could be inconspicuous enough that you could move around as needed and they'd never notice. Christian tried it, but he's too big to move around stealthily. Once he gets into place, he's stuck there until no one's around."

"Ok," Georgia said resignedly. "So do we want me to do this before or after I lean on Austin a bit and see what I can glean from him."

"Whatever you prefer would be fine," Christian said, and she got the feeling he was trying to pacify her. She both appreciated the gesture and was annoyed by it. She tried to focus on the positive aspect of things; she had spent far too long dwelling on the negative as of late.

"Well, I think if there is a chance I can get close enough to him to get information, that might be better to do up front. That way, if something bad goes down at the ravine, I'll at least have been able to get *some* information."

"What bad things do you think might happen?" Jordan asked, a hint of nervousness in her voice.

"I hope nothing. But we all know things can happen that we never would have imagined. Even the best laid plans have unexpected twists. I just figure if I get detained or something, you'll still have all the available information to work with."

"I agree with Georgia," Victoria chimed in. "It is best we all have as much to work with as possible. Thank you for thinking of it."

"Ok, so the newest plan is for Georgia to talk to Austin, figure out just how much evil we're working with, get whatever information she can, and share that information with us before going to the ravine town to see what she can hear." Sawyer listed off the tasks.

"And you all will do… what?" Georgia asked, trying not to sound too annoyed.

"Christian's going to get together the things we need for dyeing the water in the well," Jordan said. "Sawyer and I are going to go back to the mill and try to see if there are any vulnerable spots, ways to see what's going on or hear what's going on, and we'll watch the people going in and coming out. We need to determine travel patterns to know when would be best to infiltrate if it's ever needed."

"You may want to locate whatever road the mill uses to take deliveries to the ravine town as well," Georgia said, relived they had additional plans and tasks for themselves. She didn't feel as alone in the whole thing when the others had tasks to complete and weren't waiting on her to be able to continue their plans.

"That is a very good idea," Christian agreed. "I have visited the ravine town and a vast majority of the woods in the area, but I have never traveled the road they use to get from the highway to the town. If we know how well that is traveled, we may be able to find vulnerable points as well as places the road could be disabled." They all stood except Christian who, even seated, was taller than all of them. "Georgia, thank you for all you have done. You have shouldered your burdens well and you have put in significant effort and thought." They all verbalized their agreement and Georgia was thankful that, for once, her blushing wasn't visible.

"You're welcome. And thank you for saying that. It's been hard and we have a long way to go. The encouragement is nice. I don't know how much time it's going to take to do all this, but I'll try to be back as soon as I can." She turned and began walking toward the brush and the path that would lead her home. She turned and looked over her shoulder. They were all still standing there this time. "Stay safe everyone," she said, and pushed through the brush and disappeared from their view.

Chapter Fifteen
Test Drive

Georgia finished the display of new merchandise at the store and stood back to admire her work. Organizing a fun way to display books or products had always been Jordan's strong point, but she felt even Jordan would have been proud of what she accomplished with this one. The display, which she had placed right in the middle aisle of the store so it could even be seen from outside the store on the sidewalk, covered three tables; the tallest set in the middle and the rest cascading from it in various heights like arms on each side. The colors and different stack sizes drew attention and, while she had a feeling it was going to be a pain to keep up on, it was worth it if it brought people into the store and increased business. After the slow winter they had, a boost in revenue was something they needed.

The bell above the door jingled and she turned around to see Austin pulling the door shut behind him. They both gave a wave and Georgia stepped to the side so Austin could see the entire display. He walked up to it, put his fists on his hips, and took a moment to absorb everything. "This looks absolutely incredible," he finally said, looking at her with admiration and amazement. "How long did this take you?"

"About an hour and a half to draw up the plan and set up the base, then another hour or so to set everything just right. You really think it's amazing? Like amazing enough to draw people in?"

He looked at it again. "I really do. If I hadn't already been on my way in and I had walked by and seen this, there's a really good chance I would've come in to check it out."

"Thanks," Georgia said, standing next to him and admiring the display again. "I'm really happy with how it turned out. I have some high hopes for it."

Austin leaned to the side and bumped her shoulder. "It's going to be great."

She instinctively bumped him back and walked toward the circulation desk. "So hey, you came back into town again," she said. "Any reason for the quick return? More errands to run?"

He followed behind her and stopped at the counter as she walked behind it and turned away from him to check the order ledger. "Well, honestly, I was hoping you'd be free after you got off and we could do something together." She smiled widely down into the ledger and marked off the people she had called to pick up their orders before turning to face him.

"So, I'm the errand?" she said, her eyes wrinkled in silent laughter. Austin's laughter was much louder and her eyes flitted to the dimple again.

"Well, sure, if you want to think of it that way. Although I would like it to be understood that I hold you in higher regard than an errand. I tend to think of errands as something that *needs* to be done, but I'm not particularly excited about. I've been looking forward to seeing you again."

Georgia had all but given up being self-conscious of blushing in front of Austin at this point. He seemed to be able to make her do so pretty easily. "Well, thanks. That's nice of you to say. I've been looking forward to seeing you, too."

"Glad to hear it," Austin said. "So, am I lucky enough that you're free tonight and able to hang out?"

"Today's your lucky day. I'm free as a bird. What did you have in mind? Do you want to go to the restaurant again?"

"I'm not opposed to that," he said. "But I was wondering if you might want to mix things up a bit."

"I can't imagine what else there is to do in this town," Georgia wondered. "But if you have something in mind, I'm open to suggestions."

"I completely understand if you aren't comfortable with it, but you mentioned my car the other day, so I thought maybe you'd like to go for a drive for a bit. You know, get it out on the road, open it up, see what it can do."

Georgia's eyes widened. She was feeling equal parts apprehension and excitement. In the back of her mind, Christian's voice played and she remembered she was supposed to be finding out if Austin was a threat. In the moment, however, he seemed like a guy who was just looking forward to showing off his four-wheeled toy.

"Well," she said, a slight note of hesitation in her voice.

Austin took his keys out of his pocket and set them on the counter in front of her. "You can drive, if it makes you feel better." She didn't realize how long she had been staring at the keys on the counter until Austin let out another loud laugh. "It appeared I've peaked your interest."

She joined him in the laughter. "It's beyond temping," she admitted. "But I don't think I'd be comfortable driving that expensive of a car."

He tilted his head to the side slightly. "Georgia, the car was made to be driven. You're going to hurt her feelings if you don't want to use her for what she's made for."

It was Georgia's turn to let out a loud laugh at that. "Well, I wouldn't want to do that." She put away the ledger and grabbed her jacket from under the counter. "I tell you what, I'll take a little turn around town and then you can take us out on the roads and show me what she can do. Just… please don't kill me." She knew he would think she was being facetious, but a part of her was quite literal about the request.

"I think that sounds completely reasonable," Austin took the jacket from her hands and opened it to help her put it on.

"Hey, Ryan, I'm outta here," Georgia called down the hallway. "See you tomorrow. If you have any questions about the display, the diagram is under the register. If the diagram doesn't answer them… make something up I guess."

"Will do. Have a good rest of your day," they heard faintly from the back office as they opened the door and exited the store.

They stood next to Austin's car. Austin held the door open and Georgia looked down at the leather seats and shiny, black interior. "So," he said, "are you getting in?"

She looked at him. "I have a condition," she replied.

Austin leaned against the fender, still holding the door. "You have a condition to driving my car? Ok, let's hear it."

"We're going to chat while we drive, I assume. I want to have a deal where if one of us asks a question, the other has to answer it, even if it's unpleasant or uncomfortable." She could see the look of confusion on his face and she hurried on. "We have the understanding that neither of us is going to intentionally ask an unpleasant question, but sometimes you don't know what emotions a question might drudge up. I really want to get to know you, so the condition is a no holds barred, open Q&A. If you agree, I'll try driving your car."

He thought about it for a moment and then leaned away from the car. "I accept your terms. Now, get in the car!" he said in mock forcefulness.

Georgia took a deep breath and lowered herself into the driver's seat. She sank into the leather and Austin shut the door and walked around to the other side. She noticed the interior of the car smelled faintly of the same subtle cologne he wore. It was spotless inside, not even a window smudge. He clearly took good care of the vehicle.

Austin opened the passenger door and got in. He buckled his seatbelt and adjusted the seat to accommodate his long legs. Georgia looked over at him.

"What?" he asked. "You're in now, you can't back out."

"No, I'm not trying to back out. It's just… I can't reach the pedals. I know some people are really particular about their settings, so I…"

"I wouldn't have asked someone who is six inches shorter than me to drive my car if I didn't expect the seats and mirrors to be moved," he laughed. "Do what you need to do."

Georgia spent a minute moving things around until she felt comfortable enough. "Ok, here we go." She turned the key in the ignition and the car vibrated smoothly, but idled almost silently. Georgia felt her breathing slow as she enjoyed the luxury of the car. She shifted into reverse, grabbed the wheel, backed onto the road, and motored off. They drove in silence for a couple blocks before Austin spoke.

"So, what do you think of her?"

"She's amazing," Georgia answered without hesitation. "It's like we're floating over the roads, not rolling over them. I can see why you wanted this car for so long."

"I've named her Artemis."

"Goddess of the moon, the hunt," Georgia said, barely above a whisper. "That's appropriate."

Out of the corner of her eye, Austin grinned, obviously pleased she knew who that was. "She's black like the night and having her is my own form of vengeance against anyone who ever told me I wouldn't be anything?"

"Why would anyone tell you that?" Georgia asked. He didn't respond right away and she gave him a side-glance. "No avoiding answers to questions, remember? You agreed."

He took a deep breath and shifted slightly in his seat. "When I was young, I got a lot of grief for being a Neff. The name isn't exactly synonymous with pleasant people. My dad's a great guy, but my uncle Dale doesn't have the best reputation. Neither did my grandfather. Actually, I think my dad's about the only decent Neff out there, at least according to popular opinion. Anyway, I grew up hearing about bad blood so much I almost started believing it. Mama Landry never let me feel that way though. Then, Dad and Uncle Dale had a falling out when I was about ten or so and Dad didn't want me coming into town anymore. He was afraid of the influence Uncle Dale would have on me.

Fortunately, in the ravine town, most people seemed to like me, and I didn't hear the negative things like I did in town. I stayed away from town for a lot of years. When Uncle Dale started working at the mill, my dad had me do town runs instead of spending much time inside it. I think he still doesn't want me to be around him much." He shrugged and looked over at her. "So, that's why I decided to get the car. When I did come into town, I wanted everyone to see I could do respectable hard work, make something of myself, and I wasn't destined for the 'Neff blood'."

"That's ridiculous," Georgia said, irritated. "One thing I hate about small towns is that everyone thinks they're entitled to voice their opinions about everyone else. Bad blood…" she scoffed and shook her head. She thought back to the story Victoria had told them about the blood used to forge the amulets from the Onirus and Nephyrion families to house their magic. Ok, she thought to herself, so maybe blood power was a thing, and maybe Austin was descendent of a pretty terrible family bloodline. She gripped the steering wheel tighter and furrowed her brow a bit. That still didn't mean he deserved to be treated like a bad person when there was no evidence at all he was one.

"Uh, did I lose you?" Austin asked nervously.

"Hmm?" Georgia said, and looked over at him. "Oh! No, you absolutely didn't. Sorry, I just got lost in my thoughts for a second. I don't like people being judgy, that's all. I'm glad you're doing what you're doing and making people see you're a great guy. We're more than just our blood," she said and she realized it sounded a little more forceful than she meant it to, so she smiled at him.

"I couldn't agree more," Austin nodded. "Ok, my turn to ask a question. You said the other day you just moved back here with your mom not that long ago. Where did you live before?"

"We lived in Fauset, New Hampshire. It was a tiny town, even compared to this one. Just one road went through it and it was forty minutes to the closest grocery store." She looked over at Austin and saw he was looking at her expectantly. She let out a small laugh. "I'm sorry if you were hoping for more, but that's really the extent of it. I was technically born here I guess, but we moved before I can remember anything from this place. I grew up there and went to school there. I had eleven people in my graduating class." She shrugged. "That's it."

"What did you do for fun there if it was so small? Were you friends with everyone? Was it hard to move?" Austin prodded.

"I feel like that's a lot of questions," Georgia teased.

"Well, if you aren't going to give me anything to work with when I ask the first one, then I get a couple follow-ups."

"I guess that's fair. Let's see, what did I do for fun? I read a lot, I went for hikes in the woods, and I played cards with my mom. No, I wasn't friends with everyone. I actually wasn't really friends with anyone. The girls my age were all obsessed with fashion and trying to keep up with the trends in places like New York and Boston, and I just really couldn't be bothered. I never really got close to anyone. My mom was always my best friend. So, no, it wasn't hard to move. I wanted Mom to be wherever she would be happiest in the end. She grew up here, and this is where she wanted to spend the rest of her days. I'm glad she got that." She turned slightly to Austin and raised an eyebrow. "Enough?"

"I'll accept it," he responded. "Although, it blows my mind you didn't have any friends. You're an amazing girl, smart, super sweet, friendly. Those other kids were crazy not to pursue being your friend."

Georgia hoped her face didn't look quite as red as it felt. "Thanks," she said softly. "That's sweet of you. You're… um… I think you're really great, too." She swallowed and tried to steady her voice when she continued. "Jordan and Sawyer were the first real friends I ever made. It makes me sad I had so little time with them. Maybe having regular, normal friendships just isn't in the cards for me." She realized she was bringing down the mood again as well as slightly skirting a subject best not touched on, so she gave a halfhearted laugh at the end, and sat up straighter in her seat.

"I don't think that's true," Austin said quietly. "I think you're absolutely a friendship kind of person. You obviously have a lot of compassion. From what I've seen, you have so much to offer. You deserve that back."

Georgia shook her head. She knew there were awful people out there who had strong powers of manipulation, but she couldn't believe Austin was one of them. "People didn't know what they were doing isolating themselves from you because of your last name. It's their loss," she whispered.

"I'm glad you feel that way. See what I mean; sweet girl."

"All right," she said, pulling to the curb on the edge of town. She was anxious for a subject change. She loved the things he was saying, but she had no idea how she was supposed to react. "I think it's time you took the reins on this bad girl. I've done three laps around town. Time for you to stretch her legs."

Chapter Sixteen
Side Mission

Austin unbuckled his belt, got out of the car, and waited for her to get in to the passenger seat so he could shut the door for her before going around and getting in the driver's seat. He adjusted the seat and mirrors before buckling his belt and putting the car in gear. "Anywhere specific you want to go?" He asked, maneuvering the car along the paved road leading out of town. Georgia was in awe at how smooth the car rode and suspected they were probably going much faster than it felt.

"I don't really know what's around here other than the town. I'd love to see where you live sometime, but I know it's an ordeal getting there in this car, so I'll leave it to you. I'm just along for the ride."

"Have you ever been to the quarry?" Austin asked.

"No. If it's not in town or a small part of the woods behind my house, it's pretty safe to assume I've never been there or seen it. I didn't even know the town had a quarry."

"Well, it doesn't really anymore. The mill and the quarry used to be the main businesses in the area. The mill used the aggregates from the quarry to make their products. Then the quarry went defunct and the mill switched to other types of manufacturing. This was all long before either of us was born. So, now the quarry is just this big hole in the ground. Part of it's overgrown and part of it's a lake. It's actually really beautiful at dusk, and at night you can see a whole sky full of stars since the top of the crest on one side is above the tree line."

"I think that sounds great. I'd like to see it," Georgia said.

After a couple minutes, Austin turned off on a side road and began driving along a paved but not well maintained road Georgia never knew existed. They drove for a few minutes in silence and then Austin spoke up.

"I think it's your turn to ask a question."

"Oh, right. Let me think." She paused for a moment to try to think of a benign way to get some information about the mill. "You've seen where I work, so tell me about your work. What's it like in the mill? What are the people you work with like?"

"It's kind of boring," Austin said and she could sense a hint of evasiveness in his voice.

"Well, I thought my hometown story was pretty boring, but you pressed me about that. Indulge me," she said in a teasing manner she hoped would keep the atmosphere light.

"Ok. Well, like I said, I just run transport between the ravine and the mill. So I go to the mill when they want to send us stuff like supplies. Or if there are people being transferred out to us, I bring them out. There isn't enough room for everyone to have cars, so only a few people do. I also bring some materials and food items to the mill that we make/harvest in the ravine. We keep bees at the ravine.

The mill uses their wax for some things. We also have sheep, and the wool can be used."

"And the people? The workers and your bosses. What are they like?" Georgia asked.

"The people are fine. The mill hires people who are good workers, follow directions well, and are strong. It's a physically demanding job that's also dangerous at times what with the machinery and all. So obedience, strength, and intelligence are all key requirements."

"So, if it's a hard working, dangerous place, does that mean the bosses are like drill sergeants to keep people safe?" Georgia pushed.

"I guess you could say that," Austin replied. "My dad was a supervisor before he got moved out to the ravine. He isn't a particularly strong man, but he's smart and obedient. He got made the head of the ravine operations before I was even born. Family obligation is what pulled me into working for the ravine and the mill, like it does most of the kids in our group.

I've heard my dad say the mill supervisors have to be good at leading a large group of people and moving people up the line for advancement. They are really focused and dedicated to the CEO. I've never met him. I just know his name's Ed. The supervisors keep in contact with him and do whatever he requests they do. I've overheard people say he lives in an estate set way back in the woods. I don't know that he ever actually goes to the mill, but he provides instructions to the supervisors about what needs to be done and how. The process seems to work fine, since the mill's always doing well."

"You said your uncle works there now, right?" Georgia said, looking out the window at the trees flashing by. She had a feeling she knew who Ed was, but she needed to not focus on that. Keeping things light and the conversation flowing was important. "What does he do?"

"I don't see or talk to him much because of my dad, but I know he works in recruiting. He actually just got a promotion recently. He's advanced pretty quickly since starting there. They seem to like him."

"That's good, right? You said he was one who had a bad reputation. Maybe the fact he's doing so well in his job means he'll show people he's dependable and competent and not what they think he is." When Austin didn't respond, she turned to look at him and saw his face was stony. "Are you ok?" she asked tentatively.

"Let's just say working at the mill isn't a good way to bolster your reputation. I know you haven't lived in town that long, so you may not be aware of it, but the mill isn't known for being the nicest place or employing the nicest people."

"You sound like you agree with that assessment," Georgia said.

Austin considered that. "There are things about the politics of the place I don't like."

She could tell she was now getting the most basic answers out of him and felt like she had probably exhausted her chances at getting any more real information out of him for the day.

"Life's too short," she said, staring out the windshield. "Family obligation or not, if you really don't like it, you should find something else; somewhere else."

"You might be right," Austin agreed. He didn't say anything for a bit and Georgia had just settled into the silence when he asked. "Why the interest in the mill?"

Georgia was taken aback for a second. "Oh. I mean... I guess it's just because I'm new here and don't know much about anything. Just trying to get caught up on things."

"Your mom never told you anything about her hometown until she just decided to move back?" he asked.

"Not really," Georgia answered. "Mom focused on our life in Fauset. She was more of a live-in-the-here-and-now kind of person. All I know about life before Fauset is that she met my dad when they were in high school together. When she graduated, she worked cleaning houses and my dad worked grounds for the mill. They got pregnant with me, and before I turned two he died in a work accident. She moved shortly after that happened. When I got older, she told me we moved because she couldn't stand being in the same town with the bad memories being so fresh. I guess over time those bad memories faded and the memories from happier times must've come back. And here we are. Well, here I am."

Austin nodded but didn't say anything. They drove the winding road in the fading light. The car had a very smooth ride and Georgia was comfortable with one arm on the center console and the other resting in her lap. "You were right; the car is really great," she finally said after close to ten minutes. "The ride's so soft it's soothing. I've needed to get out and relax a bit for a while now. The town feels so small sometimes, driving out on these roads makes it less… I don't know…"

"Claustrophobic," they both said at the same time. They looked at each other and Georgia smiled, nodding. "Exactly. You get it." She said.

She felt something bump her hand and saw Austin's was resting next to hers on the center arm rest. His eyes moved down then back up to the windshield. He turned his hand over and slid it under hers, their fingers intertwining. Georgia was starting to like the familiar cool sensation of his touch, followed by the warmth of his skin. They rode the rest of the way in silence.

After another ten minutes, Austin slowed and pulled off the main road onto a packed gravel one. They drove slowly and Georgia sat up straighter trying to take in the view in the dim light from the sun just barely above the horizon. Austin took his hand back and used it to steer the car over the uneven road, around a bend, and up to the crest of the quarry. He parked the car, turned the key so the car turned off but the instrumental music that had been playing quietly the whole ride continued. He turned it up.

"Come on," Austin said as he got out and walked around to open Georgia's door. Austin shut the door behind her and followed as she walked to the front of his car. With the headlights off, the quarry looked like a black abyss in front of them and snaked around to the side, out of sight through the edge of the forest. It was a bit unnerving. She looked around at the trees and empty rocky space surrounding them.

Austin stopped next to her and leaned back against the hood of the car. "You're looking the wrong direction," Austin said on a laugh and he gently hooked a finger under Georgia's chin and directed her face toward the sky. She inhaled a soft gasp as she took in the deep purple, velvety colored expanse in front of them, dotted with what seemed like innumerable silver twinkling stars.

She leaned back against the car next to him so close their sides were touching from arm to knee. "It just makes you think anything in the world could be possible, doesn't it?" she whispered. "We're so small and insignificant in the grand scheme."

Austin put am arm around her waist and pulled her closer to him. "Not so insignificant," he whispered back, and she turned to him and smiled. He smiled back and leaned down to gently kiss her. A flash of heat shot from her lips through her body. She closed her eyes and leaned into the kiss, ignoring any apprehension and letting herself enjoy the moment. She turned, putting her arms inside his open jacket and around his waist. He turned as well, his other hand gently brushing her face and moving into her hair. His lips were soft and his touch was so gentle, she couldn't imagine feeling anything but safe in his arms.

They stayed like that, pressed together, Georgia didn't know how long.

When they finally broke apart, Austin looked down into her eyes. "I've been wanting to do that since that first day in the bookstore. You know, when you told your boss you couldn't help him because you were going to go do something you actually wanted to do."

Georgia laughed softly and pressed her forehead to his chest. "I was so hoping you hadn't heard that. I didn't want you to think I was over-eager in a creepy way." He placed a soft kiss on top of her head then rested his chin there. "Not in the slightest. I was already pretty interested in you. It was good for my ego."

She laughed again and leaned back, sighing heavily. "I guess I could have saved myself some stress, then, couldn't I? I kept worrying I was saying the wrong thing or making you uncomfortable. It's kind of my MO most of the time."

He pulled her tight to him again. "You definitely didn't need to stress. You can always feel relaxed with me." And he kissed her again.

Chapter Seventeen
The Ravine Town

Georgia jolted awake in a panic. She looked around at the familiar sight of her room, and leaned back against the pillow, willing her heart rate to slow down. She hadn't been able to sleep for hours after she had gotten home the night before; not that the reasons were much of a hardship.

She and Austin had stayed at the quarry for another hour before he became the voice of reason and suggested it was probably a good idea he get her back to her car so she could get home before the Marens started to worry about her. They held hands the whole way home, but didn't talk much. It was a comfortable silence, and she reveled in replaying the events of the evening in her head the whole way.

When they got back to the bookstore, he helped her out of the car, kissed her again, and said he'd be back to visit in a couple days. They both got in their vehicles and drove away. She didn't even remember her drive home, but somehow she had found herself sitting in bed, cross-legged, her blanket wrapped around her, writing the things she had learned from him during their conversation interspersed with doodles of hearts. When she finished writing it all, she laid there for hours, basking in the happy glow from the evening.

After sleep finally reached her, however, she had been thrown into fitful dreams of kissing Austin and him suddenly turning into a large, black raven and chasing her while trying to steal an amulet from around her neck. She had run through town, past Mama Landry, Auggie, the Marens, and Mr. Neff before crashing into the woods. She had run and run through the trees and brush before breaking through the other side to find herself right on the ledge of the quarry. She tried to stop in time but couldn't and, just as she lost her balance over the ledge, she jumped awake, squeezing her blanket in a death grip.

Now she laid, looking at the ceiling while her heart rate returned to normal and the cold, terrified feeling in her core subsided. She tried to bring back some of the happiness and safety she felt last night. She felt like the dreams were telling her she had no time or place reveling in her happiness about Austin returning her affections when what she needed to focus on was finding something that could help them prevent this possible war. And besides, it wasn't like she was going to be able to live any kind of normal life with things the way they were now. She needed the threat with Edmund to be over so Christian could focus on making her solely human. Then she could think about what the future might be for her and Austin, if there even was one. She hoped there was …

She sighed heavily and got up. While she showered, she made a mental game plan. Today she would venture to the ravine town. Christian had told her some landmarks and the general direction to go to find the town. The sooner she could get there the sooner she could hopefully find out something they could use to help them move forward. She made a deal with herself that, if she could get some kind of solid information today, she would allow herself to have a good time the next time Austin came to town to visit. She may have several tasks to complete, a war to possibly fight, and a major secret to keep, but that didn't mean she didn't deserve to have something positive in her life in all the murky garbage she was dealing with.

She toweled off, got dressed, threw her hair into a loose ponytail, and grabbed her bag and jacket. She wouldn't need them where she was going, but she wanted to keep up appearances that she was out doing normal things in case Judy and Gordon looked into her room as they passed by. If her things were missing, they would assume she was out being a responsible adult, instead of roaming the countryside as a bobcat looking for a ravine town to spy on. She rolled her eyes as she contemplated the ridiculousness that was her life.

She threw her things in her car and got in. She had decided last night she would drive her car back to the quarry and leave it there before transforming and making her way to the ravine town from there. No one would come across her car way out there and wonder where she had gone or what she was up to. The road looked different in the daylight and her car wasn't nearly as nice as Austin's so the ride was rough enough that, by the time she reached the packed gravel road that would bring her to the quarry, her back was hurting and she couldn't wait to stand up. When she arrived, she got out of the car and stretched her arms over her head reaching backward, half of her vertebrae cracking. She made sure the doors were locked, tucked the keys behind her driver side front tire, and closed her eyes.

Once she was in her feline form, she assessed her options and took off at a gentle lope in the direction she felt pretty sure would take her to the ravine town. After what had to be close to thirty minutes of travel, she recognized a rock formation Christian had mentioned and knew she was approximately two miles from where she needed to be. After what she estimated was close to the two-mile mark, she slowed her speed and became stealthier with her movements and noise making. She didn't know how far into the wooded areas around the town the people travelled and she didn't want to come across anyone unexpectedly.

Every now and then she would stop and listen, trying to ascertain where the location of the edge of town might be. Finally, she thought she heard the sound of distant hammering. She didn't know if it was the town or something else, but she decided to investigate. She climbed a tall tree and made her way slowly from branch to branch of the trees until she saw a small cottage below her a few hundred feet out in front. When she shifted her position, she saw a few more similar looking cottages behind it and felt confident she had found the town. She made her way through the trees behind the line of houses and came to a large building that looked as though it was likely used for storage. Anything from machinery to merchandise could have been housed in the building. She used her keen eyes to look around and finally found a pair of women in the backyard area of a cottage four houses in. She lowered herself a few feet and made her way closer to them.

The women were dressed in homemade long dresses with thick stockings, sweaters, and leather aprons. The brunette woman looked to be about fifty years old, had a rotund build, and was wearing ear muffs to block the brisk wind that was cutting through the trees and ruffling Georgia's fur. The red haired woman was closer to Georgia's age, mid-twenties or so, and wore a stocking cap pulled down so far her eyes were barely visible below the brim and her red hair stuck out only a few inches at the bottom. The women looked to be cleaning game and cutting it into portions. She pricked her ears and listened.

"It looks like Gary had a great evening," the brunette woman said. "You should be proud of that boy. Even with you all just moving here less than two months ago, he's already working his regular production schedule and still finding time to have a successful hunt. He's going to be a great provider."

The red-haired woman nodded, pulling the skin off a rabbit and tossing it over a log already laden with furs. "He's working so hard to please everyone and set a good example for little Gabe. We didn't know what we were going to do when our milking barn caught fire and we lost all our equipment and more than half the stock. We were so underinsured that the money we got from it plus selling off the rest of the stock was just barely enough to pay off the loans we had on the equipment we lost. With a three-year-old to take care of and no money left, we didn't know how we were going to survive. We were sure we'd lose the house. Then Gary got approached by Dale about a position at the mill and it was like a godsend. He was willing to do anything it took to give us a home and, when we heard our home would be provided and all we had to do was contribute to the town on top of Gary's mill duties, he jumped at it. We're so grateful for the opportunity, Marissa. We really are."

Marissa nodded. "It's no problem at all, Jill. We're happy to have you. You're both good workers and that son of yours is a good boy. He wants to help just like his daddy. It won't be long before he'll be hunting and fishing and bringing in food for the town as well. You're nice folks and hard workers. We appreciate that around here. Dale knew about your husband from before and said he didn't think it was much of a risk bringing you on. He's usually right about those things."

"It's nice to be well thought of. I didn't even know Gary knew Dale before. Glad to know he made a good impression."

"Oh, Dale Neff knows everyone who lived in town for the most part. It's why he made his way up through the ranks so quickly. He's very persuasive at getting the kinds of people the mill needs through the doors." Marissa leaned closer to Jill and Georgia leaned further down to try to hear what she was whispering.

"Between you and me, it's a little eerie just how much Dale knows sometimes. He almost never comes out here, but he's able to sell this place on almost everyone it seems. His recruiting powers are unparalleled in anyone I've ever seen, and I've been here since this town started. I don't know what all methods of persuasion he uses, but sometimes folks come here so scared you'd think they were told we would eat their young if they didn't join us. He isn't the friendliest of fellas either. It's like he's a robot programmed to do one thing and any other conversation or interaction is a struggle for him."

Jill gave her a curious look and Marissa sat up straight again and shrugged her shoulders. "But the fact is, since he started pulling more people from the town and the mill to help us out here, things have gotten much easier. Everyone has less work to do, and the kids are finally able to have some time to themselves. Kids should be able to be kids."

"Oh, I agree!" Jill responded. "Gabe has been able to experience so much more out here than he would have in town. He loves that there are cows here. He missed ours when we sold them off. And he has so many kind, hard-working male role models around here. It's good for him. As for Dale, I can't say as I ever spoke to him before. Everything I heard was just pillow talk. But Gary seems to like him fine enough. Maybe he's just one of those men who likes to keep to himself outside of work." Marissa nodded and they continued their tasks in silence. Georgia was about to climb further up and move on when Marissa called out.

"Now speaking of good male role models, if it isn't Austin Neff himself."

Georgia whipped her head around and looked in the direction Marissa and Jill were looking. Austin walked through the gate next to the house and up to them. He turned over an empty bucket and sat next to the women, picking up a rabbit and an extra knife. "Hello, ladies," he said with his one-dimple smile. "How are you doing this morning? Busy I see."

The ladies smiled back at him. "We're fine, thanks," Jill responded. "I was just telling Marissa how grateful Gary, Gabe, and I are to have been given the opportunity to join you all here. She was telling me about how effective your uncle has been at increasing the population here so people have less work to do and the kids can relax more. Have you had more free time, Mr. Neff?"

Georgia saw Austin wince at being called Mr. Neff. "Please, it's Austin ma'am. Mr. Neff is my uncle… and my father come to think of it." They all laughed.

"Raymond Neff, Ray, is Austin's father," Marissa explained and Jill's face lit up.

"Oh, him I've met!" she exclaimed. "He's a wonderful man. He showed us to our home the first night we were here and brought us a home-cooked meal that lasted us for days. And that means Charlotte is your mother! She's one of the nicest ladies. She pulled Gabe right up into her lap and showed him all kinds of things she'd brought that you make here while your dad went over the schedule of things with us and what our duties would be. Gabe adores her."

"That sounds exactly like Mom," Austin smiled. Georgia could hear the strong affection for his mother in his voice. "And I agree, they are great people. I'm lucky to have them." The last sentence held a bit of tension and forced kindness, Georgia thought.

"So, if Ray is your dad, and you said Dale was your uncle, that would make Ray and Dale brothers?" Jill asked.

Georgia could tell she was simply being inquisitive, but the force with which Austin ripped his rabbit's fur off the hide showed how displeased he was with the topic. "Yes," he said quietly. "Uncle Dale is dad's older brother. They haven't been friendly in the past few years though. Other than now and then when their paths cross for work, I don't think they've talked much for close to twenty years."

"Oh, I'm sorry," Jill said, clearly shaken she had brought up such a negative subject. She looked at Marissa for reassurance.

"Austin has a similar opinion of his uncle as what I mentioned before," Marissa said in a comforting tone. "Don't worry about it. You aren't expected to know all of this yet for goodness sake."

"Yes, I'm sorry," Austin apologized. "Please don't let our petty family drama be any of your concern. But, hey, we're definitely glad to have you and your family here. I plan to take Gabe out to look for arrow heads sometime this week because, to answer your earlier question, yes, we definitely are starting to have some more free time now that more people are arriving here."

"Oh, he would love that!" Jill said appreciatively. "He wants to go out in the woods so badly, but we don't want him wandering out there alone when he doesn't know his way around."

"That's smart," Austin agreed. "We get a lot of different animals wandering around out there too and not all of them are friendly when startled. I'll be bouncing around from place to place for most of today, and I won't be around tomorrow, but maybe the next day he and I can go for a walk and see who can find the most pine cones." Jill smiled and nodded

"You haven't been around much lately," Marissa said to Austin. "Where have you been disappearing to?"

"Oh, I've actually been spending some time in Shamore," he responded and Georgia was pleased to see his face darken a couple of shades.

"Found something, or some*one* to occupy your time there, have you?" Marissa teased, and the women smiled at each other.

Austin rose, tossed the cleaned rabbit into the bucket with the others, and reached into another bucket to wash his hands. After he dried them, he reached out and squeezed each woman's shoulder affectionately. "That I have," he winked and walked away, hands in his pockets, still smiling.

"He's such a nice guy," Jill said, watching him go. "I think Gabe will like spending time with someone Austin's age; not so old as to be like a dad, but not his own age either. He'll feel so special someone like Austin wants to spend time with him."

"They don't come much better than Austin," Marissa agreed. "He's had to endure a lot growing up the son of the man who runs the ravine. He had to grow up much faster than most kids should. The tension with his dad and uncle has been hard on him and I think he's felt caught in the middle. I know Mr. Grey and Mr. Tucker at the mill wanted him to come work for them years ago, but his daddy wouldn't hear of it. He told them he needed to mold someone to take over the ravine if and when he wasn't able to do it anymore. He finally convinced them. I don't know why he didn't want Austin to work in the mill, especially since Mr. Grey and Mr. Tucker are the highest level supervisors there, other than Ed of course. Most would have thought those men wanting his son to work for them would've been a source of pride, but it seemed to really worry him."

"Maybe he just didn't want to be separated from him," Jill offered.

Marissa nodded. "That could be, too. Something about it just doesn't sit right with me. But regardless of the reason, we are lucky to have all the Neffs." Jill nodded and the women lapsed into silence.

Georgia made her way back the way she had come until she was out of view of the cottages. She climbed back down to the forest floor and shook herself, extricating the pine needles from her fur. She was pleased with herself having gotten what she felt was pretty important information. She debated for a while whether she should try to make her way to the actual ravine and see if she could see what was going on there, or if she should rush home and deliver the information to her friends. She decided that since she was here, she might as well get as much as she could. She took off to the Northeast where she knew she would find the ravine.

Before she knew it, the ground started to get rocky and the trees became thinner. She looked around to try to determine the best way to get close without being seen. The tree cover wasn't going to be as good of an option as it had been at the ravine town. She saw large groups of boulders spaced around and decided to slink from pile to pile, hoping there would be a crevice she could lodge herself in when needed. Three piles in, she saw two men standing at the top of the ravine looking down and gesturing. She backed her way into a crack between three large rocks and hunched down, making herself as small as possible to blend in.

The two men wore heavy overalls over long sleeved shirts, work boots, hard hats, and little flashes of color near their ears made her think they must be wearing ear plugs as well. She didn't quite understand that as there had been no significant noise since she had arrived near the town, but she ignored it. She listened hard to what they were saying. Even on the same level with them, she was much farther away than she had been with the women and the men's lower voices made it hard to pick up everything.

The larger of the two men gestured toward the bottom of the ravine, making wide arcs with his arm. "See that hilly area down there, Steve? The one with new trees and fallen rocks? Ed says we're gonna reactivate the ravine and use it for the hydro-electric power source. We're gonna need to clear all that down there, reshape it a bit, then fill the majority of it with water. After that, we'll build the mechanism to keep the water pumping through and that should take care of the power shortage they think we have at the mill. All we gotta do is keep it to ourselves what he actually wants extra power for. The people at the ravine won't think to question it when we tell them it's just for a more economical form of power so the mill can run more efficient. All they're gonna hear is it means they can have consistent power to their homes and work spaces. They'll be over the moon about it."

"Hey Don, what *does* Ed need the extra power for anyhow?" Steve asked. "I mean, I thought he was only focused on building up his recruit numbers and finding guys smart enough, quick enough, and strong enough to join him out at his compound. What does hydro-electric power have to do with any of that?"

"Dunno," Don shrugged. "We get told to do something and we do it. The paper says the blasting's for gold to fund the project for the hydro-electric dam due to an energy crisis, but I ain't heard talk of any energy crisis. I s'pose he might need a more reliable source of power for something he has planned. Or he might just want a source of power he's in control of. Wouldn't be good to try to take over an area and still be dependent on the people from the electric company, now would it?" They both laughed stupidly, patting each other on the backs as though they had just made the world's funniest joke. Georgia fought the urge to roll her eyes and leaned a little closer. "Anyway, all I know is Ed said it wouldn't be long now until he had the number he needs to move to the next step, whatever that is. Recruitment's been at an all-time high now that Dale joined the team."

"The guy was always such a straight-laced guy back in town," Steve said thoughtfully. "Never broke a rule, always did his work. Who would've thought he'd have it in him to do a job like this one?"

"People'll do almost anything if the price is right," Don said flippantly. "Plus, he's a Neff. I mean, what are the odds two of them would turn out to be fine, upstanding gentlemen? Ray has the lock on that one; Mr. Perfect. Dale's one of us; it just took him a while to figure it out."

"I guess so," Steve conceded. "So, think Joe has those charges set yet? He was supposed to lay them and give us a signal they were about to…"

An enormous explosion wracked the entire ravine. The ground under the men and Georgia's feet shook and she jumped. A crumbling sound behind her made her whip around and she bolted from the crevice just as the larger of the boulders split and crashed onto where she had just been standing. She looked around and saw the men were nodding and giving each other a thumbs up. They turned and started walking but stopped short when they saw her. She paused for a second, let out the most menacing growl/snarl/yowl she could muster, and tore off toward the woods. It was the most natural reaction she could think of and she doubted they would think anything of it.

She didn't stop running for close to ten minutes. When she did, she tore up a tree as fast as she could and crouched, looking behind her to see if there was anyone or anything on her heels. After a few minutes, she was convinced there wasn't, so she climbed down and oriented herself. Her head was swimming with everything she had heard and she made her way back to her car on autopilot, trying to decide what to make of it all.

Chapter Eighteen
Confrontation

She caught a glimpse of her car through the thinning trees and was relieved. She paused before exiting the woods and looked around. She didn't see any movement, so she transformed quickly and walked the rest of the way to her car. She bent down to grab the keys from behind her tire and her heart stopped. They weren't there. She dropped to her belly and reached all around under her car. Nothing. She knew the chances of an animal coming by and picking them up were next to none, but she couldn't rationalize any other way they could have disappeared. If a person had found them and taken them, why not steal the car? She put her fists together in front of her and rested her forehead on them. The road to town was miles back through the woods and then town itself was another long jaunt and she didn't want to think about how late it would be by the time she made it home.

The sound of twigs snapping immediately next to her made her jump. She turned her head toward the sound and from under the car she saw a pair of dust-covered boots.

"Need some help?" asked a familiar voice, and Georgia didn't know whether to be relieved or apprehensive when she recognized who it was. She backed her way out from under the car and rolled to her side. Austin was standing there, his hand extended. She reached for it slowly and he lifted her with no effort. His other hand reached into his coat pocket and pulled out her keys. He held them in front of her and jingled. "I feel like we should talk," he said.

She took a calming breath and placed a bemused look on her face. "Oh? About what?"

"Well, I guess I was actually hoping *you* might have some things *you* wanted to talk about," he said. His gaze was so intense she had to look down.

"Um, I don't think so," she said evasively. "I'm glad you're the one who has my keys and not some woodland creature." She reached her hand out to take the keys and he pulled them back.

"What I'd like to know is why *you* don't have your keys. Why weren't they in your pocket?"

"I dropped them?" she said, and cursed herself that her voice went up slightly at the end so it sounded almost like a question more than a statement. "I drop stuff all the time." That part, at least, was true.

Austin nodded. "That would make sense. Except for the fact that they were tucked behind your tire. And you walked straight to where they were when you came out of the woods. If you'd dropped them earlier and you knew where they fell, it seems like the logical thing to do would be pick them up."

Georgia didn't say anything. She didn't know how to explain the situation to him. How do you explain to someone that when you change into an animal, sometimes the things in your pockets don't survive the transformation so it's easier to stash items somewhere and come back for them later?

"What do you want to hear exactly?" she asked, crossing her arms. She knew he had every reason to be curious, but she didn't enjoy interrogations. She'd had enough of them recently to last her a lifetime.

"Anything other than a lie would be great," Austin replied in a flat voice.

Georgia's face reddened, but this time it wasn't from embarrassment. "So, truth is what you're looking for, is it? That sounds good. Why don't you give me some truth first? Why don't you tell me why Ed is recruiting so heavily? It's not really just for hydro-electricity, is it? Why does he need the numbers, Austin?" Austin's eyes widened. She looked at him, her eyes equally as wide with over-exaggerated curiosity. "Come on. You're so about the truth right now. What's the big plan?"

After a solid minute of them staring at each other, Austin's shoulders slumped a bit and he gently reached forward and put her keys into her jacket pocket for her. "I don't know," he said quietly. Her eyebrows knitted together and some of the fire she had been feeling moments before died out.

He turned and leaned against her car, blowing out a sigh. "They really are getting ready to build a hydro-electric facility in the ravine. But there's something else going on and I don't know what it is. I've had a feeling about it for a while now. I think my dad knows, but any time I ask about it or hint at it, he gets really evasive. He won't tell me anything. I've been trying to spend more time at the mill lately to see if I could pick up on anything people might be talking about, but the bosses aren't outside their offices much and the sheep that work there don't know much."

"What makes you think there's something else in the works?" Georgia asked gently this time. She leaned back against the car too, her hip and elbow against his.

"Probably similar things to the things that make *you* think it," Austin replied. "I see an influx of people on the books slated to be working in the mill or sent to our town. That would mean you are seeing an influx of people leaving yours."

"But a hiring boom isn't out of the ordinary, especially if they're starting a hydro-electric facility," Georgia reasoned.

"That's true," Austin agreed. "But the numbers they've hired and the numbers we've seen come to the mill and to our town don't add up. There are a large number of people who are going... somewhere else."

"The compound," Georgia said softly without thinking.

Austin cut his eyes sharply to her. "What did you just say?"

Georgia was about to say "nothing" but stopped herself. They were sharing the truth, after all. She knew Christian and the others would kill her if they knew what she was considering sharing with this young man whom they were convinced had the potential to be very dangerous to them. But they didn't know him like she did.

"I overheard some people talking about it earlier," Georgia said.

Austin looked at her, waiting for more information. She didn't provide any. He looked down at his boots. "Where did you go when you were in the woods, Georgia?"

"I wanted to see your town. And the ravine."

"And?" he asked.

"And… I saw them," she replied.

"What else did you see?"

She put her hands into her jacket pockets. "I saw two men out at the ravine doing some blasting for the hydro-electric facility. They were talking about the plans and stuff and they mentioned the compound. I also saw some women in your town cleaning game. One of them was fairly new to town and she talked about how nice it was to be there. The other one doesn't seem to be much fonder of your uncle than you are." He looked at her. "And I saw you. You were helping the women clean the game and… they adore you."

"How could you see us and we never saw you?" he asked.

It was her turn to look down at her shoes. "I was hidden. I didn't want anyone to be able to see me."

"Why?"

"I didn't know if I'd be welcome there. I didn't know if you wanted me to see where you lived."

"If you wanted to see the town, all you had to do was ask," he said, reaching his hand into her jacket pocket to lock his fingers with hers. "Of course I want you to see where I live. And I'd love to see where you live someday." She smiled down at the ground. "But Georgia, there's no way you could have hidden somewhere you couldn't be seen that was close enough to hear all that."

"I climbed a tree." So far she hadn't lied. She was beginning to think she might be able to get through this conversation without having to divulge her secret. Telling Auggie had been a pretty easy decision. He already basically believed in the magic and knew something seemingly illogical was going on.

But she also remembered how Sawyer had reacted when he found out about Jordan. He had been completely thrown, rightly so, and listening through the fence to Jordan trying to explain things and keep Sawyer from leaving, Georgia hadn't been convinced he wouldn't. Fortunately, Sawyer had been able to accept it in the end, but Georgia couldn't help thinking that wasn't going to be the typical reaction. She couldn't bear the thought of losing Austin just when he had come into her life.

"A tree?" Austin said.

Georgia nodded. "I'm good at climbing trees. I've been doing since I was a kid; ever since I can remember." Again, not a lie.

"And the ravine? There aren't any trees anywhere near close enough to have been able to hear the men doing the blasting."

"I hid in the rocks."

"You know; you could have gotten hurt out there, or worse. Blasting tends to cause falling or flying rocks."

"I didn't know they'd be blasting," Georgia countered, looking into his eyes and feeling horrible at the look of fear and concern she found there. "But you're right, that part wasn't safe."

"The tree wasn't safe either. You had to have been incredibly high. Actually, if you were high enough for us not to see you, there's no way you could have heard us." He let go of her hand and turned to face her almost toe to toe. "I don't feel like you're outright lying to me anymore, but I don't think you're telling me the whole truth. Why? Do you not trust me? Have I done something to make you think you can't tell me things?"

That last question hurt and she winced before looking down again. "No," she said, barely above a whisper. "You've been wonderful. I think that's part of it. If I tell you the whole truth... I'm scared I'm going to lose you. I feel like you'll leave."

Austin reached his hand under her chin and tilted her face up to look into her eyes. "I've seen a lot; been through a lot. I doubt there's anything you could tell me that would make me leave. Please," he pleaded. "Confide in me."

Chapter Nineteen
Common Ground

Georgia sucked in a deep breath. "There's something you don't know about me. Something almost no one knows about me. It is going to sound ridiculous, but I assure you, it's true. My mom called it a gift. I think that's a little generous. I think of it as more like... an ability."

Austin took a step back. "Go on," he urged. His face and posture seemed calm and Georgia was slightly reassured.

She ground her teeth a few times before pushing on. "When I moved here, I met Jordan. After a few months of being friends, she and I found out we shared this ability. She was the only other person in the world I ever met who was like me. For the briefest of windows, it was truly like having a sister. And then..." she trailed off. She didn't want to go into those details. This was supposed to be about her, after all. She looked at Austin. He was all patience, waiting for her to work through her confession.

"Austin, I can... change. Transform, I guess you might say. Into something other than," she looked down and gestured at her body, "this."

He scanned her body quickly with his eyes, his head and body not moving. He showed zero reaction and she was almost convinced he hadn't heard her when he simply said, "Transform?"

She nodded. "Yes."

"You can transform. From what you are now." He repeated.

"Yes."

"And, what is it you become, exactly?" he tilted his head ever so slightly when he asked.

She bit her lower lip and looked straight into his eyes. "A bobcat," she whispered.

The sound of the wind through the leaves of the trees and the occasional call of a bird were the only indicators that time and life were still passing. Austin was still as stone, as was Georgia. It was torture for her, waiting to see what his reaction would be. Would he run? Would he call her a liar? Would he tell someone? She began to doubt whether telling him was the right decision when all of a sudden his mouth broke into a wide grin and his dimple deepened in his cheek. "I knew it," he said, reaching for her and pulling her into a crushing hug.

Georgia just stood there, arms tight at her side. This was not at all the reaction she had been expecting and she started to question whether she'd had a stroke and said something completely different than what she'd meant to say. "You…. What? You knew it? How…"

He held her out at arm's length. "I could tell there was something different about you the first time I saw you. It was a feeling. And then the first time we touched… the sharp shock. That cold feeling. It was like electricity. I told myself it couldn't be true; that there aren't any more of us around that aren't part of the family line. But here you are."

"Any of you? Family line? God, my head is spinning," she said and wobbled a bit.

Austin's face immediately registered concern and he grabbed her keys out of her pocket, opened the driver's side door, and sat her down on the seat, her legs still outside the car. He pushed her head down toward her knees. "Take deep breaths," he said calmly. After a minute, her head cleared and she sat back up slowly. He knelt down in front of her. "Better?" he asked, his eyebrows still pinched in concern.

She nodded. "Yeah, thanks. So…" she paused and looked at him "are you saying… you…"

Austin nodded. "I can do it too."

Georgia pressed the heel of her hands against her eyes. "This has to be a dream. This entire day has been too surreal to be… well… real."

Austin took one of her hands, his thumb rubbing her palm gently. "Can't you feel it too?" he asked quietly. "The cool sensation when we touch."

She nodded, almost imperceptibly. "I can. Before the heat follows, anyway."

Austin laughed and tried to cover it by coughing into his fist. "Yeah, well, I don't think that part has anything to do with the first part. That coolness happens when we come into contact with someone like us."

"I felt it the first time I shook Jordan's hand. And any time we hugged," Georgia remembered. She looked at Austin's hand holding hers. "And the first time we touched. And when we…"

"Kissed." Austin finished, smiling. "It's always there with people like us."

"People? As in multiple people? Like, more than you and me people? How many people do you know who can do this? Wait…" she trailed off. "Family line. You mean?"

Austin's face darkened a bit and he looked down at their hands too. "Yeah, the Neff family line. We can all do it."

"So, it's true," she whispered. "You're his descendent, aren't you?" She could see Austin's jaw working and his eyes narrowed. She had never seen him look so angry. She quickly reached out her hands and gently held his face. She leaned down so her face was at the same level as his. "It doesn't matter," she said. "We're more than our blood, remember? I don't think any less of you, I swear."

He didn't pull back, but raised his eyes to meet hers. She could see his jaw relax slightly. His breathing slowed a bit and he looked back down. "I hate it," he said. "I hate being associated with him. I hate that I'm expected to be a certain way because of who I come from."

"I know," Georgia said. "But you know you're nothing like him. I know you're nothing like him. Mama Landry, your dad, those ladies in town… they all know what a good man you are. Look at all the wonderful things you do for everyone; that you've done for me! I was worried about freaking you out with my secret, and somehow you're here helping me get through this."

The corners of Austin's mouth turned up ever so slightly and, even with all the feelings she was trying to process, she loved that he could smile so easily. It only further convinced her he wasn't the least bit evil. He just couldn't be.

"Well, to be fair, I've had twenty-nine years to process this and my family can all do it too, whereas you grew up alone with it. Which, remind me at some point to come back to that because I have some questions," he said as an aside. "Are you feeling ok, now?"

"I'm much better, yes. It's kind of a relief," Georgia said. "Thanks for being there for me."

"I will be there anytime you need me."

"And I will be here for you anytime you need me." Georgia responded.

"I'm glad to hear you say that," he said. "Because I think we can both agree, if the things we suspect are true, we may be needing each other quite a bit soon."

"You're right," Georgia agreed. "But, do you mind if we save some of the heavy stuff until tomorrow? I know it's important, and I already have a group of people breathing down my neck and giving me loads of things to do for this, and I could really just use a break for the rest of the day."

Austin stood and pulled her up to stand with him. "Of course." He hugged her gently and they stood there for a bit, just enjoying the warmth of each other's bodies. When Austin finally broke the hug, he looked down at her. "So, a bobcat, huh?"

She nodded, a small smile on her face. "A bobcat." A thought crossed her mind suddenly and she grabbed the sides of his jacket where her arms had been hugging him. "Hey, you can do this too! What do you transform into?"

Austin pushed her hands slightly until she released him and he backed up a few steps. "See for yourself," he smirked.

His eyes closed and his body began morphing. Even though she had done it herself thousands of times, it was always a bit bizarre watching it happen to someone else. Only when she had met Jordan and discovered they had the same ability had she seen it happen to someone else for the first time, and she hadn't had time to get used to it before Jordan had made the permanent change to her animal form to be with Sawyer. Her eyes followed his form as it shrank down, elongated, and darkened into a truly beautiful grey fox. He looked up at her and, even though it wasn't possible, she could almost see him smile back.

"It's not fair, you know, that you can be handsome even as a fox." She sat on the ground, her knees pulled up to her chest, and held out her hand as he walked over next to her. She stroked his soft fur and was surprised how similar it felt to his hair. He sat and looked at her expectantly. She sighed and closed her eyes, rested her forehead on her left knee, and felt her body slip fluidly through her transformation for the second time that day.

She opened her eyes and was on almost the same level as Austin. "Hi there," he said in a soft bark-like way.

"Hi," she responded. "This is still completely crazy to me."

"I'm sure, but doesn't it also feel kind of natural? I mean, I feel like we've clicked so well since the beginning. Shouldn't it kind of make sense we share this too?"

Georgia shook her head and looked down. "If I'm being honest, even after twenty-five years, it doesn't feel natural that *I* can do this, much less anyone else. All this has ever caused me is isolation and secrecy. I didn't have friends or family that could do this. I had to stay distanced from everyone. I wish I couldn't do it."

Austin looked almost sad as he walked over, turned, and sat next to her, leaning against her slightly. "I'm so sorry it's been hard for you. I wish you had grown up feeling better about who you were and what you could do. It's a beautiful thing to have this magic in you. A long time ago, only the strongest bloodlines could do what we can do."

Georgia let out a derisive snort, which sounded more like a hiss in this form. "This coming from the guy who's been talking about how much he hates being judged for his name and all that's associated with it? Doesn't your name equate to your bloodline."

"I suppose," Austin reasoned. "But the name only generates negative connotations because of how a lot of my relatives have behaved in the past. And present, I guess. But the magic that runs through us isn't good or evil. It's just magic. It's what we do with it that counts. People like me and my dad have always used it to try to help people or to improve situations. We're lucky to be able to do what we can. It has helped us."

"So, you are more in tune with the Onirus way of thinking than the Nephyrion way." Georgia stated. "I have to give you kudos for that."

Austin tilted his head. "I thought you didn't know anything about where you came from because your parents didn't have this ability. How in the world do you know about the Onirus and Nephyrion families?"

"Ah," she said uncertainly. "That's going to take a bit of explaining. Do you have a while? And can we maybe do this as ourselves? I'm more comfortable that way."

He stood and walked a few feet away and they both closed their eyes at the same time. A few seconds later they were looking at each other in their human form once again. He closed the space between them, put his arm around her shoulders, and walked her toward her car. He opened the driver's side door, shut it after she got in, and walked around to get in the passenger's side. "I've got all day and all night," he said, sliding the seat belt into place. "Shoot."

Chapter Twenty
Missing Pieces

During their ride back to town, Georgia told Austin about Jordan and her meeting Victoria in their clearing. She talked about them discussing the stories Georgia's mom used to tell her at bedtime and Victoria telling them the stories were true. She talked about learning Victoria and Christian's story, their being direct descendants of Bernard Onirus and Edmund Nephyrion respectively, and learning she, Georgia, was likely descendent of Bernard Onirus while Jordan was given the power due to contact with magically altered water. Austin grabbed her arm to stop her at that point.

"What do you mean she was *given* the power?" he asked, a bit forcefully. He saw her wince and immediately loosened his grip on her arm and rubbed his thumb over the spot he had just squeezed. "I'm sorry," he said softer. "It's just, I've never heard of that kind of thing happening before; someone with no magical background or magical blood being able to transform. How did the water become magic? And how did she come in contact with the water? Did she drink it?"

"Whoa, whoa," she said, slowing his line of questioning. "That's a lot of questions at once. It looks like the water became magic because of the Nephyrion amulet Christian threw in the pond to keep Victoria alive. It's been hidden at the bottom of it for centuries. Since Edmund's blood was used to make it, besides keeping Victoria alive, it seems to have taken on his magical properties. Apparently, so does anyone who comes in contact with it because, no, Jordan didn't drink the water. She just put her feet in it as far as I know." Georgia raised one eyebrow as she turned to look at him. "And now I'm confused. I thought it seemed like you knew about the recruiting process."

He shook his head. "I knew there was a hiring influx and the people had to be going somewhere other than the mill and our town. I figured that meant Ed needed them for something else, and whatever else it might be had me worried; still does. I even thought he might be building up some kind of brute force squad based on rumors I've heard about what happens to the people from the mill who don't perform well enough. But I had no idea people could be given this ability by simply coming in contact with magically altered water. I grew up hearing stories about those amulets, but we didn't think they were real. And even if they were, the stories say both of them were destroyed." His voice trailed off as he got lost in thought. She knew he must be considering all the new horrible options this news opened up for him. After a while she reached over and put her hand on his knee, squeezing it gently; comfortingly.

He looked down at her hand, grabbed it, and looked straight ahead again. "He's building an army," he whispered.

Georgia nodded. "That's what we've been worried about as well. Last year, when Sawyer went to see if he could get a job there so he could do some investigative work from the inside, he apparently tipped off some of that 'brute squad' you mentioned. He was able to escape the mill, but they followed him to the clearing and nearly killed him. Jordan sacrificed her human form and provided blood for Christian to mix with a potion. By doing that, they were able to save him and now Jordan and Sawyer are both in their animal form permanently." Austin's eyes were wide at the story. She continued on. "So, that's why I was at the mill the first time you saw me. I'm the only one who can go out and talk to people. What I was trying to do was figure out who all worked at the mill, then decide if maybe I could get some information from one of them. That's also why I was at the ravine town today." Austin looked over at her. "I did want to see where you lived," she said quickly. "And I really do want to meet your family and friends at some point. But the things we've heard about the goings on made it too likely a source of information to stay away."

"I get that," Austin conceded. "You said you heard Steve and Don eluding to the fact Ed might want the power for something other than economical and consistency reasons for the town?

"They seemed to think he might want it for something he has planned or maybe to not be dependent on anyone else for a source of power."

"Oh, man," he groaned, rubbing his eyes with his free hand. "This is ominous as hell."

"That's why we've been working so hard to block the well in the mill. We have good reason to believe one of the outlets of Victoria's pond leads to the well via an underground spring. If that's the case, he's almost positively using that water to give his recruits his abilities. Christian's working on setting dye into the outflow, a different color in each, and then sealing them so it'll change the color of the water in the mill to the color of the dye in whichever outlet leads to it. Part of the reason I was trying to find a mole at the mill was to have someone check the water and tell us if it had changed color and, if so, to which color."

"I can check that," Austin said quickly. "We definitely need to get that plugged."

"We?" Georgia said, a hint of a smile on her face.

Austin looked over at her. "It may be my family line, but this town, both your part of it and the ravine town, are my home. There are people I love deeply there and a war isn't going to do anyone any good. Lots of lives are lost in wars. This has to be stopped. If that means I join forces with people who might cause me to be considered traitorous, then that's a price I'm willing to pay."

Georgia gripped Austin's hand even tighter. "For this and so many reasons, I'm incredibly glad I met you. You've been a light in what's been a seriously dark time for me."

Austin squeezed her hand back. "I feel the same way." He waited a few moments then continued on. "You have to let me meet them, you know?" He said it more as a statement than a question.

"I know," Georgia replied. "I'm taking you to them tonight."

They rode on in silence for some time, both seeming to try to put the new pieces of information together with what they had already known.

Georgia broke the silence. "What did you mean when you said that thing about the brute squad forming based on rumors about people who didn't perform well at the mill?"

His jaw tightened and relaxed a few times before he responded. "It's something else we kind of thought was just a story told to make sure everyone gave a hundred and ten percent at their job. Some of the older guys would say things like the under-performers were pulled off the line and used for really unpleasant tasks for as long as it took to make up the salary they were paid but didn't earn. I overheard one guy saying what actually happened was they were used for training bait for a brute squad; some kind of troop. Once their sentence was up, if they survived, they were relocated out of state. Some were even brainwashed so they wouldn't remember anything about the mill and couldn't try to come back. It sounded ludicrous at the time, but now…"

"That's despicable!" Georgia exclaimed. "Using people as human punching bags or whatever it was they were having done to them? Didn't anyone ever think to check out the stories?"

"That's not really how things work around the mill," Austin said, softly. "We're told what to think and what to believe and how to behave and, if we go along with it, everything is sunshine and rainbows. If we don't, well, things like those stories might happen. It's easier to just go along with it and keep your head down."

"But you weren't keeping your head down anymore," Georgia said, urging him to continue.

"I'd heard and seen enough that I began to worry. And, with my dad being kind of in charge in the ravine town, I have a little more wiggle room with what I can get away with. So… I exploited it. I decided to do some investigation myself."

"I can respect that," Georgia said with a smile. Austin winked.

"But even checking out the mill, I wasn't able to get anywhere near the amount of information you were. I'm impressed and really grateful you shared your information with me, but please… you can't go back there. Who knows what might happen if they see you? You might not be so lucky next time." Georgia nodded but didn't say anything. "So, do you think your friends will be receptive of me joining in your efforts?" Austin asked.

Georgia chewed on her lower lip. "Um, well, I did mention to them I had met you and hoped you'd be able to provide some information about things because of you and your family members being involved in the higher positions at the mill."

"You told them my name," he said, leaning his head back against the headrest.

"I didn't have any idea about your family at that point," Georgia said apologetically.

"And I assume they weren't excited about consorting with the enemy."

"They were cautious," Georgia admitted. "But they weren't against it. They just told me to use discretion and to be careful what I shared and…"

Austin let out a bark of laughter. "That didn't end up working out very well, did it?" His dimple deepened as he smiled at her.

Georgia couldn't help but smile too as they pulled into the driveway of the Marens' house. She shut off the engine and turned to him. "Hey, to be fair I didn't intend to tell you literally everything I knew and could do. At least not this soon. But I never had exactly the same reservations they did. They haven't met you. They have no way of knowing how genuine you are. It's like, I don't know, I can feel that you aren't trying to manipulate situations. You want good things. Once they meet you and get to know you, they'll see you the exact same way I see you." Austin pursed his lips as if to keep from smiling too big, and hung his head a bit. Georgia leaned down to try to look at his face. "What?"

He took a deep breath and looked up into her face. "I was just thinking I hope they don't see me *exactly* the same as you do." He leaned forward and kissed her softly. She gently cupped his cheek in her hand, her thumb gently brushing over his dimple.

After a minute, Georgia pulled back a few inches and whispered, "Right. Not exactly like I do." He leaned back in and kissed her deeper, his hand finding its way into her hair. They stayed locked together like that until a gentle knock on the back window startled them apart. Georgia whipped around and looked out the back driver's side window. She could see the mid-section of Gordon's brown

Carhartt jacket. She pressed her hand to her heart and took a steadying breath. "It's just Gordon," she said, relieved. "Jordan's dad."

Chapter Twenty-One
Meeting the Family

"You brought me to Jordan's house?" Austin said, eyebrows raised.

"It's my house, too. After my mom died, the Marens invited me to move into their home. They've treated me like a daughter since the day I met them. I think of them as my parents."

"Oh, great." Austin wiped his palms on his thighs. "So your pretty-much dad just caught you making out in your car with a guy. I'm sure this'll go well."

"I can assure you, it'll be fine," Georgia laughed, amused by how uncomfortable Austin was. "Gordon and Judy are the greatest. And look," she gestured back to the window where Gordon was leaning casually against her back fender, facing away from the car and toward the house. "He's not even looking in here. He's respecting our privacy." She unbuckled her seatbelt and reached over to do the same for Austin.

"Plus, I'm twenty-five years old. I'm hardly a child. I think I'm allowed to kiss my boy… uh… a boy." Austin raised an eyebrow and opened his mouth to say something, so she grabbed her bag out of the back. "But, it *will* look bad if we stay in here much longer even after he knocked. Come on, it'll be fine, I promise." She opened the door and got out. Austin followed suit.

"Hey, Gordon," Georgia said, keeping herself completely casual in hopes it would assuage Austin's worries. "I didn't know you were home. I didn't see Judy's car or yours when I pulled in. Is it acting up again?"

"That rust bucket isn't worth the time or effort anymore," Gordon said, shaking his head in disgust. "This is the second time I've taken it in for repairs in the last six months. I'm seriously considering junking it and getting something new, or at least functional." He looked at Austin who had just stopped next to Georgia.

"Gordon, this is Austin. Austin, this is Gordon Maren. He's Jordan's dad, and mine for all intents and purposes." She could see that pleased Gordon as he extended his hand to Austin who took and shook it firmly.

"Nice to meet you, Mr. Maren," Austin said, flashing his dimple. "Did I hear your vehicle's on the fritz?"

"Please, call me Gordon. It's nice to meet you too, Austin. And yes, you unfortunately heard correctly. The truck's close to thirty years old, has almost two hundred thousand miles on it, and I fear it's starting to give up the ghost. I've replaced everything I can on it other than the engine and I'm afraid it's expenses have long ago surpassed what it's worth."

"Gordon's sentimental about his truck," Georgia teased.

He nudged her playfully with his elbow. "I had that truck even before I married Judy. We've been through a lot together. But, this seems to be a year of changes, so perhaps it's time to move on."

Georgia looked to Austin. She hoped he wasn't uncomfortable with the allusion to Jordan's passing, but his face didn't register sadness or discomfort. In fact, it registered interest and excitement. She knitted her brow a bit but then Austin spoke.

"If you're looking to get something newer, I know a guy a few towns over. His name's Drew and he has the best deals you're ever going to get and the largest number of options. I researched cars for months before buying and he never tried to pull any slick business. I'd love to put you in contact with him."

Gordon looked very interested. "Really?" He reached over and put his hand on Austin's shoulder, guiding him slowly toward the front door of the house. "That's an intriguing proposition, son. Why don't you come in and we can talk more? What kind of car did you finally decide on?"

Georgia watched as they walked away, discussing the bells and whistles of Austin's car and whether Gordon needed those luxuries as well. She smirked and followed a few feet behind them, feeling particularly lucky to have such great men in her life.

Georgia closed the front door behind her and walked toward the kitchen where she could hear Gordon and Austin's voices discussing cars at length. They had already seated themselves at the kitchen table. Georgia walked to the coffee maker. "Sorry to interrupt you guys and your very important car discussion, but would either of you like coffee?"

Not looking away from Gordon, Austin reached over and squeezed Georgia's hand quickly. "Coffee would be great. So have you thought about something a little more versatile? Maybe something with off-roading capabilities? It's a great way to blow off some steam and kill some hours."

Georgia shook her head and started preparations for a full pot of coffee. She could tell they might be there a while and, if car talk was going to be the main discussion topic, she was going to need it. She had just pushed the button to start brewing when the sound of the front door opening and closing met her ears. She turned to the entryway of the kitchen just as Judy walked in.

"Well, look here, it's a party!" Judy exclaimed, smiling at Georgia, bending to kiss Gordon on the cheek, and turning to Austin. "I don't believe I know this one."

Austin stood and extended his hand. "My name's Austin, ma'am. I'm Georgia's friend. She's told me so much about you and Gordon here. It's really great to finally meet you."

Judy shook Austin's hand and her face flushed with delight. "Well, aren't you sweet? There's no need for the ma'am, though. We're pretty informal here. Just call me Judy."

Austin let go of her hand. "Do you want to sit, Judy?" He pulled out the chair he had been sitting in and gestured toward it. "I'm more than willing to find a comfy piece of counter to lean on."

"Actually, I was thinking Austin and I might go over to Paul's garage and check out the beast," Gordon said, also rising. "That's what we've been calling my old truck the past few years. Its growl is getting louder and louder with each season it seems. The garage is only about a mile down the road. You can give me your opinion about whether I should finally let it go to that big junkyard in the sky. And you can also let me know if you think Paulie might be trying to sell me a junker disguised as a sensible truck." It made Georgia happy to see Gordon and Austin bonding so quickly over their love of vehicles.

"That'd be great!" Austin said excitedly. "You don't mind, do you, babe?" He looked inquisitively and expectantly at Georgia whose stomach had just leapt at being called such an affectionate name. He obviously hadn't even realized he'd done it, because he was practically vibrating with excited energy to leave and go to the garage with Gordon, but somehow that made it even sweeter. What people did when they acted without thinking tended to say a lot, and that one word made Georgia's day.

"Of course not," she said. "You guys run off and do manly things. Judy and I'll stay here and be girly."

"Oh, great! You're the best! I don't think we'll be gone long so, as hard as it might be for you, save me a cup of coffee, will ya?" He dropped a quick kiss on top of her head and followed Gordon down the hall and out the front door.

Judy looked across the table at Georgia, her eyebrows raised slightly. "So… that's Austin."

Georgia tried to reign in her smile, but failed miserably. "Yeah. That's Austin."

"Why have you been hiding him from us? He seems like a wonderful young man."

"I haven't been hiding him," Georgia laughed, pouring two mugs of coffee and grabbing the cream from the fridge. "I just met him fairly recently. It's… new."

"Well, I think that's wonderful," Judy said, taking the mug Georgia extended to her and sitting in Austin's vacated seat. "Tell me all about him!"

Georgia sat across from her in Gordon's empty seat and they spent the next hour discussing the vaguer points of Georgia meeting Austin and how they had gotten to know each other. "And then Gordon knocked on the window while we were kind of kissing in my car out front and here we are," Georgia finished, taking a sip of her third mug of coffee. She had already started a new pot so the guys would be able to have some when they returned.

"Oh, that man," Judy said, rolling her eyes in exasperation. "He just couldn't leave you two alone for a bit, could he?"

"I didn't mind. It was kinda funny how nervous it made Austin." They both giggled at that. "Anyway, it worked out ok because now apparently they're besties."

"Well thank goodness for that. Maybe now Gordon will talk his ridiculous car talk with someone else for a change!"

"I'm glad my knowing Austin has worked out well for you," Georgia winked.

"So, how serious are things?" Judy asked. Jordan had always looked exactly like a younger version of Judy, and the way the woman was leaning forward now, chin in her hands and elbows on the table, reminded her so much of Jordan. It was almost like she was sitting at the table talking to her best friend again as they had done so many times before. She wished it really was Jordan she could talk to about this, but Judy was a pleasant enough substitute.

"Well, I don't know exactly. We haven't really talked about it much, but I know how he makes me feel, and I love being with him. I almost called him my boyfriend when I was introducing him to Gordon today, but I caught myself. I mean, I think of him that way, but like I said, we haven't really discussed it."

"That's so exciting!" Judy said encouragingly. "You haven't dated anyone since you moved here. You're a wonderful young woman. You deserve a good guy, and Austin really does seem like a good one. Do you think he'd want to stay for supper tonight? I'd love the chance to get to know him more and possibly talk about something other than cars."

Georgia shrugged. "I don't know for sure what his plans are for the rest of the evening but I can ask him."

"Lovely!" Judy clapped her hands and stood up, walked to the fridge and opened it up to look inside. "I pulled a roast down the other day. How does a roast with veggies, salad, and bread sound?"

"It sounds amazing. I know he wouldn't want you to go through any trouble though."

"Nonsense," Judy said dismissively as she pulled out the meat and produce. "We'd have to eat whether he's here or not. A roast will make plenty for everyone. If he can stay, wonderful. If he can't, we'll still have supper."

"Can I help?" Georgia asked, rising and moving next to Judy. Judy handed her a peeler and pushed the potatoes and carrots to her.

The ladies kept busy for the next half hour preparing supper. They had just put everything in the oven when the front door opened again. The sound of Gordon and Austin's voices preceded them. They entered the kitchen and stopped.

"Wow, it looks like you two have been busy," Gordon said, taking in the sight of the ladies in aprons, vegetable peelings in the garbage, bread sliced and buttered on a baking pan and the bowl of salad on the counter.

Georgia tossed the last of the chopped red cabbage in the salad bowl and picked up the tossing tongs. "That we have." She turned to Austin. "Judy offered to have you for supper if you're free this evening."

"I'd love to," Austin replied appreciatively. "If it's not too much trouble."

Judy and Georgia looked and each other and let out a good laugh. Austin looked at Gordon with a bemused look on his face.

"Don't mind them," Gordon said, giving a small flip of his hand. "Women."

Austin walked over to stand next to Georgia. "This looks great," he said, reaching into the salad bowl, pulling out a cherry tomato, and popping it into his mouth.

Georgia elbowed him lightly in the ribs. "You leave that alone until it's supper time. Only the people preparing the meal are allowed to be taste testers."

"Austin, how about you and I have a pre-dinner aperitif? Can I interest you in a whiskey sour? A Manhattan?"

"A Manhattan sounds great, Gordon. Dry please. Can we bring you ladies anything?"

"I'd love a spritzer," Judy said over her shoulder, pulling a cutting board out of the dishwater and handing it to Georgia.

Georgia took the cutting board and started drying it. "I'll just have my coffee," she said. Austin walked to the fridge, looked around for a bit, then pulled out a small bottle. He brought it over to her mug, tipped a bit of the creamy liquid into her mug, and screwed the top back on.

"Now it's an Irish coffee," he said, grinning, returning the bottle back to the fridge. "Wouldn't want you to feel left out." He winked and followed Gordon into the den.

Georgia took a small sip of the coffee. "He knows what he's doing, that's for sure." The ladies laughed again and continued their dishes.

A while later, they all sat at the dining room table and scooted in their chairs. "This looks like a Thanksgiving meal," Austin said, the look on his face projecting deep admiration. "This had to be a lot of work. I hope it wasn't all on my account. I really am ok with peanut butter sandwiches too."

They all chuckled at that and Gordon reached for the salad, placing a healthy serving on his plate before passing the bowl to Austin. "My wife has always cooked for a crowd. Thankfully, she's amazing at it. It's a big reason why I married her." He cut his glance sideways to her.

"That's lovely, Gordon," she replied, eyes rolling again. "Thank you, Austin. A nice meal is more than fitting for someone Georgia seems to be very fond of. Thank you for joining us tonight."

Georgia reached for her water glass and hoped somehow the clear glass might hide how red she was turning. She was really looking forward to the day when she wouldn't blush every time she was in Austin's presence. He seemed to know she was uncomfortable and chimed in. "Well, I'm a pretty big fan of hers too and I'm honored to be invited to join you all. This is a far more delicious spread that we would've had at home."

"And where is home, exactly?" Gordon asked, shoveling roast onto his plate. "You don't look familiar so I assume you don't live here in town."

"I don't, no. I haven't been here for any length of time in about twenty years. I used to come here often when I visited my uncle, but he and my dad had a falling out so I've spent almost all of my time at home in the ravine town since then."

"That's a shame about your dad and uncle. It's too bad when adults' disagreements affect the youth of the families," Judy said sympathetically. "We might not know your dad if he's at the ravine town, but who's your uncle?"

Austin forked into a potato and popped it into his mouth. He chewed slowly, almost as if he was hoping the conversation would continue on without his answer. When it did not, he swallowed and fixed his eyes on Judy. "Dale Neff."

The riot or hissing and jeers he seemed to be expecting never came. Judy's face remained neutral and Gordon took a drink of his water before commenting "Decent guy. Not very chatty, but always did good work. The porches on some of the newer houses here in town were done by him and they're works of art. Shame about him getting hurt and having to work in the mill. He was always more of an outdoorsy kind of man from what I remember. I'm sure he's not as happy there, but at least he was able to find work."

Judy nodded in agreement. "He was a grade ahead of me in school. People seemed to keep their distance from him because he came from a shady family, but he never treated me with any unkindness. I never saw him treat anyone unkindly as a matter of fact."

"Sorry you weren't able to spend more time here growing up," Gordon continued. "It would've been nice to have a nice young man like you around town."

Austin looked beyond humbled at their words. "Thank you. I would have liked that too," was all he could say, and they all continued eating.

When supper was over, Georgia tried to help Judy again with the dishes, but Judy wouldn't hear of it. "You've done enough today and you have a guest. You two go with Gordon into the sitting room and chat. I'll get these finished up in no time and join you when I'm done.

The men retreated to the sitting room and Georgia reluctantly followed them. Gordon sat in his favorite leather chair and Austin pulled Georgia down next to him on the loveseat across from the chair. "That was an amazing supper," Austin said, leaning back with his hand on his stomach. "I don't think I've eaten that much at once since actual Thanksgiving. I can understand why you married her," he said to Gordon, who laughed the deep laugh Georgia always loved.

"It was always hard staying lean when I was on the force. But now I can let myself go slightly to seed and really indulge in her cooking."

"Wait 'til you try her pastries," Georgia said, leaning back as well. Gordon nodded emphatically.

"I look forward to it," Austin smiled. "And I want to thank you for not judging my family line. I know most people in town aren't a fan of the Neffs and it's been a trial growing up with the name. You are the first folks who haven't flinched or grimaced when they learn my name. It means more than you probably realize."

"Son, when you've seen as much as I have, you learn people are far more than their name or who they're related to. I don't make any judgements until I see how a person behaves, how they present themselves, and the decisions they make. If you leave your judgements to the opinions of others, you're going to miss out on a lot in life, and miss out on some great people. We might not have raised Georgia, but we think of her as our own, and it makes me very proud to see she seems to have the same values."

"Gordon," she said, giving him an embarrassed look.

"No," Austin said, taking her hand. "He's right. And I appreciate that about you as well." He lifted her hand and kissed the top gently.

Judy walked in and sat in the leather chair next to Gordon's. "What have I missed."

"I was just telling Austin not to worry about his family line. We don't judge until we see what a person is truly like, and we're very pleased Georgia is the same way."

"Absolutely," Judy agreed. "I didn't know Amy by more than name, but she obviously did an amazing job raising you, and we're lucky enough to reap the benefits of the wonderful person you've become.

"This is embarrassing," Georgia mumbled, looking at her knees. They all laughed.

"Ok, so more car talk?" Gordon asked.

"No!" the ladies responded together. They all laughed again.

Chapter Twenty-Two
Combined Forces

"I don't think I'll ever be hungry again!" Austin moaned. He and Georgia had gone outside and were sitting on the top step of the back porch to the house. He laid back and held his stomach with both hands.

"I should have warned you about the pie," Georgia said, rubbing his arm comfortingly. "But you know, you didn't have to eat it. He turned his head to look at her skeptically. She let out a loud laugh. "Ok, yeah, you kinda did."

"She'd never have taken no for an answer, and honestly, I didn't want to say no. That was the best blackberry pie I've ever had."

"Told you," Georgia giggled and looked up at the sky. She sighed.

Austin sat up and put his arm around her shoulders. "What's the matter?"

"It's just… things feel so good right now. Why can't this be my life?"

"This *is* your life," Austin said quietly.

"No, I mean all of it. Why can't this," she gestured broadly "be all of it? All I want is to work in the bookstore, spend time with my… you… and occasionally spend great evenings with people who are the closest thing to parents I have. Why does there also have to be this giant cloud of doom hanging over my head and a giant secret I can't tell anyone I love? Can things ever just be all good? Is that even a thing?"

"Oh, Georgia," Austin said, pulling her sideways to him and wrapping her in a hug. "I don't know why bad things happen. And I don't know if things can ever really be all good. All I know is that, since meeting you, things have been more good than bad in my life. Things are always going to be complicated, but that doesn't seem so heavy when I know I have you in my life."

She buried her face into his neck. "You're amazing, you know that? How do you always know exactly what I need to hear?"

"Isn't that what boyfriends are supposed to do?"

She jerked her head up and looked into his eyes. Even in the dark, she could see the shadow of his dimple and she smiled back. "Yes," she said, leaning in closer to his face. "That's exactly what boyfriends are supposed to do."

After a few minutes, they broke apart and Georgia stood. "So, do you think you're ready for this?" she asked, holding her hand out to him to help him up.

"The meeting your friends part, sure. The standing up part, I'm not so sure about. I really am stuffed." He reached up and reluctantly grabbed her hand. She laughed as he groaned the whole way up. "Ok, the worst is over," he said. "I know meeting your friends will be… tense… at first. But after the great reception I got from Gordon and Judy, I think I can handle a little wariness."

"They'll warm up to you," Georgia assured him. "Once they hear all the information you provided and hear your concerns, they'll have to believe that you're on our side.

Austin nodded, not completely convinced, and they looked over their shoulders to make sure Judy and Gordon weren't looking out the window before they made a run for it into the woods.

In no time at all they were within feet of the clearing. Georgia put her hand out to stop Austin and they paused before the high bushes that blocked their passage.

"We have to change here," Georgia said. "Since Jordan and Sawyer are only able to be in their animal form, it'll be better for us all to be able to communicate freely from the get-go."

"Absolutely," Austin said, stepping a few feet away from her. They closed their eyes and transformed. Once complete, he stepped back behind her. "Lead the way."

She pushed through the dense brush and into the clearing. Austin followed and stayed next to her once they were through. The clearing looked empty, but Georgia knew better. They took a few more slow steps and Georgia stopped and sat. Austin sat next to her and looked around.

"This place is beautiful," he breathed. "The soil around my town is so rocky there's really no undergrowth in the trees. I've never seen anywhere around there so green and full of life."

"Environments tend to display whatever the creatures who live in them contribute to them," a deep voice said from behind the willow curtain by the pond. "Tell me, young master Neff, what are you and your people contributing to your ravine town?" Christian's giant bear form stepped through the curtain and moved slowly toward them. Victoria glided through as well on the pond's surface, barely making a ripple as she moved.

"We contribute everything we can, sir." Austin replied. "We hunt and gather food, and we put the scraps back into the soil. We use the trees to make things, and we plant more. We raise bees and use the wax for manufacturing as well as providing honey to our town as well as this one. We waste nothing, and we don't deplete more than is necessary."

"Hmm," Christian grunted. "And the blasting you do? The permanent disruption to the land by building a man-made dam to control power? What of that are you putting back into the Earth?"

Austin looked at Christian, then past him at the two wolves who had emerged from the woods on the other side of the pond.

"Jordan and Sawyer," Georgia explained.

Austin looked back to Christian. "I know you know who I am and where I come from. I also know you know the things my family has done. However, based on the little bit Georgia has told me, I feel like you can understand not entirely agreeing with your family on how things are being handled." Christian's eyes flashed to Georgia and she lowered her eyes. "Don't be angry with her for sharing what little about you that she did," Austin said assertively. "She gave me something to work with since I'm pretty sure you all know more about me than I do about you. And you need to understand I'm on your side, no matter what you've heard about my uncle. Have you heard anything about my father?"

Christian stared, not responding. The tension in the air was palpable and it was everything Georgia could do not to jump in and start babbling about the information she had obtained and gloss over the unpleasantness of family lineage. Finally, Christian took a deep breath. "I have heard only that he runs a respectable town and does not live under the thumb of the mill directors."

"He also wouldn't allow them to bring me on as a mill worker. He doesn't agree with how things are handled there. He runs the ravine town separate from the mill. It's a good town, with good people."

"A town, as I understand it, which is now being filled by people your uncle is recruiting."

"Some of them," Austin agreed. "However, a large number of the people my uncle is recruiting aren't working in the mill, nor are they coming to our town."

Christian's head tilted slightly at this information.

"Austin's come up with a theory on why that might be," Georgia interjected. "Based on the information I shared with him, and the information he had gleaned from his own investigations, we have an idea of what might be happening."

"And it isn't good," Austin finished for her.

"What do you think's going on?" Sawyer asked, stepping forward.

"We think Ed's assembling a brute squad; an army of sorts." Austin replied.

Christian, Sawyer, and Jordan let out huffs of exasperation. "We already knew that," Jordan said, irritably.

"Yes, but we think he's training them using weaker workers as bait or involuntary training partners. We also know he's sending people to the ravine town to work at blasting and creating a hydro-electric dam." Austin said.

Georgia pushed on. "At the ravine, I heard two workers talking about how the news article about blasting for gold to fund a hydro-dam for the energy crisis doesn't seem to be the real story. One of them said there was no energy crisis and they think Ed just wants to have control of his own power so he has as much as he needs and no one to answer to."

"That sounds like Edmund," Christian growled, barely audibly.

"Edmund?" Austin asked, confusedly. "As in Edmund Nephyrion? He's been dead for hundreds of years. Ed is the one running the mill now."

"Who did you think Ed was, boy?" Christian said, condescendingly. "Use your head."

"You don't know it's the same person," Austin said, defensively. "It could just as easily, and more likely, be a great grandson or someone carrying on his legacy."

"May I interject here?" Victoria's soft voice inquired from the edge of the pond where she had been listening to the interactions.

"Please," Christian said, and they all walked closer to her and sat around her in a half-circle. She briefly re-told the story of Edmund and Bernard's battle and then she re-told the story of Christian's position with Edmund many years ago and the events leading to her living in the pond.

"So, you were serving Edmund after he was supposedly killed?" Austin asked Christian, who nodded. "And even after everything he did leading up to and during that war, you still found a way to take his amulet and get out of the castle." Austin stared at Christian, then looked at the others in turn before looking back to Christian again.

"Talk about guts!" Christian blinked at him and Jordan and Georgia stifled laughs. Sawyer turned his face into Jordan's side, presumably hiding his own laughter. Austin ignored them. "I'm serious! You just threw off hundreds of years of servitude to do what you felt was right. I wish I had the nerve to do that."

"It appears to me," Christian said carefully, "you are doing the same thing." Austin shook his head and Christian continued. "Are you not going against your father's wishes and spending time in the mill outside of your assigned duties?"

"Well, I suppose…"

"And are you not also going against what everyone assumes you will do by not working for the mill and continuing the rest of your family's… less than admirable duties and tendencies?"

"I am," Austin said quietly.

"Then you are doing the same thing, if not as dramatically, as Christian did," Victoria finished. "You are an honorable man who is doing what he believes is right. It is commendable."

"Thank you, ma'am."

"Please, call me Victoria."

"Victoria," Austin repeated. "So… does this mean you can trust me?" He looked at all of them expectantly.

"Trust may take a while," Jordan responded. "But I feel like if Georgia trusts you, then we should all give her, and you, the benefit of the doubt."

"I trust him completely," Georgia said, leaning so her shoulder was touching Austin's.

Jordan looked at her, assessing. "Is there more going on here than you led us to believe last time?"

Georgia looked at them all. "Well, when we spoke last time, I hadn't had much interaction with Austin."

"We've since interacted," he chimed in, and a snort of amusement came from the far end of the half circle. They all whipped their heads around and stared in amazement at Christian.

"It appears we cannot always control the deepest desires of our hearts," Christian said amusedly. "It also appears that Onirus women can be exceedingly... entrancing."

Victoria flapped her wings indignantly, but the rest of them smirked. "He might have a point," Georgia said to Victoria. "We can't help being irresistible."

"When you phrase it in that way, I cannot help but agree," she said, somewhat haughtily, and they all laughed in earnest.

After the sounds of their amusement died down, Austin spoke. "In all seriousness, I want to share everything I know with you and I hope you can feel comfortable doing the same. A war seems imminent, and if we don't work together, our chances aren't great. Even together, with Edmund's numbers where they must be and steadily growing, we're going to need bigger numbers ourselves if we stand a chance."

"I agree we need to work together," Sawyer nodded. "And like Jordan said, if Georgia trusts you, we should trust you. I do."

"As do I," Victoria added.

"Me too," Jordan agreed.

"And I," Christian said.

"Thank you," Austin replied softly. "That means more than I can say."

"What we need now, my boy, is less talk and more action. We need a plan."

Chapter Twenty-Three
Widening the Circle

"Fortunately, the matter of Edmund's numbers growing should no longer be of much concern," Christian said, his voice pleased. "We placed the dye in the underground channels and sealed them last night. As long as one of them does, indeed, lead to the well, they will no longer have access to the water. Once they deplete their resources, they are out of options."

"That's great!" Georgia exclaimed. She turned to Austin. "You said you'll be able to check the well and see if the water has changed colors and to which color, right?"

"I'm sure I can, but if the access has been blocked, what's the point of knowing which path it's taking?"

"We discussed it and, if the dye makes it to the well, then anything else we might want to put in there could as well. We could put something far more aggressive in their water supply as a means of attack." Jordan said.

"I suppose that's true," Austin said. "But as far as I knew before hearing your theories, that well's been out of use for years. I don't think they regularly drink from it. The mill has running water, so I think it may just be used for the recruits. Which also reminds me, if the water's been colored, they're going to notice pretty quickly. What do you think will happen then?"

"The colors we used are a very pale yellow and very pale blue," Sawyer said. "If the yellow reaches the well, they might not even notice unless they put it on a white rag. The same with the blue. Speaking of which, I think that's how you should check the coloring; take a white cloth and dip it in."

"What if both passages feed into the well?" Austin asked.

"Then it'll be green," Jordan answered.

"Makes sense," Austin said. "I'll check tomorrow. I need to bring a truck of products to the mill soon anyway. I was going to do it today, but I got distracted with one thing and another. Tomorrow seems like a good day to do it." They all agreed.

"So, now for the trickier part. What are we going to do about our numbers?" Jordan asked.

"I don't know who, if anyone, would believe what we have to say about what's going on," Georgia said, discouraged. "I have a hard time believing it half the time and I'm living it."

"Is there no one in town you feel you could trust with the information?" Victoria asked. "Someone who, while they may find it hard to believe, might trust you and possibly be able and willing to assist?"

"Well, you all know I told Auggie," Georgia said. "And I said I thought Mama Landry basically already knows too, but they are... old," she said, trying to find a better word, but failing. "I'm sure they'd like to help, but what could they really do?"

"Remember the difference between Bernard Onirus and Edmund Nephyrion," Victoria said knowingly. They all looked at her. "Edmund felt no one who was not his magical equal, or at least close, could be of any use. Bernard knew better, and it was because of his placing value on all people he was able to win the battle." They all nodded.

"Victoria's right. There has to be something they can do. We'll think on it," Austin agreed. "And hey, if we can get enough great minds together and figure out Ed's plan, we might be able to even prevent an all-out war from happening at all."

"Hey, Georgia," Jordan said and Georgia looked at her. "What do you think about telling Ryan?"

"Ryan?!" Georgia yowled in shock. "You're not serious. Can you think of anyone less likely to believe in all of this? He only believes in 'facts' and 'numbers' and 'business'. He would have me committed for suggesting any of this!"

"I know he seems an unlikely comrade, but he has a lot to offer. He's smart, he's logical, and he doesn't think magically. It's the opposite of how Edmund will be approaching everything. I think what he has to offer is invaluable." Jordan reasoned.

"Even if you're right, what could she say to get him to believe her?" Austin asked.

"I think this is going to be one of those cases where actions will speak louder than words." Jordan said, and Georgia could almost hear the grimace in her voice.

"Oh, God," Georgia whispered. "He's either going to have a stroke or have himself committed."

"If the old man did not have a heart attack, I do not believe Ryan will," Christian interjected. "Often times, seeing is believing. If you offer Ryan visual proof of something, it sounds like he is the kind of man who will not be able to deny the truth, though he may need time to consider what he believes to be any other alternative possibility."

Georgia sat for a few moments, considering. "I guess I can try it," she finally said. "But what happens if he decides to tell people? It would spread through the town like wildfire."

"It's likely if there's a war coming, they'll all be forced to come to terms with what's really going on in the world," Sawyer pointed out. "But I don't think he'll tell anyone. He'd be too afraid they'd think he's the crazy one."

"Good point," Georgia and Jordan said at the same time. They looked at each other with a hint of a smile at the edges of their mouth.

"Then it is settled," Victoria said. "Georgia will tell Miss Landry and Ryan about her abilities, the existence of magic, and our quandary. We will reconvene after this happens and determine the next best course of action. Meanwhile, Austin will check the well at the mill and determine which tunnel, if either, leads to it and report back here as well."

"What will you all be doing?" Austin asked.

"They can't do much of anything at this point," Georgia said, trying not to sound bitter.

"Actually," Christian said, "Jordan, Sawyer, and I will be scouring the woods in the vicinity of Edmund's old compound to see if we might be able to find where he is hiding these days. I do not believe he would have gone far from where he was most comfortable. If we can locate his new dwelling, we may be able to find a way to infiltrate that would cost the least amount of lives if it comes to such a situation."

"That's a great idea!" Austin exclaimed.

"It is," Georgia agreed. "Thank you Christian."

"You are most welcome. I know you are greatly burdened. Do not think I have forgotten our deal, Miss Georgia. I have been working on it and will continue to do so." He stood. "I hope to see you both again soon," he said to Austin and Georgia.

"Yeah, please let us know as soon as you have something to report," Sawyer said, he and Jordan stood as well, followed by Austin and Georgia.

"We sure will," Austin said. "And thanks again, everyone. It's nice to have support in this."

They all nodded and left the clearing, except for Austin and Georgia. "Are you ready to head back?" Georgia asked.

"Almost. Can I run something by you first?"

"Of course," she said, sitting again.

Austin did not sit. He began pacing the line of bushes. "You have people you're going to tell about this, and that's great. They very well may have something to offer in this whole thing. But they aren't magic."

"That's true," Georgia said. "But you heard Victoria. Bernard believed everyone had value, and I honestly do too."

"Oh, so do I!" Austin said earnestly. "And if they're people you're close to, I think that means they may have even more to offer. I was just thinking, maybe I should consider telling people I know too."

"Oh?" she asked, her interest peaked. "Who do you feel confident telling?"

"Confident? No one," he laughed. "But I think I need to bring my father in on this."

"Oh, wow" she said, softly. "Austin, do you think that's a good idea? You're going to be asking him to pit his loyalty to the mill against his loyalty to his family and his town. If things escalate and he has to make a move, who would be left to run the ravine town?"

Austin continued pacing. "I don't know," he replied. She could hear the conflict in his voice. "All I know is I can't stand to be doing all this and not involve the strongest force I know in the magical world, especially when that force seems to be against the mill, at least in part. I feel like he has a right to know his possible fears and suspicions are justified."

"Of course. If you feel like telling him is the right thing to do, you should do it."

"Thanks," Austin said, appreciatively. "And that brings me to one other thought I had." Georgia waited expectantly. "I think you should tell Judy and Gordon."

"Huh," Georgia let out an amused huff of air. "That's funny."

"I'm serious," Austin pressed. "Think about it. If a war breaks out, do you want them going into things completely unprepared. What kind of service is that doing for the people who have done so much for you?"

"That's not fair," Georgia whispered angrily.

"Nothing about any of this is fair! Do you think everyone survives a war? We both have a very good chance of losing people we care about by the time this is all said and done. Haven't you lost enough? Why wouldn't you want to protect the people you care about as best as you can?"

Georgia stood, turned, and walked through the bushes out of the clearing. Austin gritted his teeth and finally followed. He stayed a few feet behind Georgia while they walked back toward her house. He wanted to apologize, but at the same time, he couldn't bring himself to say he was sorry about something he believed to be true. When the trees began to thin, Georgia stopped. So did Austin. They stood there for a while, not moving; not talking. Finally, Georgia turned around to face Austin and transformed. Austin did the same. When he opened his eyes, he saw hers were filled with tears, some leaking down her cheeks.

"Georgia," he said, closing the distance between them and pulling her into a tight embrace. He was relieved when she held him back. "I never meant to hurt you," he whispered. "Sometimes I can be too abrasive with my delivery."

"You were right," she said into his neck, her voice catching slightly. "They have to know at some point. But they just got past the worst of their grieving period for Jordan. What are they going to think when I tell them, not only was that a lie and they grieved in vain, but that their daughter is actually still alive, but in a form in which they'll never be able to communicate again? Oh, and on top of that, magic exists and there's a war coming. One I'm disturbingly involved in and there is a chance we all really *could* die? How do you tell someone that?"

"I don't know," Austin admitted, stroking her hair. "But I know you'll find a way."

"Because I have to," she stated, not bothering to hide the bitterness in her voice this time.

"No," Austin said, pulling back and looking into her tear-stained face. "Because you know it's the best thing for them; the best chance they have at surviving." He wiped a tear from under her eye with his thumb. "Do you want me to come with you when you do it?"

She sniffed and nodded. "When I figure out how and when to do it, that would be great."

"Done," he said smiling.

She leaned up and kissed him lightly on the lips.

Chapter Twenty-Four
Suspected Truth

Georgia put the idea of telling the Marens the truth about the situation their world was in out of her mind. She needed to focus on how to tell Mama Landry and, even more tricky, how to tell Ryan. She knew she needed more time to work out a plan for him. For some reason, it felt like it had been ages since she had seen Mama Landry and, if she knew the woman at all, she would be wondering where she had been. Although, she had also been the one trying to push her and Austin together. Since she seemed to know everything going on even before it happened, she may already have an idea.

It was torturous getting through her shift at the bookstore with her task looming over her, but she managed to get most of her tasks done. When Ryan came in, she knew she was acting strange toward him and the harder she tried to be normal, the worse things got. She was fidgety and evasive and, even with his generally oblivious nature, he finally grabbed ahold of her arm as she was skirting by him to get to the stock room and spun her around to face him.

"What the heck is going on?" he asked.

"What do you mean?" Georgia asked, evading again.

"I just asked you how you managed to find time to get the new signage posted. Your response was 'I'll call them on Friday so I can just make all the calls at once'."

"Oh," Georgia said, looking at a spot on the wall over his left shoulder. "I guess I was just thinking about needing to make those calls. I didn't hear what you asked."

Ryan looked over his shoulder and back at Georgia. "What are you looking at?"

"You," Georgia said, focusing on a small freckle by his right temple.

"No... you appear to be focused on everything else but me. Is there something you need to tell me? Have you gotten involved with something... shady?"

She did look him in the eyes at that remark. "Shady?"

He leaned in. "Georgia, are you doing drugs?"

She let out a bark of laughter. "Drugs?! Do you think I'm the kind of person who'd do drugs? Come on, Ryan, you know me better than that."

"I thought I did," he agreed, leaning back to a normal standing position. "But I don't know. You start hanging out with this new guy from out of town and now you're acting really bizarre. I thought it might be..."

"I'm not doing drugs, Ryan, and neither is Austin. I really am fine. I just... I need to talk to you about something, but I don't have the time to get into it now. I have to be at Mama Landry's for supper soon." She saw his look of concern and hurried on. "It's nothing bad! Well... I mean, it's not great. It's... it's really hard to explain, ok?" She walked back to the front desk, put the forms she had been working on in their binder, and slid them under the counter. "Just trust me, you don't have to stress about it. I'll tell you all about it soon. Do you want to maybe meet for coffee or something soon? Are you free any time this week?"

He looked at her, one eyebrow raised. "We've never had coffee."

"That's true," she agreed. "But does that mean we never can?"

"I guess not," he said hesitantly. "I'm going to wonder what this is about until we get together."

"Well," she said, grabbing her bag and jacket from under the counter and squeezing past Ryan. "Then we should get together soon. Plus, I told you not to stress about it. I can't control what you do from here." He smiled at that. She knew that, even though he griped about her attitude all the time, he enjoyed their banter, and this was more along their usual line of dialogue.

"Ok, let's do tomorrow. That seems soon enough. Where do you want to meet?" he asked as she opened the front door.

"How about your place?" They both froze at that. She had never been inside Ryan's house, although she knew where he lived. She had dropped things in his mailbox before. He wasn't much of a social creature, but she knew he would be much more comfortable dealing with the bomb she was about to drop on him in a familiar and relaxing setting.

"I'll bring s'mores bars." He had never been able to resist when she brought in the s'mores bars her mom had always made when she was little.

She could see his discomfort melt into intrigue and a small smile played on his face. "Ok," he said, still a bit guardedly. "I'll see you at my place at three."

"Can't wait," she beamed back and left the store quickly before he could change his mind.

Great, she thought to herself as she got in her car and headed over to Mama Landry's restaurant. Now all I have to do is find a way to tell him by tomorrow afternoon. She pulled to a stop in a space in front of the restaurant, turned off her car, and thumped her forehead on her steering wheel.

She took a deep breath, grabbed her things, and headed toward the door. As she reached for the handle, it swung open from the inside and standing in the doorway was Dale Neff. Georgia started at him, her mouth partly open. He looked at her with squinted eyes, forehead furrowed, as if wondering what her problem was.

"You comin' in, or what?" he asked roughly.

"Oh, uh, yeah, thanks." Georgia stammered and stepped through the door past him. He walked out and shut the door hard behind him.

She walked to her booth and watched out the window as he walked to the parking spaces in front of the restaurant. She saw him stop and look at her car for a second, his head tilted, then he turned to look back at the restaurant. She looked away quickly and sat down, opening a menu and pretending to look over what she already had memorized. After what felt like an eternity, she shifted a sideways glance toward the window. He was still looking at her. Just then, Mama Landry arrived with her mug of coffee.

"Now, I was gettin' ta thinkin' ya fo'got 'bout ol' Mama Landry," the woman said, setting the mug down in front of Georgia. "I'm bettin' a certain young man's been occupyin' ya time, am I right?"

Georgia smiled up at Mama Landry in spite of the incredibly creeping feeling she had from Mr. Neff looking so intensely at her. "You know I'd never forget about you, Mama. But, yeah, Austin's been taking up some of my time."

"Well, ain't that good ta hear," Mama Landry said, smiling widely.

"Hey Mama, what was Mr. Neff doing in here? I thought you said a while ago you only saw him coming out through town at night since he worked all day at the mill."

"That's true 'nuff," Mama Landry said, her face tightening slightly. "His schedule musta done changed though, 'cause he's been in here a couple times now in tha last couple weeks. Always talkin' real quiet ta someone or otha' in here, they heads bent low like they havin' a real private talk. Then he up an' leaves. Never orders nothin', never talks ta Mama Landry."

Georgia looked out the window again and was happy to see Mr. Neff had finally gotten in his truck and driven off. "He was looking at my car when he left just now and then stared in at me for a while. He's kind of…"

"A odd duck," Mama Landry finished, nodding and looking out the window as well. "That he is, darlin'. That he is. Always has been, but it's got worse these last few months." She turned back to Georgia. "What sounds good ta-night?"

"I was actually hoping you'd join me for supper again," Georgia said in what she hoped was a casual tone. "I wanted to talk to you about some things."

Even though she thought she had sounded completely nonchalant, Mama Landry's face registered a more serious expression. "Sho' 'nuff, honey," she said. "I feel like this chat might need some good ol' fashioned comfort food. I'll be right with ya."

Georgia watched as she walked away and to the kitchen. She looked down into her cup at her rippled reflection in the brown liquid, thinking the movement of it reminded her of the beginning stages of watching a transformation. She felt more confident from the subtle symbolic nature of it all and took a long drink, letting the drink warm her.

When Mama Landry returned, Georgia took the plates of fried chicken and mac and cheese as well as the basket of warm bread and butter that were handed to her. She waited while Mama Landry got herself settled. They both unwrapped their silverware and took a few bites, savoring the deliciousness of it all.

"Man, this is great," Georgia sighed. "Your cooking is pure magic, Mama."

"Thank ya, sweets. There's all kindsa magic in this world. I'm glad I can be a parta one of 'em."

Georgia couldn't hardly pass up such an easy segue so she set her fork down, picked up her mug, and looked over the top of it at Mama Landry while she took a sip. "Speaking of magic…" she trailed off to see if Mama Landry would take the bait.

The old woman's eyes looked up to meet hers and the depth of their brown was almost as warm and inviting as the coffee in her mug. "What 'bout it?" She asked, her voice hushed but anxious.

"What all kinds of magic do you think there is out there, Mama?"

"Oh, chil', there ain't 'nuff numbers out there, I reckon. There's magic in almost everythin' an everyone. There's magic that moves people ta do certain things an' say certain things. There's magic in music and stories. There's magic in death an' after."

"What would you say," Georgia said, interrupting the list and leaning forward over the table, setting her mug aside, "if I told you there was more concrete magic out there? Something more… tangible. Something you could see clear as a bell and know you'd seen something that couldn't be explained any other way. Would you be scared? Excited? Nervous?"

"I think I'd feel like all my years a believin' without needin' ta see woulda led ta that moment."

Georgia nodded. "I thought you might feel that way." She looked around the dining room to make sure they really were the only ones in there. "Mama, there's real magic out there, right now." She shifted her eyes in the direction of the woods. "You said you didn't believe Jordan and Sawyer were dead. You were right. They're out there."

Mama Landry clasped her hands together and held them against her chest, her brown eyes pooling with tears, her smile so big it split her face almost in half. "Oh, lawd, thank ya," she said, and closed her eyes, two tears floating down her cheeks from under her dark eyelashes. "Thank ya for not takin' them young'uns away from this Earth." Georgia let Mama Landry process the news quietly. Finally, the woman opened her shining eyes and looked at Georgia. "And they ok, ain't they Miss Georgia?"

"In a manner of speaking, yeah, they are. But that's part of the real magic I was talking about, Mama. They aren't like themselves anymore. See, before the accident happened, Jordan and I shared a special ability; something no one else we ever met could do."

Mama Landry never broke eye contact, but shook her head slowly. "Don't surprise me a bit," she said. "Ya two was always special; ya two and Mr. Austin. I felt it from tha first time I met ya. What kinda ability, Miss Georgia?"

"Well, Mama, we can kind of… disguise ourselves. Really well. So well no one would know it was us, in fact. We can change how we look. We can change… into animals." She expected this pronouncement at least to be met with at least a small level of shock, like it had with Auggie.

To her surprise, however, Mama Landry just nodded slowly.

"Miss Jordan an' Mr. Sawyer out there as animals then, ain't they?" she asked, almost inaudibly. She looked out the window as if she could see them. "They tha ones everyone been seein' 'round town." Georgia nodded. "They been comin' close ta Mama's backyard too, I reckon. It's why I sense Miss Jordan now an' then."

"Probably," Georgia agreed.

"It's strange," Mama Landry pondered, and Georgia thought that was probably the understatement of the year. But then the woman continued. "When I met Mr. Sawyer, I did' get that sense 'bout him. But I guess he might-a just slipped unda my radar."

"Oh, no," Georgia interjected. "You're right. He wasn't able to change before. Not until the accident. But there's a little more to the story that leads up to that."

She spent the next fifteen minutes regaling Mama Landry with the stories her mom used to tell her, of meeting Victoria and Christian, Sawyer almost dying, and the new mission they were on. When she was done, Mama Landry finally did look shocked. "So, now we're trying to prevent this war from happening, but we need more people who might have something to contribute and who want to help the cause."

"A war," Mama Landry whispered, her eyes focused on something over Georgia's shoulder she was sure she wouldn't be able to see. "Say it ain't so."

"I'm sorry, Mama. It is so. And we need help."

Mama Landry's eyes came into focus again and she looked at Georgia. "'Course ya do, chil'. Whatever Mama Landry can do for ya, just say tha word."

Georgia reached out and took Mama Landry's hand. "Thank you," she whispered.

The woman put her other hand on top of Georgia's and squeezed it tightly.

Chapter Twenty-Five
Eye-Opening

"This is exhausting." Georgia was lying back, her head on Austin's lap, staring at the blue sky over the quarry.

"Looking at the sky? Lying down? Spending time with me?"

"Shush," Georgia laughed. "Spending time with you and looking at the sky is the most relaxed I've been in days. I just mean finding ways to tell everyone. And the actual telling. It's stressful."

Austin stroked her hair and she closed her eyes and sighed. "I'm so sorry you have to do all this," he said, and she could hear the sadness in his voice. "I'm constantly in awe at how well you handle things having grown up with no one in your life who could do this stuff. I can't imagine what that would've been like. You're amazing."

Georgia didn't respond for a minute. It struck her how, for the past few months, she'd been so focused on how alone she felt in this whole thing and how much resentment she'd been carrying about it. Hearing those words from Austin seemed to be just what she didn't even realize she needed to hear. She smiled. "Thank you. That means so much. It's been hard, but I don't feel nearly so alone now."

"You aren't alone, now. You won't have to feel that way ever again."

Georgia sighed and sat up. "I really like what we have going here. And I know I still have Jordan and Sawyer to talk to about things if I need to. But Austin… if there really is a war coming, the likelihood of us all making it through this…"

"Stop," he said. "You can't think like that now."

"I have to think like that! It's real. I don't want to lose any of you. I already lost part of my best friend due to this stupid conflict. I hate that we're in this situation; a situation we didn't have anything to do with in the first place. We're cleaning up other people's messes; fighting thousand-year old people's wars. It isn't fair. I've lost enough. I don't want to lose more."

"You stand to lose much more if you do nothing," Austin reasoned. "You know that."

"I know," she said on an exhale, leaning her shoulder against his. "But it doesn't make me feel any better."

"Once it's all over and we come out on the other end, you're going to feel so much better knowing you did what was right. We're going to win this."

"How do you know?" she asked.

"Because we did last time," he shrugged. "The good guy almost always wins. The odds are in our favor."

"Oh yeah, that's rational." She rolled her eyes but couldn't stop from grinning.

"Nothing about any of this is rational," he smiled back. "And yet, here we are."

She reached over and rubbed her thumb gently over his dimple. "Yeah, here we are."

He leaned in and kissed her forehead. "And we'll be here when it's over."

"I'm looking forward to it," she said, pulling her knees toward her and standing.

"Oh!" Austin exclaimed, standing as well, and she jumped slightly, pressing her hand to her heart. "Sorry," he apologized. "I just remembered, I was able to get into the training room yesterday and I pulled up the water bucket in the well."

"Really?! What color was it?!"

"Yellow. And not only that, but when I pulled the bucket up it was only about a quarter full. So blocking the outlet seems to have stopped it from filling pretty quickly. We might want to tell Christian if he doesn't want to raise suspicions, he either needs to open it back up or fill it some other way."

"That's a good idea," Georgia said. "We can think about that and discuss it when we see them in a couple days. But for now, I have to go tell the most logical, rational, stoic guy I know that there's magic in the world."

"I'd offer to join you but..." he paused and she looked at him, eyes brows raised. "I'm trying to come up with a good reason... but I really just don't want to."

She smacked his shoulder and they both laughed.

"Charming," she stuck her tongue out at him and walked toward her car.

"Mature," he responded, jogging after her and opening her door for her. She turned and kissed him again. He began to pull away and she reached up and put her hand in his hair, holding him in place gently, not ready to be out of the security of his presence just yet. He let go of the door and reached his arms around her waist, pulling her to him. The kiss deepened and Georgia knew that, even though she didn't want to, if she didn't stop now, she wouldn't end up making her meeting with Ryan. She finally broke the kiss and tucked her forehead against Austin's chest. "If I don't leave now, I won't leave at all."

"You're not giving me much reason to encourage you to go," he whispered into her hair.

"I'll be back at my house by six," she promised, looking up and kissing his dimpled cheek before turning and getting in her car.

"I'll be there at five after," he said, waving and shutting her door. She waved back and turned the key in the ignition, backed down the side road, turned around, and drove away before she lost what little motivation she still had.

*****

Georgia pulled up in front of Ryan's house and shut off her car. The white cottage with green shutters looked like many of the other houses on the side street. She thought the uniformity of it all suited Ryan well. She grabbed the baking dish with her s'mores bars and walked up the path to his matching green front door. She used the silver knocker and stood waiting.

The door opened and Ryan looked out at her. "Hey," he said, and she could tell he was as uncomfortable as she felt. This wasn't a good way to start what promised to be a rough afternoon, so she tried to look as relaxed as she could.

"Hi," she said, cheerily. "I brought sustenance." She held up the bars and he smiled back, stepping to the side.

"Come on in. I have a pot of coffee brewing."

"Music to my ears," she said walking into the house and taking in her surroundings. Whatever she might have been expecting, this wasn't it. There were medieval flag tapestries, swords with an armor helmet mounted above the fireplace, and a rug with a crest comprised of lions and feathers on the floor in front of it. She turned in slow circles, taking it all in. She noticed Ryan standing in the doorway between the living room and the kitchen, looking at her.

"This place looks really cool," she said.

"I kind of have a thing for medieval history," Ryan said in an apologetic tone.

"I think that's great," she said, enthusiastically. "How come you've never mentioned it before?"

"I don't know. I don't want to bore people with things they aren't interested in."

"Jordan and I used to talk about books set in this time period all the time! We would've loved your input."

His face reddened as he walked over and took the s'mores bars from her. "Well, the books you guys read are fantasy. They aren't the real thing. I'm more focused on the actual events, not what's made up just for entertainment value." She watched him walk into the kitchen. She couldn't have asked for a better transition into what she needed to talk about. She followed him in and leaned against the counter as he took six of the bars and put them on a tray before setting the tray on the table between two mugs.

"You know, sometimes the things we think are so fantastic can actually be more real than we might imagine."

He shrugged one shoulder. "Maybe, sometimes. But the whole Merlin magic part of the King Arthur stuff kind of turns me off the stories. I like to read stuff I can believe in."

"What would it take for you to believe in something you didn't believe in before?" Georgia lead.

He looked at her, and the expression on his face told her he was completely lost. "Um, I don't know. Proof I guess."

"How do you know what you read about medieval history is real? What proof do you have of it?"

"It's history," he replied, as if that explained anything.

"History used to tell us the world was flat," she countered. "Then someone took a boat ride."

"That's true," he conceded, sitting at the table and gesturing for her to do the same. "However, that boat ride was proof, and so I believe the world is round."

"But if you had lived before the boat ride, you would've believed it was flat, right? Because that's what the history books told you?"

"I guess. But with the medieval stuff, they've found physical evidence of these items being used as well as written text about *how* they were used. To me, that's proof."

"I get it. That makes sense." Georgia nodded, taking a sip of the coffee and picking up one of the bars.

"Why the line of questioning?" Ryan asked, also taking a bar and dipping the corner into his mug before taking a bite.

"I just wanted to know how you process things; your reasoning."

"Is this leading into what you wanted to talk to me about?" he asked, one eyebrow arched slightly higher than the other.

"It is. So, my next question is this: What would you do if someone showed you proof of something you previously believed to be fake, non-existent, or even ludicrous?"

He considered her question for a second, chewing thoughtfully. "What, like aliens or something?"

She tilted her head slowly from side to side, eyes raised in contemplation. "Sort of like that, I guess."

"I think a lot of the 'proof' out there can be faked. Unless I saw something I couldn't refute, I still don't think I'd believe it."

"Fair enough. So what about magic?"

He groaned softly. "Georgia, magic is so… speculative. It's subjective. People see something they can't explain and they want to believe that automatically means it's magic. I tend to just think of magic as a blanket term to cover anything that doesn't have an easy answer or explanation."

"In most cases, I think that's a good approach," Georgia agreed. "Although I think you could also consider the entertainment aspect of it. I think a lot of people don't actually believe in magic, but they pretend to because it's fun."

"For some people, probably. Not me." He popped the last bite of bar into his mouth, wiped his fingers on his napkin, and reached for a second bar.

"But, if you sat and watched something happen you never believed could happen before, you'd have to believe it, right?"

He looked at her appraisingly, then set his bar on his napkin, folded his hands on the table in front of him, and leaned forward. "Georgia, what is it you want?"

She blew out a sigh, took the last bite of her bar, and chewed slowly, delaying the inevitable. She swallowed, took a sip of coffee, and leaned back. "I need to tell you something. And possibly show you something. But I need to know you aren't going to 1.) Freak out and 2.) Tell anyone. And I really need you to understand how important this is; you have to open your mind."

He continued to stare at her and she stared back. They sat that way for a while before Ryan finally leaned back as well and crossed his arms. "Ok," he said. "What do you need to tell me."

"You're guarded," Georgia said, shaking her head. "You cross your arms when you're ready for an argument. I can't tell you like this." She leaned forward as far as she could and looked directly into his eyes. "This isn't our usual banter anymore, Ryan. This is real and this is serious. People are in danger and I need you to hear me and understand and, more than anything, I need you to believe me."

After a beat, she was relieved to see a hint of concern cross his face and his arms untighten and finally uncross until his hands were resting on his thighs. "I don't want to scare you, Ryan, and I don't want to rock your world. But with things the way they are right now, you need your eyes opened."

She proceeded to tell him the whole story from the beginning as she had twice already; her and Jordan discovering their shared abilities, Sawyer almost dying, the mill, Bernard and Edmund… all of it. He sat quietly and listened to it all. When she finally finished, she leaned back and let him process. She rose, poured herself a second mug of coffee, and sat back down. Ryan still didn't move. She had just opened her mouth to see if he was ok when he slowly shook his head.

"Georgia," he said in a tone one might use when speaking to an unpredictable mental patient. "You know I can't believe that. There's absolutely nothing logical about any of it. People don't turn into animals, they don't live to be thousands of years old, and even if both of those were possible, if there was a war coming, someone would know about it." He reached across the table and touched her hand. "I know losing Jordan's been hard on us all, and particularly on you. But making up a story like this to justify her death isn't healthy. Maybe you should talk to someone."

Georgia ground her teeth and took deep breaths to keep from launching across the table. She would have gladly gotten questioned by the police again before being talked to like a mental case. She pushed her chair back and stood.

"I'm not making it up, Ryan. I would never make up something like this. I hate that it's true. I've never wished I could think like you more than I've wished it these past few months. I've never wanted to be wrong about something more than I do about this. But it's all true, and I can show you, but I need to know you can handle it without freaking out."

"Show me... what exactly?" Ryan said, still in a little more of a placating tone than she cared for.

"Show you that people can turn into animals."

"Am I to understand you intend to turn into an animal…
here in my kitchen?"

"Yes, if you can promise me you won't have a heart attack
or run out of here screaming to the police or something
else equally asinine."

She felt a pang of satisfaction as she saw his nose wrinkle at
the insults. "Ok, fine," he said resignedly. "Show me this
magic of yours."

"When it happens, I can understand you, but you won't be
able to understand me. Please… please… try to process
calmly. I'll wait until you come to terms."

He shook his head and smiled unbelievingly at her. "Sure,"
she said, again with the placating tone.

She took a deep breath and closed her eyes. She was
frustrated enough the change didn't happen immediately,
but she finally felt herself shifting forms. When it was
complete, she opened her eyes and wished she could laugh
the same as she could in her human form.

Ryan had jumped out of his chair, backed to the counter,
and was sitting on it, his knees pulled up to his chest. His
eyes were so wide she could see white all the way around
them. She sat and then laid down on the cool floor, her tail
flicking lazily. After five minutes she hadn't seen him move
or blink and her emotions started to cross over to concern.
She debated on changing back, but she didn't want to
throw more at him. Instead, she rolled onto her side in the
most submissive form she could think of and pawed gently
at the air, purring softly in her throat.

Finally, Ryan relaxed his grip on his knees, letting his legs dangle over the edge of the counter, but didn't get down. He stared at her and she stared back. She rolled back onto her stomach and inched toward him, reaching her paw forward gently. She saw him swallow and slowly move forward and slide his feet to the floor. She stayed where she was as he walked a full circle around her, as far away from her as he could be. When he reached his starting point, he moved a bit closer to her, crouched down, and squinted his eyes as if trying to see whatever "trick" she was pulling on him.

"You said you can hear me and understand me, right?" he finally said, his voice both tight in his throat and hoarse. She lowered her head and purred a bit louder. He stood up again and laughed nervously, pacing back and forth, one hand rubbing his eyes, the other in a fist on his hip. "This is insane," he finally said. "You almost have me believing this crazy trick of yours." He spun around and looked at her again, before sinking back into his chair at the table. "There has to be another explanation." He said, pleadingly.

Georgia rose and walked slowly toward him, pausing for a moment when he pulled his feet closer to the chair as if trying to keep some distance between them. When he relaxed, she continued her forward movement until she was close enough for him to touch her if he chose. She sat and reached out to paw his foot gently before pulling back and looking up at him. He shook his head, eyes closed, not looking at her. She purred as loudly as she could and he took a deep breath and looked down at her. She tilted her head to the side and he laughed again, this time more genuinely. She leaned forward and butted her head lightly against his knee. He reached down, almost involuntarily, and touched her shoulder.

"You're warm," he whispered. "And your fur feels more like hair." Her gaze met his and he sucked in a small gasp. He leaned a bit closer to her and looked deep into her eyes. "Geez, your eyes are exactly the same."

They stayed as they were for a while, her letting him touch her and talk through what he was feeling, him trying to work through the disproving of almost forty years of disbelief in magic. After a few minutes of silence, she rose and walked back to the spot where she had transformed before. She sat and looked at him, head tilted again. "Yeah," he said. "I'm ready."

She lowered her head again and felt her body shift back to her human form. When she opened her eyes, she saw Ryan's mixture of relief and amazement. "I know that was hard for you, but thank you," she said, sitting back in her chair and picking up her mug again. "Thank you for finally understanding."

"Oh, I don't think I understand any more than I did before," he said, sounding drained. "But, you convinced me that maybe magic isn't only an easy out. There's nothing easy about what just happened here today."

She couldn't help but smile at that comment. "And the situation we're facing is even harder for me to believe," she stated. "But the more people we can get to believe and the more people who know what's coming, the better position we'll be in. We need you."

"Need me?! For what?! I'm not magic. I'm still not even a hundred percent sure what I just saw is actually magic. What could I possibly offer?" he asked, his voice an octave higher than usual.

"Your support is more valuable than you can possibly understand," she said calmly. "Right now, Austin and I are the only ones who can be in both forms. We can only talk to so many people within a certain amount of time. There may well come a time when we need other people to deliver messages or do things only people can do. Will you help us if we need it?"

He shook his head, not in disagreement, but in continued disbelief. "Please, Ryan. I know this is hard. But I wouldn't ask if it wasn't important. I didn't sign up for this war, but it seems it's coming whether we want it to or not. We need to try to protect as many people as possible. We need soldiers... knights."

He looked up and she knew she had struck the right chord with him. His appreciation of the code of chivalry apparently ran deep and the idea of being a knight was obviously appealing to him.

He squared his shoulders a bit and finally responded. "I guess if there's any way I can help, then I'm obligated to do it. Yeah," he nodded, "just let me know what you need from me and I'll do what I can." She smiled at him and he smiled back, the first genuine smile she'd seen from him in a long while.

Chapter Twenty-Six
Story Recanted

Georgia was laying on the hood of her car in the Marens' driveway trying to let her mind go blank, even if just for a little bit. It had been a few days since she'd told Ryan the whole story of her life and what was going on in the town. After today, everyone who needed to know would know and she would be able to focus on moving forward. She kept thinking about the deal she had made with Christian. He was working on a solution to make her permanently human, and the more she thought about it, the better it sounded. She longed for a life without secrecy and complications. Well… less complications.

Her mind wandered to what life could be like after all this was over. She imagined herself and Austin living in a house of their own, likely away from the towns they had grown up in. A fresh start was very appealing. She let her mind move further into the future and saw children in the yard playing catch, while she and Austin sat on the porch watching. She sighed and smiled.

"Thinking happy thoughts?" a voice next to her asked softly.

"Gah!" She started, jerking so hard she slipped sideways off the other side of the car and landed heavily on the ground.

"Oh my god!" Austin said, running around to help her up. "I'm so sorry! I didn't think I'd scare you so bad." He grinned and shook his head when he saw she was sitting on the ground laughing. "And, apparently you're fine." He reached down and helped her to her feet.

"I am," she said, still laughing, brushing gravel and dirt off her jeans. "I was in the middle of a day dream."

"A good one?" he asked, brushing gravel off the back of her jacket.

"A great one," she replied. "I can't wait until all this is over and I can see how much of it comes true."

"Was I in it?" he asked.

"Of course you were."

"Good to know," he said, leaning back against her car. "So, what all did the daydream entail?"

"Just a future without magic. Being able to be normal for once. Living a regular life."

"Without magic?" he asked, his brow furrowed. "How do you figure that's part of your future?"

"I made a deal with Christian. In exchange for me doing the brunt of the work with this whole mess and talking to people and having to deal with the grief and suffering they all knew I didn't want to do, he's working on a potion to make me permanently human."

Austin stared hard at her. "Is that even possible?" he asked, shocked.

"I don't think it is yet. But he's been working for a long time trying to find a way to fix Victoria's problem. In doing that, he's come close to making a solution, along with a few others. One of them is the potion that ended up saving Sawyer's life and making him and Jordan permanently animals."

"I see," he said, and she saw a shadow of something in his face.

"What's the matter?" she asked, reaching over and touching his arm.

"I knew you said before you wished you couldn't do this, but I thought it was just an off-hand remark. I just… didn't know you planned to give up such a big part of your life. Don't you think you'd miss it at all? It's part of who you are. Who knows what else it would affect."

She shook her head. "I will always be me, whether I can change forms or not. All I know is this particular aspect of my life has brought me far more grief than happiness. You forget we grew up very differently. You grew up with this being something normal. You had others you could share it with. I grew up with this making me a freak and isolating me from ever having any friendships or relationships. Then, when I finally did get a real friend, this lead to me losing her, or at least a big part of her. I hate this part of my life. I don't want it in my life anymore."

"So, what about us?" Austin asked quietly. "I know the war is awful and things'll probably get much worse before they get better, but your search for answers is what brought us together."

"Austin." She reached out and took his hand. "I honestly believe we would've met anyway. We were meant to be a part of each other's lives. And besides, we're together now. Do you really think me not being able to transform anymore would change that?" she asked, realizing in the pause before his answer that he may have a different response than she was hoping for.

"I'm going to care for you no matter what you decide," he squeezed her hand gently. "But I think this decision is going to change things for you far more than you realize. Just think about it, ok. And please don't do anything without talking to me before you do."

"I can be ok with that," she said. She looked into his eyes, her brows knitting together. "Are you mad at me?"

He pulled her to him. "Absolutely not."

They stayed that way a while before pulling apart. "Are you ready for this?" he asked.

She took a deep breath and turned her head to the house where Judy and Gordon were likely just finishing their supper. "I guess now's as good a time as any."

"It's going to be ok," Austin said softly, his hand in the small of her back, guiding her forward. "Ultimately, you'll be telling them their daughter is still alive, and that'll be at least a small comfort."

"Maybe," she replied, doubt in her voice. They stopped at the front door and paused a beat before Austin reached out, turned the knob, and they walked in.

The smell of apple pie hit them and they both sighed in pleasure. The comfort the smell brought to Georgia made her feel a bit better. They hadn't even gotten their jackets off before they heard Judy calling from the den.

"Georgia, is that you?"

"Me and Austin," she called back, hanging her jacket and bag on the hook by the door.

"Oh, good," Gordon called. "We need his help eating the two pies Judy made this evening. They should be ready in about ten minutes. Come on in here and we can chat a while."

"Gordon, they might have other plans," Judy chastised.

"Not at all," Austin said, threading his fingers through Georgia's and walking through the doorway into the den. "We were hoping you guys would be home tonight. We're game for a chat, aren't we?" He sat on the loveseat and pulled Georgia down next to him. She smiled and nodded but didn't trust herself to speak yet.

Gordon gave her a quizzical look but didn't press. He stood and walked toward the kitchen with his coffee mug. "Can I get anyone a drink? I need a refill on my tea."

"I'll have more as well," Judy said, handing him her mug.

"Water, please" Austin said. He looked over at Georgia. "Make that two."

"Coming up," he said, disappearing into the kitchen.

"So, how has your day been?" Judy asked them. Georgia looked at her and instantly relaxed. Despite the fact she wasn't her biological mother, Judy had always been able to make her feel safe, comfortable, and secure. Her smile brought warmth into any room. Georgia leaned back and tried to relax more. She knew the calmer she was, the easier this would be for everyone, and she was extremely glad Austin was with her for this.

"I've been working most of the day, so it's nice to finally be done and relax," Austin responded.

"It's definitely good to be done with work," Georgia agreed. "Business is picking up and putting out the shipments has been tiring. I told Ryan he should be doing it since he's the man, but he just said I was being sexist." They all laughed at that. "He and I are getting along pretty well though. I, uh…I actually spent some time with Ryan at his house the other day."

Judy raised her eyebrows. "Really? I didn't realize you two spent time together outside the store. That's wonderful!"

"It's kind of a new development," Georgia said. "It was the first time I've ever been to his house. But it was nice. I'm sure we'll hang out again sometime. Turns out he's into medieval history, which is far more interesting than most of the other things he's into." There was laughter again. Everyone was aware of Georgia and Ryan's difference in interests.

"Getting to know more about people is always a fun experience," Judy said. "I love learning things I never knew about people."

Georgia saw Austin slide his gaze sideways at her. She knew he had recognized the opportunity to bring the subject around to what they had come here for that night. He had no idea it was the second time in a matter of days the perfect opportunity had presented itself. With all the hardship she had to endure over these few months, she was grateful for these opportunities.

Gordon returned with two bottles of water under one arm and holding two mugs of tea. He distributed the beverages and sat back in his chair. "I agree," he said in response to Judy's comment. "Being on the force, it's amazing how many times people surprised me. You might think you have a person completely figured out and then they shock the hell out of you. It got to the point I never assumed I knew anything until I had proof."

"That's a smart way to operate," Austin nodded. "In fact, I think we might be able to add to your cache of stories in that vein, don't you?" He looked over and Georgia and squeezed her knee gently in encouragement. Judy and Gordon's faced registered intrigue at the same time and they shifted their gazes back and forth between the Georgia and Austin.

Georgia nodded, leaned forward, and cleared her throat. "So, I feel like I need to preface everything that's about to be said by telling you we're very aware it sounds impossible and insane."

"Noted," Gordon replied and Judy nodded. A bit of the intrigue had been replaced with concern, but they still seemed to be in a receptive place and Georgia felt encouraged.

Georgia looked at Austin. He turned to Judy and Gordon. "Before we start, I'd actually like to ask you a question. It's probably going to seem vague, but it'll work itself out through the course of our conversation. Is there anything about this town, or maybe life in this town, that doesn't make sense to you? Maybe something you've always wondered about but never gotten a satisfactory answer to?"

They considered this for a while. Judy shook her head slowly. "I can't think of anything. Gordon?"

Gordon's eyes weren't quite in focus as he started across the room, deep in thought. Finally, he shifted slightly. "I know this is a very small town, and yet people generally don't seem to know a whole lot about each other. Some do, but people tend to keep to themselves more than I think makes sense or more than is common in other small towns. Otherwise I can't think of anything off the top of my head."

"Ok," Georgia said, nodding. "I agree with that observation. The town I lived in before here was smaller than Shamore, and I think that's accurate. They all seemed to know each other, but since we were 'outsiders' we weren't in that group."

"I think it's an accurate observation as well," Austin agreed. "Let me try a slightly different question. What are your thoughts on things or events that can't be explained logically? If you saw something you couldn't explain, how would you process that? Would you search for scientific answers? Would you assume it was something supernatural? Would you ignore it and hoped you were mistaken?"

Again, they considered the question. Gordon spoke first this time. "I *have* seen something I was never able to explain. It happened a long time ago on the force." Judy leaned back, ready to listen to a story she had clearly heard before. Austin and Georgia sat back as well, ready to listen.

"It was about six months before the first cull hunt. There was a young boy, about eight or nine, who'd wandered into the woods from his backyard. The mother had just seen him playing through the window. She went to grab something from another room and, when she came back, the boy was gone. She went out and called for him, but he didn't answer. She walked quite a distance into the woods and kept calling for him, but still nothing.

She ran to the station for help. Danny and I were there when she came in. We mobilized everyone available and did a search of the woods, each man going in about a quarter of a mile apart and heading in the same direction so we wouldn't miss anything. I'd walked for a little over a mile when I heard rustling up ahead to my left. I called for the boy, but no one answered.

I walked in the direction from where I'd heard the noise and, as I passed through a deep line of bushes, I saw what looked like a man dressed in dark clothes with a pack on his back. He suddenly bent down and then shrank impossibly fast behind another dense patch of greenery. From where he seemed to have disappeared, a rabbit took off under a fallen tree and down a hole in the ground. I ran to the patch of bushes where I saw the man disappear and found a large mound of animal hides. Inside them was the boy. He was unconscious, but seemed otherwise unhurt.

I brought him back to the doc here in town and, when he came to, he was unable to tell us anything other than a man he didn't recognize had called for him from the woods and said his dad wanted to talk to him. He told him his dad had sent this man to fetch him. The boy's father worked in carpentry and spent some time in the woods, so it didn't seem out of the ordinary to the boy that his father would have been in there. When he went to the man, he grabbed him and wrapped the animal hides around him. He felt something wet and that was all he remembered until he woke up with us at the doctor's office. Obviously the woods were searched and any strangers in town were questioned for some time after that, but no one was ever found."

At this point, Gordon rubbed the back of his neck, deep confusion rested on his face. "I told the guys on the force what I'd seen out there when I was looking for the kid; or at least told them how I couldn't explain what I'd seen. They all said it was probably just a trick of the light and shadows and no one blamed me for losing track of the guy because I ended up finding the kid and that made me a hero."

He shook his head almost angrily at that comment. "But I still dream about that day every now and then, and while the missing kid was the biggest concern for me at the time, the dream always seems to focus on the man. He disappeared right in front of me and then a rabbit just appeared in the same place and ran to hide. That's the part of the dream that always repeats. How can a person just disappear right in front of someone? And how can a rabbit appear out of nowhere?"

They all sat quiet for a while. Judy reached over and squeezed Gordon's hand comfortingly. "You *are* a hero for saving that boy, Gordon. Can you imagine if we were to lose Jordan at eight years old and someone was able to bring her back to us? You'd have thought they were a hero, too."

He patted her hand gently and looked up at Austin and Georgia. "So, to answer your question, I guess I might react in any number of ways. I ignored what I couldn't explain at the time, but I also never stopped thinking about it. I wish I could get an explanation for what I saw so I could have some peace about it, but I never pursued any further investigation of it after the search for the man was called off."

Austin nodded and looked at Georgia who had been shifting a bit uncomfortably ever since Judy made the comment about losing Jordan and someone bringing her back. She knew she could tell them Jordan was technically alive, and they would be thrilled, if they believed her at all. But once they realized they would still never be able to communicate with her, would it be like losing her all over again?

"What is this about," Judy asked softly. "Georgia, you look miserable. Please, just say what you need to say. We're listening." Gordon nodded his agreement.

Georgia slid forward to the edge of the loveseat and rested her elbows on her knees, her hands dangling in front of her. "I'm just so scared of hurting you both all over again."

"Oh, honey," Judy said. "You were never the one who hurt us! Losing Jordan was a tragedy, but we knew you suffered that loss just like we did. We never looked at you as the one who hurt us! It was a horrible accident."

"Judy's right," Gordon said. "You should always feel like you can tell us anything. This is a safe space," he gestured widely. "Come on, hun. Get whatever it is off your chest."

Austin put his hand on her back supportively. She looked into their faces. "We can explain what you saw that night, Gordon."

She once again began the story of how she and Jordan had met and become friends and, in the course of their spending time together, discovered their unique shared ability. At the mention of shapeshifting, Judy's whole body tensed, but Gordon reached over and squeezed her arm as if asking her to stay quiet and calm for the story. Georgia continued, sharing the stories her mom had told her about the history of magic and how Christian and Victoria had confirmed the stories were true.

Her voice cracked a bit when she got to the part about Sawyer's attempts to penetrate the mill for information and the resulting events in the woods that caused Jordan and Sawyer to no longer be able to come home. She looked up briefly and saw tears cascading down Judy's face and the pools of liquid in Gordon's. She didn't think she could continue, but Gordon nodded to her gently and she gathered every last ounce of determination she had to move forward.

Finally, she talked about the investigative work they had been doing since that evening, how she had come to meet Austin and learn he was able to do the same thing she and Jordan could, and that they were now working toward developing a plan to stop an impending war.

When she finished speaking, her shoulder's sagged and she leaned back, exhausted. No other telling of the story had taken as much out of her and she was exceedingly glad Austin was with her. She wished she could pause time and rest before dealing with the myriad of potential reactions the Marens might have, but she knew it wasn't possible.

"My, god," Gordon whispered quietly, after what seemed like hours of silence. He looked into Georgia's eyes and she could only imagine the thoughts rushing through his mind. She wanted to look away, but at the same time she wanted to comfort him in any way she could. Her lower lip trembled a bit and a single tear leaked out of her eye.

Georgia and Austin both flinched at the same time as Gordon exploded out of his seat and, for a second, Georgia actually wondered if he was going to hit her, but then she felt incredibly ashamed as he sank to his knees in front of her and wrapped his arms around her. She hugged him back, her head turned to look at Austin, whose eyes looked a little misty as well.

"You've been dealing with all of this on your own for months?" Gordon asked, his voice choked and slightly muffled as he spoke into Georgia's shoulder.

A soft sob escaped from across the room and Georgia and Austin looked over at Judy who had one hand to her mouth. The other still holding the mug of tea trembled precariously. Austin rose quickly, took the mug and sat it on the table next to her, before kneeling next to her and letting her collapse against his chest. They all remained in their somewhat awkward yet cathartic embraces for a while.

Gordon finally pulled back, his face damp but, ever the father, taking the time to wipe the tears from Georgia's face.

"I'm so sorry," she whispered. "I never wanted to lie to you both, but at the time we thought it'd be the best way to let you grieve and move on. We didn't realize how serious the situation would get and how badly we'd need people to know the truth and be able to help."

"Oh, honey," Judy said softly, having gotten herself together enough to speak. Georgia and Gordon looked over at her and she smiled blearily through a continued stream of tears. Austin still knelt next to her, his arm around her for support. "You've given us our daughter back. Or at least, given us the essence of our daughter back. We know she's alive in some way. That's easier to deal with than not having any closure."

"I just feel awful you can't talk to each other anymore. She misses you so much, but she didn't know how you'd feel knowing she was out there but never being able to talk with her again." Judy sniffed and nodded her understanding.

"Is she happy, otherwise?" Gordon ask, his voice breaking slightly.

"I mean, we're all dealing with some pretty heavy stuff right now, but I don't think she regrets the choice she made. She really loves Sawyer, and he loves her. They're happy together."

"As long as she's happy, we can have some kind of peace." Judy said, a small sigh escaping her and the tears slowing slightly. She looked at Gordon, who nodded.

"Can you please tell her we wish she would've talked to us first, but we understand and we love her?" Gordon asked. Georgia nodded, biting her lower lip. "I know she wanted to, but there just wasn't time in that moment."

"Wait," Gordon said, looking back and forth between her and Austin. "How is it you can communicate with her but we can't?"

Austin could see Georgia was still pulling herself together so he rose to sit in Gordon's abandoned chair, still not letting go of Judy's hand.

"We can only communicate with them when we're in our animal form as well," he said. "Technically, if they were here, you could talk to them and they could understand you, but you wouldn't be able to understand them. It's an unfortunate part of what we have to deal with."

"So, maybe someday we could talk to her again?" Judy said, hopefully. Georgia's heart contracted at the sound of relief in her voice.

"She could understand you," Austin repeated. "But it would be a completely one sided conversation," he said emphatically. "We can see how she'd feel about it. It might be painful for her to not be able to participate in the conversation, but we can ask." He looked at Georgia, his eyebrows raised. Georgia nodded again and took a deep breath.

"So…" Gordon said, rubbing his forehead with the palm of his free hand, the other squeezing the back of Georgia's neck affectionately as he had always done. "Shapeshifting?"

Georgia and Austin looked at each other and, despite all the raw feelings in the room, they smiled ever so slightly.

Chapter Twenty-Seven
Recruitment

"I guess part of me was hoping they wouldn't focus on that," Austin quipped, and the Marens smiled in spite of themselves. Judy's smile faded first.

"You said something about Jordan changing when she was ten," Judy said, her words slowly working their way from her brain to her mouth. "That means she's had this secret for over ten years! Why in the world would she keep that from us?!"

"She didn't want to," Georgia answered quickly. "My mom told me I could never tell anyone either. Can you imagine what you'd have thought if someone told you something like that? We were both told to be afraid people may want to commit, experiment on, or even hurt us because of what we could do. It was safer for everyone that we just stay under the radar."

"She shouldn't have had to go through that alone," Gordon said quietly, rising from the floor but not taking his hand off Georgia. "I can't believe she went through something like that so young on her own."

"She was trying to protect you as much as herself," Austin chimed in. "Wouldn't you be afraid it might shock someone pretty intensely if you shared or showed them an ability as unheard of as this? She's a strong girl. She did what she had to do and hoped to never have to burden you or anyone else with that knowledge."

Georgia's heart warmed at Austin's words. He'd only ever met Jordan once, but through his and Georgia's conversations, he really seemed to have gotten the spirit of who she was. And she loved that he was comforting her pseudo-parents like he was. He hadn't grown up with the fear of telling those closest to him about his abilities, but he spoke as though he understood, and that meant a lot to her.

"But, now we're in the position of having to tell you," Georgia continued for him. "This stuff is real. We're willing to show you and answer any other questions you have, but we also need to request your help and we have a couple of questions for you too."

Judy looked uneasy at this, but Gordon's face was set. "I would really like to see it. I want to see for myself what might explain what happened all those years ago. I've spent all this time thinking I was hallucinating or mistaken about what I saw. I've felt guilty for letting a criminal get away from me and never finding him." He looked at Judy. "Do you want to leave the room? If you don't want to see it, you don't have to. No one will think any less of you. It's a lot to take in and it scares the hell out of me, but I have to see it."

Judy was quiet for another minute before slowly sitting forward on her chair and clasping her hands tightly in her lap. "I think I should see it, too." She said, her voice wispy. "I don't like the idea of watching it, but I believe knowledge is power and I want to have as much information as I can when we need to move forward. Plus," she said, her voice stronger, "this is a part of our daughter's life now. I want to be as much a part of that as I still can."

Austin patted her hand and stood as Georgia did. They both walked to the middle of the room between the two Marens. "Do you think we should both do this, or just one so the other can mediate?" he asked, his hand on her shoulder.

"I've had to do this three times already without mediation. It might be nice to have someone handle that part of it for me."

"Fair enough," he smiled and took a few steps backward toward Judy.

"Wait, three times?" Gordon asked. "You've told other people about this already?" Georgia tensed at the tone of accusation in his voice.

"I have. Augustus Toole already seemed to have an idea there was something going on around town and had made that known to me before everything happened with Jordan and Sawyer. Mama Landry spoke to me a few times telling me she didn't believe Jordan was actually gone, though she couldn't explain why she thought that. I knew she'd probably be receptive to the information. And Ryan…"

"Ryan?!" Judy and Gordon exclaimed at the same time. "You thought Ryan would be more receptive to this than we would?" Gordon said in disbelief.

"No, no, no," Georgia responded, waving her hands. "He was just someone we all decided we had to tell and I just…" she paused for a second trying to find the best way to explain, but coming up empty. "I knew it would be a

pain in the ass and I really wanted to get it out of the way."
She looked at them apologetically.

A snort from Judy pulled all of their gazes toward the
woman. As they all watched her, she dissolved into
hysterical laughter and the sound was so welcome in the
tension-filled room they couldn't help but join in.

"I'll give you that one," Gordon conceded after they finally
caught their collective breaths. "My interactions with him in
the past make it easy for me to understand your line of
thought."

"He did ok, honestly. But it was nice to get the worst of it
out of the way."

"We saved the best for last," Austin added, with a smile.

"You're an unapologetic flatterer, and I like it," Judy said,
reaching out to swat his leg. "Go on Georgia, we're ready."

Georgia breathed deeply and let the change take over. She
heard a quick intake of breath from Judy as she completed
her transformation and opened her eyes. She immediately
sat and held still, only her tail moving lazily.

"My god," Gordon whispered, and she looked toward him
slowly. His eyes were wide and he was leaning so far
forward he was almost off the couch. Georgia rose slowly
and walked a few tentative steps toward him. When she was
close enough he could reach out and touch her if he chose,
she sat again.

"You can touch her," Austin said quietly. "She's in the exact same headspace now as she is when she's in her human form. She'd never hurt you."

Gordon reached out and touched her shoulder. Georgia purred softly and her whiskers twitched. Gordon smiled a bit, running his other hand through his own hair and turning his face to his wife.

"It's real! Judy, what I saw in the forest was real. It was a man and he turned into the rabbit. That's why I couldn't find him. I didn't lose a full-grown man in the woods. There really was nothing I could've done."

"Honey," she smiled, and her tone was relieved, even if her face was still tense at what she had just witnessed. "No one ever thought you could've or should've done more. I'm so happy you can finally believe that yourself."

Georgia turned her face to Judy and tilted her head slightly. Judy nodded slowly and Georgia stood. Gordon patted her once more before retracting his hand and she walked over to Judy. She stopped in front of her and stared as hard as she could into the same eyes where she had found comfort so many times. This time, she hoped she could project that same comfort through their different forms.

Judy never broke eye contact, and her body started to relax. "It's you in there, that's for sure," she breathed. "It feels like you. I'd know those eyes anywhere."

"It's absolutely her," Austin said softly, then looked between her and Gordon. "I know this is something you've been told can only happen in stories, but the truth is, this is our reality. We're dealing with a large group of pretty terrible people who can do this as well, and we need to try to find a way to meet them head on. We could really use your help. We need numbers desperately."

"I don't know what we can offer, but we'll do anything to help our daughters and their friends," Gordon said assertively. Georgia's head whipped toward him, her eyes widened. He had just referred to her as his daughter. She had never had a father figure in her life that she could remember, and his words penetrated through to her very soul. If she had been in her human form, she would have probably burst into tears, so she was glad she hadn't changed back yet. Still, her eyes must have divulged her thoughts because Gordon nodded gently before continuing.

"You've been a daughter to us since we met you. We would do anything for you." He looked to Austin whose eyes were also misty. "And you obviously care a great deal about this gentleman, and Jordan about Sawyer, so we're more than happy to help you all in any way we can."

A tremulous, deep breath from Judy drew their attention, and she dabbed at her eyes before speaking. "We don't need any more loss in this family. Her lower lip quivered a bit, and she reached out and touched the side of Georgia's face, while taking Austin's hand in her free hand. "We got Jordan back tonight, in a way, and we'll do whatever needs to be done to keep you all and our town safe."

Austin looked down to Georgia and said softly, "I think it's time to come back. We have a lot to talk about."

Georgia backed away a few feet and closed her eyes. When she opened them again she was standing close to Gordon who pulled her into a crushing hug. Still holding Austin's hand in hers, Judy rose to embrace Georgia as well, pulling Austin in to the group embrace. The four of them stood that way for a while, before Gordon stepped back, squeezing Georgia's hands before sitting again. They all followed suit, resuming their originally seating spots.

"What is it you want from us," Judy asked, breaking the silence.

"We honestly don't know," Austin admitted. "We're just working on recruiting at this point, and with your collective contacts throughout the town, we thought you might have ideas about who we can get to work with us."

"With Auggie, Mama Landry, Ryan, and us, we're only seven people," Georgia added. "Factoring in Jordan, Sawyer, Victoria, and Christian, it still only makes eleven. Christian believes Edmund's numbers are in the hundreds, possibly thousands. We're trying to figure out how best to get a more accurate estimate, but regardless, they are extremely unbalanced sides at this point."

"Even if we got everyone in town on our side, we could never match that many people," Gordon said hesitantly.

"We don't necessarily need to match the numbers," Austin responded. "We definitely need more people, but if we find people who can help to circumvent Edmund's plan or plans of action, it may not have to come down to an actual war. That's what we're hoping for. And in that case, our numbers being smaller might not matter quite as much."

"Do you have any idea what Edmund's plans might be?" Judy asked.

"We're in the really early stages of planning and investigating at this point," Georgia said apologetically. "We just started telling people we knew we could trust and who might have ideas about how to contribute. Auggie has a long history with the mill, Mama Landry seems to know all about this town and is receptive to all kinds of ideas of magic. Ryan thinks logically and is basically the antithesis of magic-minded. And you two have met pretty much everyone in town and know about them and their families because of your jobs. Then there's Christian who knows a bit about how Edmund operates."

Gordon tilted his head. "You know, I bet there are at least a few strong guys on the force who might believe what happened with the man disappearing and what really happened. It wouldn't hurt to have legitimate soldiers on our side."

"And I know a few people from the school I could talk to about this. Joe is a military history buff and Vanessa teaches about folklore and mythology in her classes. She might be receptive to the story and maybe even have some information to contribute."

"That all sounds amazing," Georgia said enthusiastically.

"I agree; that could be incredibly helpful," Austin agreed. He looked to Georgia. "I think the next step is to talk to my dad. He might be able to help with some insider information that could help us."

"You said he works in the ravine town, right? What does your father do?" Gordon asked.

"He's basically in charge of making sure the ravine town is running efficiently; that everyone's needs are met, supplies are stocked, and he supervises most of the jobs in town. We supply things for the mill, so he checks orders and delegates tasks as needed."

"So, he's kind of like the mayor of your community," Judy said, impressed.

"Pretty much," Austin said.

"Impressive work; a lot of responsibility," Gordon added.

Austin nodded. "So, since he interacts with the mill a bit, he may have information that could be useful. And he may have an idea of what's going on if I can lean on him a bit. It won't be a comfortable conversation. He's never been keen to share any information about it with me before. I feel like he's been sheltering me from whatever he does know, but it's time it all comes out." He took a deep breath and looked at them all, a bit embarrassed.

Gordon reached behind Georgia and squeezed Austin's shoulder. "A parent never likes to admit when their children are old enough to take care of themselves. Sometimes we try to protect them longer than we need to. I have a feeling once you tell your father your concerns, he's going to have to come to terms one way or the other. Good luck."

"Do you want me to come with you?" Georgia asked. "Having you here tonight really helped keep me centered and focused. Plus, he may be more diplomatic if someone else is there with you."

"I appreciate the offer, and I'll definitely think about it. I need to figure out the best way to approach the topic and what questions I need to ask. It's not going to be as easy as tonight was." Austin took Georgia's hand and squeezed it. "I may well take you up on that though. He and mom'll at least start the evening on their best behavior if I bring my girlfriend. I'm just not sure how the evening will end…" Austin trailed off.

Georgia looked at Judy, who winked and smiled knowingly at her. She smiled back. "Sounds like my boyfriend and I have some planning to do, eh?" Austin forced a smile and leaned his shoulder into hers.

Gordon chuckled softly and rose, gesturing to Judy to join him. "Come on, Judy. Let's leave these two alone to do their planning. I'm going to grab a piece of pie and start working on a list of people I want to talk to on the force." He looked down at Austin and Georgia as Judy stood and joined him by the couch. "I won't talk to anyone until we discuss how exactly we want to proceed, but it'll make me feel like I'm doing something to at least get started."

Georgia stood up and hugged him again, reaching past him with one hand to squeeze Judy's. "You guys are amazing," she whispered. She broke the hug and looked down at Austin. "We should have a better idea of what's going on in a few days. We'll probably be meeting with Jordan and the others soon to hopefully get some more information and determine the best way to proceed."

"Will you please tell Jordan…" Judy's voice caught and she took a minute to continue. "Will you tell her we love her and we're glad she's ok."

Georgia nodded, not quite trusting herself to speak.

"We absolutely will, Judy," Austin responded for her. Judy patted Austin's shoulder as she and Gordon left the room and headed toward the kitchen.

Georgia sat heavily next to Austin and leaned back, exhaling deeply. He reached around her, pulling her to his chest, resting his chin on her head. "You did amazing," he said softly.

"That was really hard, but it went better than I could've imagined. It's just been a really heavy couple of days."

"I know. And I do need you to know the conversation with my parents likely won't go nearly this well."

She hugged him tighter. "I hope you're wrong, but if you aren't, it doesn't matter. I'm going to be there for you and we'll get through this together."

He kissed the top of her head and they stayed in their comfortable embrace, both wondering what the future held, but content to enjoy the moment while they could.

Chapter Twenty-Eight
Meeting the Neffs

The following Friday found Georgia and Austin at the edge of the quarry again. Austin had picked Georgia up after he shift and been determined that this was the day he was going to lay it all out for his father and demand information. During the ride to the quarry however, Georgia had noticed some of the wind seemed to have left his sails. When they arrived, he had moved to the front of his car and leaned against it, staring down over the still water at the bottom of the giant hole in the earth.

"Would you mind if I just tossed these keys down there?" Austin asked contemplatively.

"Um, considering you're the one that drove us here, yes, I do mind," Georgia said, snatching the keys from his fingers and giving her head a small shake. "I'm fast as a cat, but that's still a hell of a trek back home." She bent and tucked the keys behind his front tire.

Austin sighed heavily and stuffed his hands deep into his jacket pockets. He stared at the ground, toeing the dirt with his boot. Georgia walked over to him, feeding her arm through the crook in his and guiding him slowly toward the edge of the trees. "Come on. For better or worse, it'll all be over in a little bit."

"Oh, for worse... Definitely for worse," he mumbled.

Once they were deep enough in the woods that they wouldn't need to worry about anyone seeing them, Georgia squeezed his arm affectionately before letting go and stepping to the side a couple of feet. She looked at him silently until he took a deep breath and closed his eyes. She did the same and willed herself to change, feeling the familiar sensations flow through her. She opened her eyes and saw him standing next to her, staring into the woods in the direction she knew would take them to the ravine town. She didn't want to push him when he was so obviously tense about the encounter with his parents, but she really believed he would feel better once it was done and out of the way.

"Ok, let's get this over with," Austin sighed and broke into a swift lope through the woods. Georgia matched his speed staying at his side. They ran for quite a while before Austin slowed to a walk and then stopped. When Georgia had visited the ravine town she hadn't come from this direction, but she could tell from the smells of meat and vegetables cooking they were close. She saw Austin transform back to his human form and she followed suit. He grabbed her hand a bit tighter than usual and started toward a break in the trees.

Within a few hundred feet, they emerged from the forest into a large clearing. Georgia stopped and looked around. It looked like a meadow, but a large house lined with beautiful wildflowers on the far end of the clearing told her it was actually a yard. The lawn was extremely well landscaped for being in the middle of the woods, and she could also make out a swing set and small shed near the house.

"Home sweet home," Austin said softly and she could tell, even though he was dreading their pending conversation, being in this place made him happy.

"This is beautiful," Georgia breathed as Austin started walking toward the house, pulling her along behind him. "I've never seen anything like this; not even in books. Those flowers are incredible, and this yard is bigger than any I've seen. You live on a plantation!"

Austin laughed. "Mom loves her flowers. These aren't even native to the area, but she can make anything grow anywhere." He looked around a bit as they walked. "I guess I just got used to it growing up here, but it is kind of pretty, isn't it?"

"Gorgeous. You're so lucky to live here."

"Dad always said being the guy who runs the town has its advantages. He never made a big deal about it, but I think he really likes it here. I broke my arm falling off those monkey bars," he said with a grin, gesturing toward the swing set. "Mom threatened to get rid of it for years, but it's still here. I think now she imagines grandkids playing on it someday." Georgia looked at him and he blushed before rushing on. "You know, someday far, far in the future." She grinned as they reached the steps leading up to the enormous wrap-around porch.

She had only gone half way up the stairs when Austin stopped and swung around to face her, grabbing her upper arms tightly in both hands. She put her hands out to avoid crashing into him and knit her eyebrows together.

"I know this isn't the most charming time or place to do this, and of all the ways I imagined this moment, none of them involved getting ready to walk into the lion's den that is likely to be this evening, but I needed you to know it, no matter what happens tonight or how this all goes…"

"Needed me to know what?" Georgia asked, her stomach contracted with apprehension.

Austin's shoulders relaxed and he reached up to cup her face in his hand, his thumb brushing gently over her cheek. He smiled. "I need you to know how in love with you I am."

Georgia's eyes went out of focus for a moment and when they refocused on his face she could feel them filling with tears. Austin bend down a bit so his face was level with hers. "Georgia? Are you ok?"

She leaned forward and wrapped her arms around his waist, her face buried in his chest. He held her tight, stroking her hair softly until she finally pulled her damp face back and smiled up at him. "I'm beyond ok." She wiped her face with her sleeve. "I never thought I'd hear those words from anyone, let alone someone as amazing as you. I'm so incredibly in love with you, too."

Austin let out a breath he didn't realize he'd been holding and bent down to kiss her softly. "I'm glad to hear it," he said. "Hang onto that thought through the evening, will ya?"

She punched his chest gently and wiped the rest of the dampness from her face as Austin turned and led her the rest of the way up the steps, across the porch, and into the house. They walked through a giant kitchen with pots and pans hanging from a rack over an island with five stools pushed against it. They walked down a hallway and into a huge foyer with a double staircase heading up to the second floor. Georgia's eyes felt like they were being pulled in ten different directions taking in everything from the pictures on the wall to the ornamental rugs on the floor, to the gargantuan chandelier hanging from the vaulted ceiling.

"Are we still in Vermont, or did we walk into another dimension and get dumped in the deep south?" she asked softly. She didn't know why she was whispering, but she felt like talking loudly might disturb the image she was taking in.

"Is that you, son?" a deep voice called from upstairs before Austin could answer. Georgia jumped at the sound.

Austin squeezed her hand and called back, "Downstairs, Dad. Georgia and I just got here."

"Wonderful," the voiced called back, and Georgia was surprised to find he sounded much more friendly than Austin had led her to believe he would be. "Head into the dining room and I'll be down in a minute. I'll have Lynette bring you some tea."

"I hope you like tea," Austin whispered as he guided Georgia into a large room with a table big enough to seat at least a dozen people comfortably. "Coffee's only consumed in the morning in this house. My mom is a huge tea drinker the rest of the day. If you want to get in her good graces, compliment her tea."

"Tea's great," Georgia said absentmindedly, still looking around at all the things on the walls and decorative figurines on every available surface.

Austin pulled out the second to last chair on one side of the table for her and seated himself next to her in the end chair. A small, white-haired woman in a black dress and white apron came into the room carrying a large tray. She placed a cup, saucer, and spoon in front of each of them as well as in front of the empty seats directly across from them. She also set down a pitcher of cream, a bowl of sugar cubes, a selection of six different teas, and a kettle with steam gently rising from the spout.

"Can I get you or the young miss anything else Mr. Austin?"

"No thanks, Lynnie. This looks great. Go put your feet up." The lines around the woman's eyes crinkled as she gave a small bow and flicked the tea towel she'd carried over her arm at him before walking back out of the room. He leaned toward Georgia. "Lynnie's been with the family since before I was born. Dad says she was the housekeeper when he was a little boy. She was basically like another mom when I was growing up. She watched me when mom and dad were busy with other obligations. I'm the only one who calls her Lynnie."

"She definitely loves it. And she's a fan of you," she added, warmly.

"It drives dad crazy," Austin muttered. "He was raised a lot stricter than he's raised me, but some of the old ways still stick with him. He doesn't think we should be friendly with the help. 'You don't want to confuse them, son, or they'll forget their place. It's their job to serve us. We show them kindness and respect, but we don't befriend them'. Never mind that I've probably spent more collective hours with Lynnie than I have with both my parents combined." He turned and saw Georgia's mild look of pity. He patted her knee quickly before grabbing a tea bag and lifting his spoon toward the bowl of sugar cubes.

"Now, what would your mother say if she saw you preparing your tea before everyone is at the table?" They both looked up at the man who had just entered the room and who was wearing a look of gentle disapproval. Austin returned the tea bag, set down the spoon, rose, and reached out his hand to shake the other man's.

"Georgia, this is my father, Raymond Neff. Dad, this is my girlfriend, Georgia."

"Nice to meet you Georgia. Please, call me Ray." Georgia started to stand, but Ray placed one hand on her shoulder to indicate she could remain seated, and reached down to shake her hand with the other. Her shoulder and hand cooled familiarly at his touch.

If Georgia thought Austin was tall, it was nothing compared to Ray Neff. The man had to be at least six and a half feet tall, and his shoulders were wider than anyone's she had ever seen. He was a formidable sight to behold and she was starting to understand Austin's concern with possibly upsetting him with their upcoming line of questioning. Still, she had valued Austin being there so much when she had told Jordan's parents, she was going to do everything she could to be there for him, even if it meant pushing past her comfort zone.

She hiked her shoulders back a bit and smiled up at him. "It's great to finally meet you as well, Ray. Austin's told me so much about you and your town. It's nice to be able to put a face to the name."

"Yes," Ray said in a flat tone, lowering himself into the chair across from Austin. "I'm sure he has. You're very kind. Depending on what my son has chosen to share, however, I hope he hasn't soured you on anything about us. We are a very devoted and proud people and do important work here. Our isolation from the rest of Shamore seems to have driven a wedge over time, but we are still happy to be associated with it."

"Oh, no," Georgia said, taken aback by his defensive response to her calculatedly benign comment. She glanced at Austin before looking back to Ray. "I assure you, he had very nice things to say. I've been looking forward to coming here and seeing this place and meeting you."

"Isn't that nice," Ray said, his gaze never leaving his son's face. Austin's eyes remained lowered to his cup, his jaw clenching almost imperceptibly. "Charlotte will be joining us shortly. She got caught up dealing with a grocery issue. One of the women had a significant decrease in productivity and had to be relocated."

At this statement, Austin looked up at his father inquisitively. Ray's tone was guarded as he continued. "Marissa will be working the looms in the clothing manufacturing barn going forward. We promoted Jill to her position in the grocery."

"Marissa got moved?!" Austin exclaimed. "She's been at the grocery for years. No one can do that job better than her. She's the one who *trained* Jill. How could her productivity be that bad all of a sudden?"

Ray cleared his throat and Austin seemed to deflate ever so slightly, but he continued to look at his father expectantly. "I agree, she is quite talented and has been a valuable asset. Unfortunately, Marissa's focus appears to have shifted as of late. It seems she has been speaking out of place about her superiors and sharing information beyond her purview. She has been relocated somewhere there will be far less opportunity for gossip. Hopefully that will allow her to regain some of her focus and to continue efficiently."

Georgia swallowed hard. She remembered listening to Marissa and Jill's conversation in the woods. Apparently she wasn't the only one who had overhead similar conversations. She could see Austin's breathing had become more rapid, but he didn't say anything else.

They sat in uncomfortable silence for a few minutes before the sound of footsteps drew their attention to the doorway. Georgia had been expecting Austin's mother to be tall and tan with dark hair, just like Austin and his father. When Charlotte entered the room, however, Georgia had to do a double take. The woman could have been her own mother. She was medium height, at least a full foot shorter than her husband, and had long, blonde hair that fell to her waist. Her eyes were almost the exact same emerald green as Georgia's and their builds were similar. She couldn't help looking to Austin, wondering why he'd never mentioned how similar they looked. She didn't know if she was imagining he was deliberately not looking at her, but after his initial look at the doorway, he had gone back to staring at his tea cup, his hands clenched tightly in his lap.

Charlotte arrived at the table and Ray stood, taking her hand and kissing it gently, before guiding her to the seat across from Georgia and sliding the chair in for her as she sat. Georgia could tell Ray adored this woman. And the flush in Charlotte's cheeks as she smiled at her husband made it clear she adored him as well. It warmed Georgia's heart to know affection could stay so fresh and real in a relationship through the years.

"Austin," the woman said softly in greeting.

"Mom," he replied. Charlotte looked at Georgia and smiled. Austin seemed to remember his manners and rushed on. "This is my girlfriend, Georgia. Georgia, this is my mother, Charlotte."

Georgia reached out her hand to shake Charlotte's. The cooling sensation penetrated her arm. Along with it, however, came a tingling that was unique and she held Charlotte's grip a little longer than she normally would have, trying to understand it. Charlotte didn't seem bothered by the extended hand shake, but a wary look crossed Ray's face and Georgia dropped her hand quickly before speaking. "It's so nice to meet you, Mrs. Neff."

"Charlotte," the woman corrected. "It's very nice to meet you too, Georgia. When Austin told us he was bringing you to tea, I was surprised and pleased. He has never brought a young lady to the house before. I was beginning to think he was ashamed of us." She said in a playful tone.

Austin looked up at her. "Not ashamed. Cautious."

"As if we are something to fear," Ray said, leaning back in his chair, his hands folded on the table in front of him.

"I didn't say…"

"Now, now, gentleman," Charlotte interrupted Austin's response. "This is a social tea. Let's keep things civil." She reached forward, selected a tea bag, and lifted the kettle to fill her cup. Georgia did the same and the men followed suit.

After they had all prepared their cups and the tea was steeping, Charlotte looked at Georgia. "So, Georgia, how did you and Austin meet? He hasn't told us much about you yet other than you work at the town bookstore."

"Well, I'd seen him a couple times around town, but the first time we really spoke to each other was at the bookstore. He came in to find a book when I was working and we got to talking. I guess the rest is history." She smiled and, despite his discomfort, he smiled back at her, reaching over to squeeze her knee.

"It is fortunate your new schedule afforded you the opportunity to go into town so often or you may have never met this lovely young lady," Ray commented, removing his tea bag and stirring in some cream. Austin nodded but didn't reply.

"I agree," Charlotte chimed in. "I, myself, enjoy reading. Austin has never enjoyed it quite as much, which is why I was surprised when he said he met you in the bookstore. When he told us where you worked, I already felt confident he made a good choice in a companion."

"That's nice of you to say," Georgia said and turned to Austin, smiling. "It's funny that you don't like reading, because one of the other places I saw you before we actually spoke was at the library." She turned back to Austin's parents. "He was going in as I was leaving. Oh, and if there are any books you're interested in reading, let me know. I'd be happy to bring you whatever you'd like; both of you."

"How sweet of you," Charlotte responded. "I may take you up on that sometime."

"Did you see a lot of each other before you finally spoke at the bookstore?" Ray asked. The question seemed innocent enough, but she thought she saw Austin stiffen in his seat.

"Um, not really. I think the library and outside the mill were the only times I saw him before we spoke. Well, at least in person. There's a fun picture of him when he was about nine at Mama Landry's restaurant too." Her smile faded as she took in the looks on Ray and Austin's face. Ray's face had darkened to a light purple and Austin's had paled at least as many shades. She looked to Charlotte for help and she gave her an almost imperceptible look of pity.

"Outside the mill, you say." Ray said, barely above a whisper. "I wonder what could have prompted you to visit the mill, my dear? Except for those who work there, I didn't think towns folk had much cause to visit the mill. In fact, I have heard it has a negative reputation; that it is a place to stay clear of."

Georgia's stomach dropped and her mind raced, trying to think of a neutral explanation for what she had been doing there. Ray's eyes bored into hers and she couldn't seem to drag her gaze away from his. In her peripheral vision, she saw Austin shift in his chair and it seemed to shift her thoughts back into gear. She tried to keep her voice casual as she replied.

"Oh, I wasn't *visiting* the mill exactly. I like to go driving sometimes, and I just used the parking lot to turn around. It's a big lot, as I'm sure you're aware, and on the way back out of the loop I drove by the front entrance and saw Austin leaving. I just figured he was one of the workers. Then I saw him at the library later that day and thought maybe he was a stalker." She winked at Austin, who looked beyond relieved at her explanation. Charlotte laughed softly at her comment. Ray looked like he didn't buy it, but didn't continue his line of questioning.

"I cannot believe Miss Landry still has a picture of you in her restaurant," Charlotte said incredulously. "It has been so long since you've been to town until recently. That is sweet of her."

"She's a wonderful lady," Austin said, finally speaking. The sound of his voice was a relief to Georgia. She had been wondering if she was going to be doing all the talking that evening. She nodded her agreement and Austin squeezed her knee, emboldened by her support. "Georgia and I actually went there for supper the day we finally met in earnest. She knew who I was the second I walked in and it was like no time had passed at all. I spent a lot of time with her when I stayed with Uncle Dale. It's the picture from the eating relay. I hadn't thought about that day in a long time. It was nice being reminded of those times again."

"I am sure," Charlotte said, and Georgia thought she heard a note of sadness in her voice.

"I am surprised you have any good memories of your time with Dale," Ray commented, his voice harsh. Austin winced. "From the way you talk about him these days, you would think the man has no redeeming qualities at all. Sinister, I believe, is the word you used in our last conversation regarding your uncle."

"Yet you didn't disagree, did you?" Austin bit back. Ray's face remained impassive and it was Charlotte's turn to shift uncomfortably. "I have good memories of Uncle Dale. But they are just that; memories. I wasn't allowed to know the man for twenty years because of your concerns, not mine. But, yes, I've come to agree with you, Father. He isn't the nicest man, and maybe I do think he has some sinister intentions, even though you've never been willing to discuss that with me. But I'm not the only one who thinks it anymore. This is bigger than you and me now. The discussion needs to be had."

Charlotte rose from the table and the conversation came to a halt. "If we are going to discuss sensitive topics, perhaps we should go into the sitting room away from prying ears." She said this quietly, but her tone seemed to affect her husband as well as her son. The men both placed their napkins on the table next to their undrunk tea and rose as well, walking out of the room together.

"Lynette!" Charlotte called, and the white-haired woman stepped into the room. "Please bring the drink cart into the sitting room. Make sure there is brandy." The woman bowed and exited the room quickly. Charlotte looked at Georgia apologetically, her arm extended toward the doorway. Georgia slowly placed her napkin on the table as well before rising and allowing the woman to place her arm around her waist and guide her out of the dining room and down the hall after the men.

Chapter Twenty-Nine
Difficult Conversation

"I'm sorry for my husband and son," Charlotte whispered in Georgia's ear as they walked down the hallway. "They usually get along well enough, but these past few years, Austin seems to have become suspicious of our life here and the circumstances which brought it about."

"Unfortunately, it might be for a good reason that he arrived at those suspicions," Georgia responded. "I can only imagine the strain it put on all your relationships, but I think at this point the more information we all have to work with, the better the position we'll be in."

"You may be right," Charlotte said, not sounding like the idea of it brought her much comfort. "Although, it could also bring significantly more strain as well."

She stopped speaking as they turned into a large room with comfortable looking furniture around most of the perimeter. The men had already seated themselves in large arm chairs at the far end of the room. They were both sitting forward on the front edge of the seat, their arms resting stiffly on the armrests. They didn't look at each other; Austin's eyes were on the pictures of various people on the opposite wall, while Ray's eyes were on his wife and Georgia. Charlotte removed her arm from Georgia's waist as they reached the chair next to Austin, and she went to sit next to her husband. Georgia looked to each man in turn, before looking at Charlotte, who shook her head almost imperceptibly, and they both remained silent.

"Why have you asked to meet with us here today?" Ray asked, breaking the silence. "Why, on the first time meeting this lady in your life, have you chosen to initiate this line of questioning which you know I don't approve of discussing?" He glanced at Georgia, then back to his son. "Do you fancy her a better interrogator than yourself? Backup, as it were?"

"Well, you've always told me there's strength in numbers," Austin responded dryly. "But no, I didn't bring her for backup or to interrogate you. Georgia has information I think you might find interesting, and she also has questions; questions that are very similar to ones I've been asking for years, and which you seem disconcertingly hesitant to answer." His father continued to look at him but did not respond. The tone in Austin's voice had changed when he spoke again; less formal, softer, almost supplicating. "Father, the time for answers has come."

Ray leaned back a bit in the chair. His fingers drummed slowly on the armrest and it felt like everyone in the room had collectively stopped breathing. Finally, with a tilt of his head, he spoke. "You may be right. It may be time for you to attempt to understand the reasons why I have chosen to guide this family as I have all these years. I do not appreciate you bringing an outsider into this house to do so, but if she has the same concerns as you and information to provide, I will trust your judgement."

"She has a name, Father. And I brought her, not only for the reasons you've stated, but also because she's a potentially valuable asset to our eventual cause and, more importantly, because she is someone very important to me."

Georgia saw Charlotte smile and Ray's face softened just the slightest degree. "Forgive me my lapse in manners, Georgia" he said. "This is a difficult topic for me and I've struggled for years to protect my family from the unpleasantness associated with it." He turned to Austin before adding. "I only ever acted with my family's safety and best interests at heart."

"I understand that," Georgia said. "Please, don't feel like you need to apologize for trying to protect your loved ones. I know our love and devotion can make us say things and act in ways which might upset those around us. But sir... I'm sorry... Ray," she corrected when he lifted his hand to stop her, "With all due respect, the signs that something horrible is coming are indisputable, and the more information we can gather to help us prepare against the worst, the better our chances are of surviving it, or even preventing the worst of it."

"And just what is it you think is coming?" he asked.

"A war."

Charlotte sucked in a small, sharp breath and Ray's mouth tightened ever so slightly. Austin looked over at her, but Georgia held her ground, never taking her eyes off Ray.

"If you are looking for confirmation, I am afraid I cannot give it to you." Ray said, barely above a whisper.

Austin sighed exasperatedly, but Georgia put her hand on his arm. "But you also can't refute it, can you?"

Another long pause passed between them before he responded, even softer than before. "I cannot."

"Then you can understand our concern. Our information leans heavily in favor of a war approaching. I'm willing to share what we've learned with you so you can prepare yourself to protect your family in the best way possible, but we could really use whatever information you might have to do the same. Please…" she trailed off.

"Dad," Austin said, all formality dropped. "Help us. Help us understand what it is we're working with. What's the truth about what's going on in the mill? With Uncle Dale? With the dam? What have you been protecting us from? What's coming?"

"Ray…" Charlotte's voice pleaded as well. "They deserve to know what you know."

"I do not know!" Ray exploded, rising from his chair and they all flinched in alarm. "I do not know anything about what is going on! I have not known for years!" As he paced the room, he seemed to deflate. He stopped by a window and looked out for a bit until his breathing returned to normal. "Everything I have done to protect this family has cost me access to the information you are looking for."

Austin rose too and approached his father slowly. "But you did know things before, didn't you? That's why you felt the need to protect us in the first place. What were you protecting us from, Dad? What was going on?"

Ray looked away from the window toward his son. He reached out and squeezed his shoulder before returning to his chair. Charlotte reached over and put her hand on Ray's arm and he placed his large hand on top of hers.

"When Ed first took over the mill, he focused for years on revenue only. Making money was the only thing he cared about. It seemed a logical focus for a businessman I was hired and worked hard to achieve those goals he set for us all. I was good at my job, and was promoted quickly. I never dealt with him directly, but the men who he had running things said he was impressed with my dedication and he rewarded those who served him well.

He had me pulled from the mill and placed me in recruitment with a substantial wage increase. I was tasked with getting workers into the mill and growing the business, at which I was also successful. After a while, he began having me evaluate mill workers for the most dedicated, loyal, and subservient workers, and he would pull them to his compound to work for him. I have never seen the compound, but from what I heard from others who have, it is expansive and it made sense to me he would need help there.

The first thing I noticed that did not sit right with me was that the people we sent to work there never returned; we never saw them again. When I asked, I was told he gave the workers their own quarters on his compound so he could better serve their needs, and so they could better serve his. It made sense at the time, but it became apparent the numbers he wanted recruited far exceeded what he would need to help him with his compound. And yet, he continued recruiting, but by that time I had learned inquiring minds were not well tolerated, so I continued my work without asking questions.

Not long after you were born, there came word a new town was to be developed to hold buildings and house workers to provide supplies to the mill. Apparently, Ed wanted to begin to cut all ties with any outside sources and become completely self-sufficient; also a bit suspect in hindsight."

"Did no one else think these things seemed odd?" Charlotte interjected, and Georgia and Austin looked at her in surprise. They had assumed anything Ray had to tell them would be known by Charlotte as well, but it seemed he had been protecting everyone in the family by not sharing the information.

"I'm sure a few did, but we all knew better than to discuss it. There were ears everywhere," Ray mumbled dejectedly. "However, with my feelings of trepidation growing, I saw a silver lining in this town being developed. Getting you all away from the mill seemed the best course of action, so I volunteered my name to run the new town and get things set up. I was notified of my appointment to the position and we relocated. This house was already here when we arrived. It had been one of Ed's old properties. Aside from a few outbuildings, the rest of the structures are relatively new construction. I purposely brought people into this town who I believed to be good of heart and not 'sinister' as you so dramatically put it. We cultivated a good community and became close, as you know. The idea we were serving a darker purpose was easier to ignore out here. Then your uncle contacted me."

Ray's face darkened at this and out of the corner of her eye Georgia noticed Austin grip his armrests tighter. "As you know, he had been injured in his construction position and he knew he would never be able to return in the same capacity. What you do not know is that he had come to me a number of times prior to his injury looking for a position at the mill. He knew I was making good money and he has always been a little deficient in his level of motivation, so he was looking for an easier way to make a living. At first I didn't help him out of principle, but later it came from concern for his safety as well.

After the injury, he came to me begging for work, and I denied him again. He called me selfish and cruel for not helping out his own brother. I told him he was the selfish one to assume I would be agreeable to nepotism and that he was foolish to not accept my views that the position would not be a good fit for him. We parted ways, him saying he would find a way to get a job at the mill without me and I should watch myself now that we were in the game of hurting each other. His threats unnerved me, and I ceased your visits to him as well as the town in hopes he would not put you in the middle of our animosities."

"That makes a lot of sense," Georgia said. "It sounds like he was a little unhinged."

"Desperation can make a person do and say terrible things," Charlotte added.

"I wish you had told me earlier," Austin said sadly. "I spent a lot of time thinking you were letting me suffer due to an insignificant disagreement between you two. If I had known…"

"It was better you didn't know any of it," Ray interrupted. "I could bear your being upset with me far easier than I could bear you being hurt or used as a pawn in one of his games." The two shared a small smile before Ray took a deep breath and continued. "As you know, my plan to keep him away from the mill failed in the end. Dale found a way to communicate his desires to work at the mill to the higher powers and I am sure he dropped my name to sweeten the deal. Not only was he given a job in the mill, he was given my former job of recruitment coordinator. Dale may be lazy, but he is a fairly good judge of character and a shrewd observer. The rest is history."

"So you really don't have any other information about what's going on behind the scenes in the mill or Ed's compound?" Austin asked, disappointment strong in his voice. "Don't you at least have suspicions about what might be happening?"

"I have told you everything I know. As far as my speculations, they are just that; speculation. I have no concrete evidence to back up any ideas I might have, and even if I did, it would be irrational and foolhardy to act on them."

"What do you mean?!" Austin exclaimed. "You've worked so long and hard to protect us, but you don't want to try to stop a potential war from erupting? Don't you think a war would be significantly more dangerous for us all?"

"You have no idea if a war is even on the horizon, Austin. The only thing you know is that Ed is bolstering his numbers. It could be for any number of reasons, all of them far less dramatic than a war."

"We have more information than that," Georgia said. "We have been in contact with a man who used to serve

Edmund Nephyrion; served him *after* he was supposed to have died. He's still alive, Ray. We're positive Ed from the mill is actually Edmund Nephyrion and the war he started over two thousand years ago is still happening." She stared into Ray's widened eyes, willing him to understand the gravity of the situation.

He blinked slowly, and leaned back in his chair. "I am sorry, Georgia, but that assertion is completely absurd. I believe the gentleman you have been in contact with has been feeding you false information."

"Dad," Austin barked, and Georgia was a bit frightened at the anger she heard in his voice. "Just because something isn't what you want to hear, doesn't mean it's absurd. We can change into animals for god's sake! That is absurd to the vast majority of the population of the world, and yet, it's true."

"Please think logically, Ray," Georgia said, in a much calmer voice than Austin's. "What purpose would he have for lying to us about something like that? Play the situation out. If he's right and Edmund is still alive and we can prepare and possibly prevent a war, we have the potential to save hundreds of thousands of lives, including the lives of the ones we love. If he's lying, we'll simply investigate and find our suspicions are unwarranted. Christian has nothing to gain by lying to us."

The wood of the armrest on Ray's chair cracked as he gripped it hard enough to turn his knuckles white. "Did you say Christian," he spat, the color in his face darkening again. "Christian… as in the alchemist who served Edmund and helped to create the very amulet that caused him to survive the blow that should have ended him, then stole it later *causing* Edmund's wrath and determination to finish the war he started?! How, and more importantly *why*, have you been in contact with that man?!"

Austin sat back, stunned. Ray breathed rapidly in his chair, but he closed his eyes, realizing what he had just divulged. "You know about Christian. And his story." The sound of Ray's rapid breathing was the only sound for several agonizing minutes.

"You sat here, and you lied to me… to all of us," Austin whispered. "You knew everything… all of it." He rose slowly and looked down at his father, who stared ahead blankly. "If you know about all of that, then you *do* know he's building an army, don't you?"

"Austin," Ray said, attempting to sound conciliatory, but also fighting the anger than struggled to push through. "Knowing all of it changes nothing. The man has proven he cannot be killed. His numbers have to be in the thousands at this point. There is no way you, I, and a handful of non-magic townsfolk have any chance of stopping him at this point. The effort would be an exercise in futility and all would be lost. If we stay out of it, keep our heads down, and let things play out, we may well live to survive under his rule and live comfortably, together." He looked over at Georgia before adding, "All of us."

Austin shook his head slowly and looked at his mother. "I'm sorry, but I can't stay and be a part of this anymore. I'm not sure where the man is who raised me to stand up for what I believe in, no matter the cost or the popularity of my decisions, but he isn't here tonight. To die protecting the ones I love is a risk I'm willing to take, and I would rather die than live under the rule of an evil tyrant."

He looked back at his father. "I've lived my entire life with the negative reputation of the Neff name on my shoulders, and I refuse to confirm those prejudices now. If this cowardly decision is something you can live with, then by all means, hide your head in the sand. But you no longer need to consider me in the list of people you need to protect. I absolve you of that obligation, because who you have chosen to be is no father of mine." He turned on his heel and walked swiftly out the door. Ray rose from his chair but made no move to follow him. He instead looked at the two ladies in the room, turned, and exited out a side door.

Georgia looked at Charlotte, whose face was streaked with tears. She reached across from her chair and took the woman's hand, squeezing it tightly.

"I always feared it would come to something like this," Charlotte whispered, her voice shaky. "They both love so strongly, but also so stubbornly. It was bound to come to a head. I do not know that either of their minds can be changed." She smiled at Georgia, but there was no happiness in her eyes. "You seem like a wonderful girl, and I truly am happy to have met you. Please know I welcome you in this house any time." She let go of Georgia's hand and walked slowly toward the door.

Before she walked through, she turned back to Georgia. "When Austin is in a temper such as this, he often runs off, sometimes for days at a time. I know your instinct will be to look for him, but I am afraid your chances of finding him are slim. I assure you, he will return when he has things sorted out. Please feel free to check back here any time and I will let you know if we have seen him. I would love the chance to visit with you again." She left the room and Georgia sat there, stunned. The evening definitely had not gone as well as the evening with Jordan's parents, and her mind was reeling with everything she'd heard.

She rose and walked slowly to the door Austin and Charlotte had left through. As she reached it, Lynnette appeared in the hallway, her face almost as white as her hair. "I can show you out, miss." She led Georgia toward the rear door she and Austin had come in earlier and opened it for her. As Georgia began to descend the steps into the yard, she felt a light touch on her shoulder. "I was asked to give you this," Lynnette said, handing Georgia a folded piece of paper. She reached up and touched Georgia's cheek gently, before spinning around and returning to the house.

Georgia reached up and touched her cheek where the woman's fingers had just been. She opened the folded note and read the words in Austin's neat script writing.

Need time. Talk to you soon. Love you.

Chapter Thirty
Origin Story

Georgia took the same path back to the car that she and Austin had taken to get to the Neff's house. She went slowly and kept an eye and ear out for Austin, even though she knew she wouldn't find him. She believed Charlotte when she told her he would be gone for a while. She had never seen him so angry, and she could understand needing time to process what he'd heard. His father had lied to his face about knowing anything significant; it had to hurt. She wasn't all that thrilled at having been lied to either, but at least with Ray's outburst, she knew beyond any doubt Edmund was still alive. That was enough to heartily refocus her on the task at hand. They had to bring everyone together to find a way to stop this war, or at the very least, to stop Edmund permanently.

When she got to the car, she debated for a moment about whether she should take it and leave Austin without a ride back to town. In the end, she decided to take it, reasoning he could be anywhere at this point and who knew if he would even be back this way anytime soon. She would take the car home, and bring it back out to the Neff house in a few days if she hadn't heard from him. Charlotte had told her she was welcome after all. She wasn't sure if Ray felt the same at this point, but she didn't really care. A man who would lie about something so important, especially to his own son, wasn't very deserving of her consideration.

When she arrived back at her house, the lights were all off and there were no cars in the driveway. She figured the Marens must be out and, while she was starting to feel tired despite it still being fairly early in the evening, she decided she didn't want to be alone right now. She backed the car out of the driveway and headed back into town. The bookstore was already closed, but Mama Landry's restaurant would still be open for hours. She pulled into one of the many empty spots out front and went inside.

The familiar smells of cooking meat, tomato sauces, and garlic filled her nostrils and she was immediately comforted. She took the booth she always sat in and leaned back, her face lifted to the ceiling, her eyes closed. It felt good to finally relax. They day had gone far from smoothly, but the last thing on their to-do list was crossed off. She felt relived there was no one else to tell; no one else to have the difficult conversations with. Now it was just time to plan. Georgia had always been more comfortable with action than she had with talking, and the time for action was approaching. Once they developed a plan, they would be able to move forward. She couldn't wait.

"Miss Georgia?" a voice said softly, and Georgia jumped, her eyes flying open. "I'm sorry, suga. I didn' wanna disturb ya, but I weren't sure if ya needed a rest or a meal."

"It's ok, Mama. Honestly, I could use both. I haven't had anything to eat or drink today except a few sips of tea."

"Tea?! Who eva heard-a ya drinkin' tea-a all things? Gracious me. I'll be right back with a fresh pot a coffee an' tha biggest mug I can find. You wait right there."

Georgia smiled as the woman hurried off to the kitchen. She looked out the front window of the restaurant at the deserted main street of the town she had grown to love.

She didn't want anything bad to happen here. She didn't want the people to be threatened by a war they knew nothing about and had very few ways to prevent or win. She took a deep breath and set her shoulders. Hopelessness wasn't going to help anything, she thought to herself. They had to think outside the box and they could defeat Edmund. He'd damn near been beaten once already. They could do it again.

"Here ya go," Mama Landry said, setting the coffee pot and two mugs down in front of Georgia along with a plate of deep fried mushroom caps.

"Thanks, Mama," Georgia said appreciatively, filling both mugs and sliding one toward Mama Landry. "I don't think there's anything your coffee and food can't fix." She reached out and popped one of the mushroom caps into her mouth, sighing at the taste.

"Well now, wouldn't that be a wondaful thing if it was true?" Mama said, sipping at her coffee. "I'd sure like ta fix what's goin' on out there in them woods. Mama'd cook 'round tha clock if it'd make things betta."

Georgia nodded and drank her coffee. They sat in silence for a few minutes before Mama Landry asked, "Where's Mr. Austin this evenin'?"

"I wish I knew, Mama. We had to go out to his house late this afternoon to try to get his dad to tell us what he might know about the things going on with Edmund and the mill. It didn't go well." She paused, but the look in Mama Landry's eyes urged her on. "We tried so hard to make him understand how important it is to share the information we had with each other to stop this war from happening. First he said he didn't know anything about a war and all he knew was that he had to boost the recruitment for the mill. Then he told Austin about the fight he and his brother, Dale Neff, had that lead to Austin not being able to see him anymore. He told us he did everything he had to protect his family. But when Austin mentioned Christian, Ray freaked out. He started yelling about how Christian helped Edmund create the amulet that let him survive and about how Edmund was determined to finish the war he had started. Mama, he knew everything; all of it! He lied to Austin his whole life and lied to all of our faces tonight.

When Austin confronted him about it, he said it didn't matter what he knew; that there was no way so few of us could ever win against him, but if we pretended we knew nothing and flew under the radar, after the smoke cleared we might be allowed to live peacefully under Edmund's rule. Austin couldn't handle it. He told Ray he shouldn't worry about protecting him from now on because he didn't think of him as his father anymore. Then he left." Georgia's eyes were swimming with tears as she finished the recap of the evening. "It was awful, Mama."

"Oh, sweets," Mama Landry reached out and took Georgia's hand in both of hers, squeezing it so tight it almost hurt. "That's awful, sho 'nuff, but there's sumthin; ya gotta know 'bout most daddys. They'd do anythin' ta protect they little-uns. Sometimes fear an' love can make a body do things that make no sense no how, but all they see's what might keep them kids safe. I know what Mr. Ray did was wrong, but it come from a good place."

Georgia sniffed and shook her head. "Maybe when he was younger, Mama. But there comes a certain point when knowledge is way more powerful than keeping kids sheltered in a box. Austin's almost thirty years old, and he's been asking about this stuff for years. He needed to know, and Ray should've told him. If you truly love your children, you can't lie to them for so long."

"Oh, now, I don' know if that's true. There's plenty a parents I know loved their youngun's but felt they needed ta keep things from em ta keep em safe." Georgia gave Mama Landry a deeply skeptical look. Mama Landry patted Georgia's hand and sat back, her hands wrapped around the mug in front of her. She took a deep breath and then looked Georgia in the eye.

"Ya mama, Miss Amy, loved ya as much as any motha I'd eva seen love a chil'. But she din' share everythin' 'bout her past, or ya past, with ya. Don't mean she loved ya less."

"What do you mean she didn't share everything about her and my past?" She leaned forward, her eyebrows knitted together. "Mama, what do you know about us that she didn't tell me?"

Mama Landry's face was unreadable as Georgia tried to look past its familiar lines and wrinkles to uncover the secrets it held. She knew the woman had known her mother before, but she didn't know they had been close enough to discuss things her mother hadn't even shared with her own daughter.

"It was neva my place to tell ya, suga. Shoulda been ya mama that done it. She was gonna. I think she musta thought she had more time. Truth is, she din' jus move back ta be closer ta where she grew up. She brought ya back 'cause she knew somethin' was brewin'; something ya might need ta be a part of."

"She knew something was brewing," Georgia repeated slowly. "Are you telling me…" she shook her head, the words catching in her throat. It couldn't be that her mother had been keeping the same secrets from her that Austin's father had been keeping from his family. "No. If she had known about a war, she would have told me."

"Well now, I think she told ya quite a bit more than ya give her credit fo'. Them stories she told ya 'bout magic an' families was all true, wasn't they? An' she told ya how ta control ya talents; ta keep tha secret and keep yaseff safe. Seems like a mama who loved ya ta me."

Georgia paused a moment to process. "Mama, she told me all that stuff as a bedtime story, not as something real; something I should be concerned about or take seriously. If she knew the stories were true and there was an evil man still alive out there plotting a war, don't you think that's something she should have shared?! She's no better than Austin's dad if she kept it all from me! And sure she told me how to deal with my… abilities. But what was she going to do; pretend they didn't exist? Let me stumble into a situation where they took me away from her and did testing on me? She told me she had a friend who was the same as me when she was younger and that's the only reason she knew anything about it at all. She told me just enough to keep me quiet about it."

Mama Landry shook her head sadly. "Miss Georgia, I know ya angry and it's a lot ta process, but ya know how ya mama was. Ya know she loved ya; I know ya do. People we love do things we don' agree with all tha time, and it always comes from love. Don' always make it right, but it don' make 'em bad people eitha."

Georgia wiped her eyes roughly and popped another mushroom cap into her mouth, more out of something to do than of hunger. She swallowed and looked at Mama Landry again. "Fine. She did what she did to protect me and out of love. So why would she bring me back here? What could I possibly have to do with all of this? How is bringing me to the heart of the battle going to protect me?"

"Well, there's mo' ta tha story a how she an' ya came ta be in this situation, and I got a feelin' it's gonna be mo' information ya don' like. But if ya really wanna hear it all, I can tell ya what I know. But ya gotta promise ta listen ta Mama Landry 'til it's all said, ya undastan? I ain't lookin' fo'ward ta sayin' it all, so ya gotta make it easy on a old woman."

Georgia leaned back, gripping the edge of the table to calm herself. "If someone's finally going to tell me the entire, honest truth, then I'm more than ready to hear you out, Mama."

"We'll see," Mama Landry said softly, shifting in her seat to get more comfortable. "Ya mama was born here in town. She started out sweet an' grew up even sweeta. She come inta Mama Landry's shop every week fo' a root beer float from tha time she was old enough ta walk all tha way up 'til afta she married ya daddy. She an' I'd talk fo' ages any time she visited, just like someone else I know." She winked at Georgia, and Georgia gave a small smile.

"Ya daddy worked at tha mill, as ya know, but he din' work inside; he was maintenance an' grounds. He loved the outdoors, ya daddy did. He neva' woulda lasted workin' inside a place. Anyway, when they married, they was tha happiest couple ya'd eva know. They wanted so badly ta have a baby, but they was havin' trouble conceivin'. So ya mama started lookin' fo'some work ta help save money ta see some fancy docta' outta town.

Ya daddy knew a man that lived way out on tha far edge-a town; even farther out than my house, past tha covered bridge an everythin'. The man's name was Alastair Kinde, Al they called him, an' he was very wealthy; old money ya mama and daddy called it. It turned out Al was outta tha house a lot. Ya daddy figured he traveled or somethin'. His wife, Henrietta, had just got pregnant an' Al told ya daddy if ya mama was lookin' fo some work, she could come clean fo them an' keep Henrietta company an' sorta keep an eye on her while he was gon'. Then, if she wanted, she could stay an' help with tha baby when it came. Ya mama always loved people, ya know that. And tha idea a being around a new baby made her happy. So, she went ta work fo' Al an' Henrietta.

Ya mama an' Henrietta got along great from tha start. Ya mama called her Hettie, an' they spent hours togetha, talkin' an' gigglin' like schoolgirls. I never got ta meet Al or Hettie, but I neva heard a bad thing said 'about neitha one-a em from ya mama an' daddy, an' I neva heard nothin' 'bout 'em at all from anyone else in town. I don' know that anyone here knew 'em ta be honest. But they sounded like wondaful people, an' ya mama was happy workin' there."

Mama Landry's face darkened a bit as she paused and took a long drink of coffee. "Wasn' long afta Hettie had tha baby, a little girl, that things started takin' a dark turn. Al came home one evenin' while ya mama an' daddy was visitin' with Hettie an' tha baby. He told 'em he found evidence that a terrible man who was thought ta be dead was still alive an' livin' deep in tha woods undagroun'. I think ya know who that man was he was talkin' 'bout."

"Edmund," Georgia whispered.

Mama Landry nodded. "He told ya mama an' daddy tha same story she told ya all them years; 'bout Edmund an' Bernard, 'bout tha war an' tha battle, 'bout Edmund gettin' killed. Turned out Al hisself was a direct descendent o' Bernard Onirus. His daddy an' his daddy's daddy had searched they whole lives tryin' ta find proof Edmund was still out there. They met a man that used ta work fo' Edmund an' he said he survived tha battle 'cause o' a amulet he helped make..."

"That's Christian," Georgia interrupted. "Christian's the one who worked for Edmund and helped make the amulet. He also stole it after Edmund survived because he couldn't bear to be a part of his evil schemes anymore. He hid the amulet where no one could ever find it."

"Did he, now?" Mama Landry said, sounding impressed. "Well, ain't that somethin'? Someone so deep inta tha dark side-a things makin' a turn fo' tha betta. Good fo' him. Anyway, afta' talkin' ta Mister Christian, Al's daddy an' gran-daddy searched fo' years but neva found nothin'. Al continued their search an' that night he came home an' tol' tha story, he said he thought he foun' somethin'.

He told ya mama an' daddy he an' Hettie'd moved far outta town ta stay outta sight. Like I said, Al was tha last o' tha direct Onirus line an', while Hettie wasn't from a magic family, he knew if Edmund learned he existed, none of 'em would eva' be safe. So, he searched as his animal se'f, a coyote I think ya mama said, day an' night 'til that evenin' when he said he found a tunnel. He thought tha tunnel lead underground ta a subterranean fortress o' some kind an' that was where Edmund was likely hidin'.

Ya daddy, bein' tha great man he was, offered ta go with Al ta try'n investigate tha site an' see what they could find. Al tried ta talk him outta it, but ya daddy was a brave an' kind man, always doin' what he felt was right. Al told ya daddy where ta find tha cave that had the tunnels an' they planned ta meet there in a few days when ya daddy was off work."

Mama Landry's eyes got misty and she dabbed a napkin to each eye. "Tha day before ya daddy was ta meet Al at tha cave, ya mama came ta work an' found Hettie cryin' somethin' fierce. She tol' ya mama Al'd been killed while out near tha cave; shot dead. His body'd been brought ta they house an' left in tha yard fo her ta find in tha mornin'. She foun' a note with him sayin' he'd been discovered by tha wrong side an she should be careful not ta disclose her existence ta tha outside world if she wanted her an' her baby ta live. She neva knew who left it, but she said there was a big bear print on it."

"That's Christian, too," Georgia whispered. "That's his animal; a bear. He must've found Al when he was out. He's been looking for a secret way into Edmund's compound for years too."

"Ya don' say," Mama Landry said, curiously. "It's really a small world, ain't it? Well, afta' Hettie got tha note, ya mama told ya daddy an' they buried Al near tha flower garden at the back o' tha property. Ya daddy told Hettie he wouldn't rest until he finished what Al started an' found tha cave an' where tha tunnels led. Ya mama an' Hettie both begged him not ta mess with it; they didn' want him gettin' hurt o' worse, but he wouldn' listen."

At this point, Mama Landry began to cry in earnest, and Georgia reached out to grab her hand in alarm. "Mama?" she asked concernedly. "Mama, if you need to stop for a bit, it's fine, really."

"No, suga," Mama Landry said. "It's almost done. This is just tha hardest part ta rememba. I try not ta think 'bout it if I don' hafta, but ya need ta know." She sniffled and blew her nose on her napkin. "Ya mama'd taken ta stayin' with Hettie at tha house fo days at a time ta keep her company an' so she felt safe. One day, afta ya mama'd taken tha baby out ta get groceries fo' tha week an' ta give Hettie a break, she came back ta find Hettie layin' on the groun', dead. She'd been shot just like Al, only this time there was no note. Ya mama ran home immediately an' took tha baby with her. She waited fo' ya daddy ta get home an' told him what'd happened. They was both scared-a what it meant, but they agreed ta stay put 'til tha next day so ya daddy could at least find tha tunnels in tha cave an' try ta fin' where they led."

"What?!" Georgia exclaimed. "Everyone kept ending up dead, but they thought it'd be a good idea to stick around?!"

"Ya daddy'd made a commitment, an tha people he made it for was dead. He felt a obligation ta tha people who'd shown 'em so much kindness ta at least finish out tha task they'd given they lives fo. Besides, he knew what could be comin', an' knowin' 'bout them tunnels could give 'em a real advantage." Georgia sighed in exasperation and waved her hand, indicating Mama Landry should continue.

"Ya daddy went out tha next day lookin' fo them tunnels, an he foun' 'em. He was in 'em when tha cave-in happened." Georgia gasped. "Ya mama was at home when a note got slid unda tha front door. By tha time she got there an' opened it, they was gone, but it was tha same writin' an' same bear print that told her ya daddy was gone an' what happened. It also told her she needed ta get outta town seein's how they didn't seem ta know tha baby existed, but if they did, they'd be sure ta come after her too. Ya mama wrote me a letta explainin' what happened an' left it in my screen door on her way outta town."

"Wait," Georgia said, after Mama Landry had stopped speaking. "Where am I in all this? Mom said dad died when I was almost two, so if she took me and this other baby to the town we moved to, where did the other baby end up?" Mama Landry looked at her with such sadness that Georgia pressed a hand to her mouth and the other to her stomach which was churning. "Oh my god," she whispered. "Did they find the baby and kill her too?!"

"No, suga. That baby's still very much alive."

"Oh, thank god," Georgia exhaled on a breath of relief. "So, what happened to her? Do you know where she is? Do you talk to her? Is she safe."

"She grew up ta be a beautiful young woman her mama an' daddy'd be proud of. I do talk ta her. An' she's not as safe as I'd like her ta be. None-a us is."

"Well, where is she? Maybe we can recruit her to the cause."

"Sweetie, she's sittin' right across from me."

All the air in the restaurant disappeared Georgia stared at Mama Landry, her heart pounding in her temples. The woman was messing with her; she had to be. After everything she'd been through today, everything she'd been through these last few weeks, she couldn't be telling her the woman she'd known as her mother her whole life wasn't really her mother. The booths and lights in her peripheral vision started swimming and black dots began to appear.

Miss Georgia!" Mama Landry said in alarm. "Breathe suga, ya gotta breathe." She hefted herself out of the booth and pulled Georgia's arm around so she was sitting with her legs out of the booth. "C'mon now, sweetie, put ya head down between ya knees an' push up on Mama's han', now," she said as she pushed Georgia's head toward the ground.

Georgia breathed and pushed up on the woman's hand and after a bit, the black dots cleared and her heart rate lowered below stroke level. She reached out and grabbed the arm Mama Landry was pushing her head with. She sat up slowly. Mama Landry bent down in front of her and held a glass of water out. "Here now, drink some wata'. Ya gave me a fright. Ya alright?"

Georgia drank deeply, the cold water feeling good on her tight throat. She finished the glass and set it down, wiping her mouth with the back of her hand. She looked into the concerned face of the woman in front of her.

"No, Mama, I'm not alright. I was just told the woman I spent my whole life thinking was my mother… wasn't my mother. What am I supposed to do with that information? I'm the daughter of the last descendent of Bernard Onirus. If Edmund ever finds out who I am, he'll stop at nothing to kill me, and yet I'm also supposed to be heading up the revolution against that very man. Oh, and not to mention I'm in love with a man who's a direct descendant of that man, and whose relatives very well may be the people who killed my actual parents! I am *far* from alright!"

Mama Landry pulled Georgia up and wrapped her in a rib-crushing hug. Georgia could feel the dampness from her tears as they soaked into the woman's shirt. "Don't ya never say that woman wasn't ya mama. She loved ya as much as any mama could. She kept ya alive when no one else could've. She gave up everythin' includin' her home ta keep ya safe. An she brought ya back here 'cause ya needed now. Whetha ya knew 'bout ya family or not, this is ya born obligation; ta protect ya home an' ta do what's right. She knew it, an' ya know it ,too. Ya birth mama an' daddy died fo' tha cause an' in service ta ya future. Ya adopted daddy died fo' that same cause. Tha right thing ain't neva hardly tha easy thing, Miss Georgia. But this is ya place in tha world, an' we all need ya if we have any chance at all ta win this thing."

Georgia ground her teeth trying hard to stay mad; to keep her emotions together, but it was no use. She crumpled against the woman holding her and sobbed. She sobbed for Mama Landry, for Jordan and Sawyer, for Christian and Victoria, for Austin and his parents, and especially for her parents; all four of them. All of these wonderful people she was linked to who had, in one way or another, paid a price toward this war. It was selfish of her to focus on her own sorrows at the moment, and yet she couldn't help it. She knew Amy was her mother, whether they shared the same blood or not. Amy would always be her mother. But she now had definitive blood ties to this war and a new mother to avenge, and a father as well; two fathers honestly. As much as she wanted the whole thing to be over, she couldn't let them die in vain.

She pulled her face out of Mama Landry's shoulder and kissed her wrinkled cheek. "Thank you, Mama. Thank you for being the first person to tell me the whole truth. I know it wasn't easy for you to relive that, but you're right; I needed to know. I appreciate you more than I can say."

"Oh, sweetie," the woman said, brushing a hand along Georgia's long, blonde hair. "Ya welcome. An' I'm sorry ta lay so much sadness on ya. I do have somethin' for ya though." She reached behind her neck and unclasped the chain she always wore around her neck. From under her apron she pulled a small, misshapen, opalescent stone encased in a silver pendant. "This was ya Mama Hettie's necklace. Ya mama, Miss Amy, took it befo' she left tha house that day she foun' her. She wanted ya ta have somethin' of hers someday when she told ya tha story. She left it with me just in case, and now it's time it came back to ya." She moved behind Georgia and draped it in front of her, clasping the chain again.

Georgia looked down at the stone which seemed to shimmer on its own, separate from the low lighting in the restaurant. "It's beautiful, Mama. Thank you."

Mama Landry squeezed Georgia's hand affectionately. "Do ya want Mama ta make ya some suppah now? Ya gotta be starvin' afta the day ya had."

"Honestly, I don't feel that hungry. What I feel is exhausted. I think I'm going to go home and sleep."

"Course ya are, suga! Let me get ya a to-go box with some chicken an dumplin's at least," and she hustled off to the kitchen.

Georgia slumped back into the booth. Sleep, she thought. That's what she needed. A full night of sleep would do her a world of good, and then she was heading back to Austin's house. She needed to see if she could track where he'd gone and find him. She couldn't wait for days for him to process his thoughts. Neither one of them had that kind of time. They both needed to get back to the woods, share everything they found with the others, and get a plan started immediately. Georgia's hands clenched involuntarily as she thought back to Mama Landry's story. She refused to lose any more people in her life due to lack of action. It was time to move.

Chapter Thirty-One
Unforeseen Alliance

Georgia woke the next morning more exhausted than if she hadn't slept at all. Her muscles were sore from tossing and turning in her sleep. Visions of her mother, Amy, screaming through thick woods had plagued her all night. Every time Georgia had tried to run to her, she'd been attacked by another obstacle; a bear, a raven, a woman in white holding her arm and begging her to come with her and leave her mother behind. In some of the dreams, Austin had run with her until just before reaching her mother, then had stopped and said he needed time and disappeared at the same time her mother did.

Georgia dragged herself to the bathroom, showered, and got ready as quietly as possible. She didn't want to wake the Marens. They would have noticed Austin's car in the driveway and would want to know about the circumstances of it being there. It would have been comforting to see them, but their questions would lead to complicated answers and she wasn't ready to talk about everything she had learned the day before; at least not with them. She knew they'd be sympathetic, but they'd also want to try to explain it from a parent perspective, and she wasn't in the mood to hear it. What she wanted was to discuss it with someone else who was having their own parental angst. She needed to talk to Austin.

She grabbed her bag and tip-toed through the house, pulling the door shut behind her with a soft click. She got in Austin's car and drove away quickly. The car maneuvered almost effortlessly and she still marveled at the power of it.

As she drove the now familiar route out to the abandoned quarry, she thought to herself how easy it would be to just keep going; leave all the deceit behind, forget the war and her obligations, and start a new life far, far away from here. She'd always wanted to see the beach.

Her eyes caught a swift movement to her left and she refocused in time to see a deer run out of the woods and across the road a few feet in front of her. She slammed on the brakes and swerved, barely missing the white tail as it passed her and disappeared back into the woods on the opposite side of the road. Georgia breathed deeply as her heart rate slowed and she was struck by how much her life had changed in the last year. Normally she would have been relieved she had missed the deer and moved on. Now, she was wondering if it had really been a deer, or if it was one of Edmund's henchmen and she should have sacrificed Austin's car to take him out and reduced his numbers by one. She stifled a frustrated groan, squeezed the steering wheel tightly, and turned on the hidden dirt road to the quarry.

She couldn't leave, she thought. Even if she was thousands of miles away, her conscience would never let her live in peace. She would always wonder what happened to the people she had come to love and know that she had abandoned them when they needed her the most.

When she arrived at the quarry, she didn't stop where they always stopped before, but continued along the narrow path along the edge of the quarry that Austin told her would take her to his house. She doubted he would have returned this soon, but she figured she might be able to find some trace of what direction he'd gone. The path was even rougher than the dirt road to the quarry, but it didn't take her as long to get to the Neff house as she thought it would. She parked Austin's car by the shed at the far end of the clearing and sat there for a minute.

She was debating whether she should knock and ask for Charlotte, or if she should just start canvasing the woods around the house when a light tap on the passenger door made her jump. She looked to her right and saw Charlotte's face smiling at her. She sighed in relief that it wasn't Ray, waved and smiled back, and got out of the car.

"Well, hello there, Georgia," Charlotte said in a genuinely happy voice. She reached out and took Georgia's hand, not shaking it, but feeding it through the crook in her arm so they could walk intertwined into the yard. "I did not expect to see you again so soon, but I must admit, I am pleased."

"Hi, Charlotte," Georgia adjusted her gait so their strides matched and they could walk more comfortably. "I didn't expect to be back this soon either, but after I left yesterday things got even more... intense."

"Did they?" Charlotte asked, concern in her voice. "What happened?"

"It's kind of a long story. I knew it wasn't likely, but I was really hoping Austin had come home sooner than expected and I could talk into a sympathetic ear, ya know?"

"I am sorry; he has not come back yet. I know mine is not the ear you were looking for, but it is available if you would like to use it. I do not mind long stories. In fact, I enjoy them."

Georgia smiled and leaned into Charlotte. She couldn't help but feel comfortable with the woman, even though she was essentially a stranger to her. Something in her manner felt familiar and maternal. Her heart panged as she thought of how similarly she had felt about her mother and remembering hearing she hadn't really been her mother. She looked over at the woman walking with her and saw a look a concern on her face.

"It's not a very pleasant long story."

"Oh, my dear, but those are the stories that need to be told the most. You do not want to let them fester inside or they become toxic. Let us not forget Ray and Austin's… discussion, yesterday." Georgia laughed in spite of herself and Charlotte smiled. They reached the top of the stairs to the porch and Charlotte guided Georgia to a glider chair. "Come, sit. Tell me what happened." She sat across from her, her hands folded in her lap.

Georgia glided back and forth gently, the motion and the beautiful view easing her a bit. "After I left here, I didn't want to go home right away. I didn't want to be alone." Charlotte nodded in understanding. "So I decided to go into town and visit with Mama Landry. She's always been so sweet to me and I figured she'd be good to talk to. When I got there, we sat down to talk and when I told her the overview of what happened with Austin and Ray, she ended up telling me a story that kind of has me shaken."

"Oh, my! What did she have to say?"

"Well," Georgia paused, trying to decide just how much to tell Charlotte. "It basically turns out that the woman I grew up thinking was my mom, wasn't actually my birth mom."

Charlotte's face registered shock and she placed her hand to her heart. "Oh, Georgia. That indeed had to be unsettling to hear. Did she tell you why your mother never told you the truth of your birth mother?"

"Not really. She said that no matter who gave birth to me, my mom was still my mom forever."

"She is correct," Charlotte agreed. "She raised you and loved you like her own. I just wonder what the reason was for not sharing your origin with you."

"Mama Landry seems to think she intended to and just ran out of time. She passed away last year."

"I am so sorry. That had to be difficult for you."

Georgia nodded. "Anyway, I guess hearing she wasn't my mom made the loss that much stronger. I mean, I lost her and that was hard, but then hearing this other lady was actually my mom and she and the man who was my dad are dead too… I guess it sort of feels like I lost another family." She saw Charlotte's crestfallen face. "I'm really lucky though," she rushed on. "The people I live with now are as much like parents as I could ever want. And I have Mama Landry, too. She gave me something of my birth mom's, so I feel more connected. I'm well cared for."

"That is wonderful. I am glad to hear you have support in your life. I hope in time you can come to think of me as a part of your support system. I know we just met each other, but Austin is so fond of you and it is easy to see why; I have already become fond of you myself. You have been through so much, and yet you carry yourself so well. I admire you."

Georgia could feel her cheeks reddening. "Thanks, Charlotte. I like you a lot, too. It's really easy to talk to you. Walking up here, I was thinking you make me feel comfortable, a lot like my mom used to. It's a good feeling."

"I am so glad," Charlotte said. "Did you learn anything else about your birth mother and father?"

"I did!" Georgia said excitedly. "My father was the last surviving direct descendent of the Onirus family. I always kind of wondered deep down which family line I really came from, and getting that confirmation was nice. It definitely prevents a potentially awkward situation with Austin." She laughed, but her laughter was cut short. Charlotte's eyes had widened and seemed to be out of focus. "Charlotte? Are you ok?"

She stared at the woman for a few moments before Charlotte shook her head slightly and swallowed hard before putting a smile on her face. "I am fine, thank you." She waved her hand in a dismissive manner. "There was never any doubt in my mind what blood line you are a part of. You are the spitting image of an Onirus. The hair, the eyes, your complexion. Beautiful and fair, the Onirus ladies."

Georgia was still concerned by Charlotte's expression a few moments previously, but hearing her speak so definitively about the family she belonged to overpowered the concern. "Oh, did you know some of the Onirus family? I didn't think descendants of the Nephyrion family associated with Onirus descendants on principle."

"That may be the general rule, but I have never been one for following rules based solely on nonsense," Charlotte said bitterly. "The feuds of old men have nothing to do with me."

"That's a good way to look at it."

"With all that is going on and the sides people have chosen to fight for, either because of or despite their lineage, I believe it can be safely deduced blood no longer means much of anything."

"I guess you're right," Georgia said, thinking of Austin and Christian.

"Did you mention you received an heirloom from Ms. Landry?" Charlotte asked.

"I did," Georgia beamed and lifted the chain around her neck, the pendant emerging from under her shirt. "This was my birth mom's. My other mom took it for me so I'd have something of hers. Isn't it beautiful?"

"Oh, yes. It is quite lovely," Charlotte responded, and Georgia noticed the smile she wore seemed a bit forced.

"Are you sure there isn't something wrong?" Georgia asked again, looking hard into Charlotte's face.

"No, nothing at all. I feel like I have seen something similar to that stone before, but I cannot remember where. Perhaps a picture in my past."

"I hate when that happens," Georgia said, putting the necklace back under her shirt. "When you know you've seen something or someone somewhere but you can't remember where. It's really frustrating."

"Indeed," Charlotte said, and she shifted in her seat. "Anyway, did you learn how your birth parents came to pass?"

Georgia winced softly at the memories of the story she'd been told. "Um, yeah. My father was killed looking for some tunnels to Edmund's compound. Someone found him dead in the woods and brought him back to my mother's house with a note saying to stay hidden because there were enemies she couldn't see out there. She stayed hidden in her house, but she was murdered there anyway shortly after that."

"My lord," Charlotte gasped.

"I know! Who would murder an innocent woman who wasn't even a part of the family line? She just *married* an Onirus?"

"Awful," Charlotte said, almost dismissively. "Did you say something about tunnels? How did he know to look for tunnels specifically, do you know?"

"Um, yeah," Georgia said uncertainly. Charlotte's focus on the tunnels instead of the deaths of her parents struck her as a little odd. "I guess my dad's father and grandfather had heard about them from someone who'd been close to Edmund and they'd spent their lives looking for them."

Charlotte stood up and began pacing the length of the porch. Georgia watched her silently, growing more uncomfortable the longer she sat. Finally, Charlotte spun around and sat on the edge of the chair she had vacated and faced Georgia, her eyes bright.

"Did he find them?" Charlotte asked in a sharp whisper. Georgia stared at Charlotte's flushed face and leaned back a bit in alarm. Charlotte seemed to realize she was scaring her and she swallowed hard, reaching out to gently touch Georgia's knee. "My dear, I am so sorry to be so forceful. It is just… I grew up hearing the same stories of these tunnels; tunnels hidden deep in the woods that could lead to a secret entrance to Edmund's underground compound. But we were told these tunnels did not actually exist; they were something to distract those who would oppose Edmund and keep them from stumbling across his true endeavors. It was said the beginning of the tunnels were in a cave, and Edmund's men would lie hidden around any cave within a good many miles. If someone came searching, they would be killed."

"That's what happened to my dad!" Georgia exclaimed. "He came home one day, told his wife and my mom and other dad that he thought he'd found the tunnels and he was going to explore them. They next time he went back there is when he was found dead and delivered back with the warning."

"It is safe to assume, then, that the story of the decoy caves is true, and they are guarded."

"But if they are decoys, how could my other dad have been killed in a collapse? He went to find them after my real dad was killed, and he got caught in a cave-in. Would a fake tunnel be deep enough for a cave-in?"

Charlotte looked contemplative. "It isn't likely. In fact, I wouldn't imagine there would be any real tunnels at all. Getting people to the cave would be enough to trap and kill them. The tunnels wouldn't be necessary."

It was Georgia's turn to stand and pace. "Do you think it's possible then that the story of the tunnels could be based on reality?" Like, all but one of the caves obviously have no tunnels, but there is one that does?"

"It might be possible," Charlotte said slowly.

"The thing is, I kind of know the guy who told my dad's dad and grandpa about the tunnels. You know, the guy that used to work for Edmund. And he didn't just work for him; he was like his right-hand man. He left because he didn't like what was happening in the compound and he bolted; took Edmund's amulet with him, too, so he couldn't use it anymore. Anyway, this guy isn't the lying type. I don't think he'd tell them they existed if they didn't."

"So it is true! The Christian you know is Christian Vihle!?" Charlotte exclaimed, then covered her mouth and looked around in alarm.

Georgia looked around too, not sure what she was looking for. "I think so. I don't know his last name, but the rest of it is what he told me and my friends about his history. Well, his and Victoria's I guess."

Charlotte slumped back in her seat, her eyes wide and her mouth open. Georgia leaned forward in alarm. "Charlotte, are you…"

"I am all right, Georgia. In fact, I am more than all right," she said, beginning to laugh. Her laughter continued until her eyes watered. Georgia stood there awkwardly, trying to decide if the woman was having a fit of insanity. "I am sorry," she said, sitting up and pulling a handkerchief out of her sleeves and dabbing at her eyes. "It is just… it is all true! The tunnels, Christian, the amulet, even Victoria! I cannot believe the stories I have heard are all true."

Georgia knelt down next to Charlotte's chair. "I know what that's like. When I was growing up, my mom told me the stories of Edmund and Bernard as bedtime stories. Something to entertain, not educate. It's surreal to say the least."

"It most definitely is, but it is also wonderful! Don't you see? If the tunnels really exist, there is a very real chance we can look for them, find them, and have a significant upper hand in surprising Edmund and his troops and potentially stopping or winning a war, if one comes to pass!"

Georgia thought for a while. It sounded ludicrous and brilliant at the same time. "But, if so many men have died looking for these tunnels, what makes you think we can find them without being killed; if they're even real at all? There's still no actual proof."

"It is true, we have no proof, but my instincts tell me they are real," Charlotte said fervently.

"Mine do, too," Georgia agreed resignedly.

"As far not getting killed, I am sure those men were very skilled at many things, but I am willing to bet nonchalance was not one of them. They likely saw a cave and immediately started investigating it, tipping off anyone around it. If we were to come across one on a stroll, make note of its location, and then scout around the area to find the people hiding and watching it, we would be able to diffuse the danger before we investigate."

Georgia looked at Charlotte in awe. "That's actually pretty brilliant." She sat thinking for a bit before continuing. "Between knowing the amulet is hidden in the pond so Edmund doesn't have it to keep himself immortal anymore, and the possibility of a secret way into his compound, there might actually be a way to end this. The others are going to be thrilled when I tell them…"

"No, Georgia," Charlotte interrupted so strongly Georgia blanched. "I do not think it would be wise to invite anyone else on this quest."

"What? Why?" Georgia asked, stunned. "The more people we have looking, the less time it'll take. Plus, strength in numbers and all that."

"Normally, I would agree with you. However, in this case I think we are better going alone. We both know what needs to be done. Two women out for a stroll is not suspect; a larger group would be. Also, should the worst happen, we are only a loss of two; there would still be many left to carry on the task. I do not want to bring Austin into this. He would likely go the way of your father and many others. I feel Christian would be a poor choice as well since he may still be well known."

"I guess you're right, but if we don't tell anyone what we're doing, if we die, no one will know to keep trying."

"That is true. We should leave a note for Austin to find." Charlotte rose and went into the house. Georgia sat back onto the porch, her head spinning. She had come to Austin's house to complain about a secret her mother had kept from her. How had she ended up agreeing to a potential suicide mission? Charlotte reappeared with a piece of paper and a pen, which she handed to Georgia. "You decide what you do and do not want to tell him." She sat back in her seat and leaned back, her eyes cast in the direction of the deep woods around the property.

Georgia stared at the blank piece of paper, at a loss as to where to start. Finally, she put pen to paper and began.

*   *   *

Austin emerged from the woods and into his yard. No matter how angry he was when he left, he was always relieved to see the place when he returned. He smiled and his pace quickened as he saw his car parked next to the shed. Georgia must have brought it back. He thought about how much he was looking forward to seeing her again. It had been four days since the conversation between him and his father. He shook his head to clear the memories of that evening. He didn't want to think about that now. Four days was the longest he and Georgia had been apart since they had met. She had to be missing him too. He stopped in the middle of the lawn, looking at the house, back to his car, and back to the house again. He should really stop in to tell his mom he was back safe, but he didn't want to risk running into his dad. He could be in there for lunch. He turned and walked toward his car. His mom would understand if he waited a few more hours. She appeared genuinely happy he had found Georgia and seemed to like her herself.

He got in the car and reached for the keys that were still in the ignition, but stopped short when he saw the folded piece of paper on his dashboard. On the outside he could see his name in Georgia's handwriting. His hand shook a bit as he reached for the paper and unfolded it.

Austin,

I hope you make it home soon and that you're safe. I've been worried about you. I came back the day after our visit with your parents. I got some really intense news about my mom from Mama Landry that night. I wanted to talk to you about it, but I ran into your mom instead. She's a really wonderful woman! I like to think you take after her. You probably like to think that too, huh?

Anyway, we got to talking and... there's really no way this isn't going to sound crazy, so I'm just going to lay it all out here. Austin, your mom knows about Christian. She knows the story about him taking the amulet, about Victoria, about all of it. She heard it all as stories when she was younger, just like I heard the stories my mom told me about Edmund and Bernard. And she knows about some of the things Mama Landry told me about my parents, but you don't know about those things yet, so I'm not going to get into that right now. You can ask Mama Landry about it. Just tell her I had to go away for a while and I told you to ask her about it all. What you do need to know is we found out some really important information that can possibly help us defeat Edmund. We're leaving tonight and I don't know when we'll be back. But we will be back. I'm not going to lose you, too.

You need to go to the woods and find Christian and everyone else. Tell him your mom and I are looking for the tunnels. He'll know what it means and I'm sure he'll tell you all about it. Tell him we're looking for them and we have a plan that will keep us safe. He's probably going to be mad. Actually, he's definitely going to be mad. I'm sure you're probably mad too, and I'm sorry. This was just too important to wait around and be talked out of. It's the most direct plan of action to putting a stop to this whole thing, and with everything I've gone through in the last year, I needed to act. I hope you can understand that. I know you and I are both tired of hearing things are being done in our best interest, but I hope you can believe me when I say this really could be the best thing for all of us. Isn't stopping a war better than winning one?

I'm depending on you. I need you to go to the woods and do what needs to be done until I can get back. Christian can't go into town so he's going to need you to deliver messages and take care of things in town until I can be back. I'm sorry to dump this on you, and I know how much of a pain it is, but please know I wouldn't do this if I didn't think it was incredibly important.

I love you, Austin. I miss you, and I'll be thinking of you always while I'm gone. Keep the faith.

All my love,

Georgia

About the Author

J. Lawson was born in Davenport, Iowa. She went to St. Ambrose University in Davenport for her undergrad work and Western Illinois University (QC Annex) in Moline, Illinois for her graduate studies.

Lawson moved to Peoria, Illinois in 2009. She is married to her husband, Don, and they have one son, DJ. They also have two dogs, Bailey and Loki.

When Lawson isn't spending her time writing, she likes to read fantasy and mystery novels, listen to 80s and 90s rock music, drink copious amounts of coffee, and discuss new book ideas with her best friend and creative consultant, Laura.

To find more information about J. Lawson visit:

twitter.com/AuthorLawson

www.facebook.com/AuthorJ.Lawson

www.AuthorJLawson.com

Made in the USA
Coppell, TX
02 February 2021